Chapter One

Batbayar Khan stood next to his father in the spaceport manager's office. The room was small. A holo-screen on the wall behind the desk played an ancient movie depicting a black and white scene with horses and men wearing guns. Posters of human women, wearing tiny bathing suits, with large breasts, hung on every available space in the office.

Bat's stomach churned. Where was Big Ping the spaceport manager? Ronald Ping, better known as Big Ping, was not sitting behind the desk. An enormous alien creature sat in Big Ping's chair. His head was round and pink, his eyes slanted, his hair a stiff, black bristle on the top of that round pink head. He had four arms and a large belly. The skin under his small chin was layered in rolls that jiggled when he spoke. A stringy black mustache drooped over a small wet mouth. Because of the eyes and mustache, he looked vaguely, disturbingly, oriental. Spit flew, and he shook with rage as he screamed at Bat's father, Toghus Khan, in Mandarin Chinese.

Bat understood most of it. The Company was getting rid of the Tong. The shady relationship the Tong had enjoyed with the Company for years was now at an end. The Smugglers Guild was taking over their contracts and providing better service, according to the CEO. The giant alien held a stack of papers and photos in one of his hands which he shook while he berated Bat's father.

"You been stealing us blind," the CEO bellowed. "Taking from the hands of those who give you food." He waved his four hands including the one holding the stack of papers. "We received these proofs of your perfidy. Contracts are terminated. Get off our property immediately."

"But revered sir," Toghus said. "We would never do this. We are honest businessmen. We've always honored every contract.

Have we ever been late? Have we ever failed to deliver? Whoever gave you this bad information is lying."

The CEO surged to his feet. He was not that tall, just wide. His bulk was vast. "No, you is the liar. Guards! Guards!"

The door flew open and two guards, who appeared human, raced into the office.

"Take this vile representation of a sentient being out of my office and murder him most grievously by strangling with rope hung from the tallest fibrous growth behind this building."

Bat and his father were grabbed by the guards and dragged out of the office. Bat struggled wildly. He was terrified for his father who looked pale and defeated. The guards hauled them out of the building. A large group of Company Enforcers waited outside. The CEO's guards secured their hands behind their backs with plasti-cuffs. They were marched behind the building where two tall, tan-colored, fungus-like trees towered above the structure. A platform was waiting there beneath the fungus. It looked like a scene from a Western movie. Looped ropes hung from an arm above the platform.

Bat and his father were shoved toward the platform. "Get away," his father whispered in Mandarin. "You can do it."

"No father, not without you."

"I am dead anyway. They will hunt me down if I run and kill my ships and our people. Run. Warn them."

"Stop mumbling in that foreign lingo," one of the guards snarled.

Bat stared at his father through a curtain of tears. His father was in his fifties, his once-black hair silver, his eyes sad, his shoulders were slumped. He realized his father's words were true. The Company had decided the Guild could and would provide more services. Services the Tong wouldn't supply. The Tong had never hauled conscripts. They'd never hauled heavy, radioactive metals. They'd maintained their integrity and autonomy no matter what the Company ordered. Their right to decide what and where they'd go had always been theirs as well. The Guild would land on planets the Tong wouldn't. Crazy planets that were dangerous for human life, but contained deposits of valuable metals or gems. The Tong's agreements with the Company were over. They were all being declared outlaws. He had to escape to warn his people.

Bat dragged his feet and the guard tugged on him. "I feel sick," Bat said in Earth basic.

"Walk," the guard ordered. "I not care about you be sick."

"No really," Bat moaned. "I'm gonna hurl." He bent over and vomited right on the guard's shiny black combat boots. The other guard stopped and stared.

The guard holding his arm let go and jumped back. "Stink! Is disgusting mess."

He kicked up a shower of rust-colored dust in his effort to remove Bat's barf. "Little, nasty, Tong cub," he shouted.

Still bent over, Bat apologized profusely. "Sorry, I'm so scared and my stomach hurts." He threw up again and both guards leaped out of the way. His lunch of noodles and soy curd splattered all over both guards. The guard with the most vomit on his shoes dropped his weapon onto the ground, let go of Bat, and bent over to clean the super-shined, military-issue, black boots.

Free of the guard's grip, the plasti-cuffs were not a problem. Bat had practiced escaping from all kinds of restraints, including this type of cuff. As a small boy with nothing to do on long space voyages with his dad, he'd learned several kinds of martial arts. Escaping from things had been a hobby. He didn't like locks or restraints and could get out of just about anything.

With the cuffs off, he lunged at the guard cleaning his shoes. He'd always had this weird ability to barf whenever he wanted. It had paid off well when he didn't want to go to school. He snatched the weapon laying on the ground beside the guard. It was something he'd never seen before. Bulky with a large barrel. He pointed it at the guard holding his father and pressed the trigger button. A blue beam hit the guard and nothing happened. He turned the beam on one of the Company Enforcers and the man dropped to the floor convulsing.

Bat threw the weapon down and attacked the man holding his father. He wasn't leaving without his dad. The guard suddenly shimmered and changed. Bat gasped. The CEO's guard was an alien like the CEO. He held Toghus Khan in one skinny arm as he reached for Bat with two others. "Run!" His father's scream was cut off by the alien's clawed hand wrapped around his throat. The guard with the dirty shoes tried to grab Bat from behind. Bat spun around, leaped and round-house kicked the guard in the head. The guard's head burst. Stinking green slime flew in all directions as the human-looking guard suddenly revealed himself as an alien.

Bat was surrounded. There were two more of the aliens. They were apparently immune to the strange blue ray. He picked up the weapon and fired at two Enforcers advancing on him warily. They fell to the ground in front of him in the throes of terrible seizures. He stepped on the chest of one, leaped over the second, and ran for the cliffs surrounding the spaceport.

Chapter Two

The alarms never sounded before. Shayna's heart pounded as she ran for the cafeteria. The dining hall doubled as a meeting room. Cain Hollyroad joined her as they entered the dining hall. He took her arm and stopped her. Shayna stared into his lined face. Hollyroad had been in the mines with Deklan Hall, Logan's dad, escaped with him, and was in the military before he was conscripted. In Dek's absence, Cain was their leader.

"I set off the alarm," he told her. "The Company is coming for us."

"How do you know?" Shayna asked.

"Mai Li has been monitoring the spaceport's communications. The Tong has been ousted by the new Smuggler's Guild. All hell is breaking loose at the spaceport. It's under new management. Mai said the CEO is actually at the spaceport right now."

"The CEO? You're kidding?"

"Wish I was. Mai said they know we're here and they're coming for us. We need to bug out."

Shayna followed him into the dining hall. "Bug out? You mean leave?"

He turned and grabbed her shoulders. "Yes, leave. We need to pack up and get out of here right now."

Shayna swallowed hard. This was so horrible, she couldn't fathom it, understand it or even deal with it. "But, Cain, we live here. This is our home. We can't just leave. What about Logan and everybody who went to Earth? We are supposed to stay here."

The dining hall was rapidly filling. Shayna stood in the center with Cain as the colony members filed in and sat down. He patted her arm as he took a firm grip on her elbow and escorted her to a seat. She fell onto a bench too stunned to speak. Ju, Mai Li's daughter, sat next to her. "What's going on?" Ju demanded. "Mom wouldn't tell me."

"Cain says we have to leave," Shayna said in a small voice.

"Leave? Where will we go?"

Shayna shook her head. "I don't know. Cain said your mom heard the Company is going to attack us and he set off the alarms."

Mai Li sat next to Shayna as Cain began to speak. He held his hands up for silence and paused as though examining each one of them. "You are all so important to me. I love you guys." His voice cracked and he took a deep breath. Tears shimmered on his lashes. Cain was a tall man with a dark complexion and short graying hair. His face was lined, but his body was as strong as his will. "The Company knows where we are. We have to run."

When the door suddenly slammed open, everyone in the quiet dining hall jumped. It was Thomas Curran, Cain's right-hand man. He'd been on guard duty on the plateau above the cave dwellings. He was dragging a boy, or more like a teenager. The boy struggled in his grasp, twisting and turning. Cain leaped off the podium and grabbed the boy from Thomas.

"He's tricky," Thomas said to Cain. "Watch him." Thomas unclipped something from his belt and handed it to Cain. "He had this on him."

Cain took what Shayna thought was a grotesque weapon and rolled it in his hands to examine it. "This is a neurolizer," he finally said. "I've only seen one before and that was held by a guard in the mines. Who are you, boy?" Cain demanded.

The boy's mouth was turned down in a sullen frown. His slanted eyes were narrowed as he glared at the members of the colony unashamedly gawking at him. "I'm running from the Company."

Cain's thin smile said he was suspicious. "Why?"

The boy suddenly cracked and sobbed into his hands. Cain wasn't buying this and jerked him upright. "I asked you a question, boy?'

"They killed my father." The boy's voice was thin and quivered with real despair. "They tried to kill me, but I got away."

Cain narrowed his eyes and tilted his head to look the boy over. "You look Tong to me."

"I am. I mean I was. Tong's out. Company's using the Guild now. They fired us." He looked up into Cain's strong face. "Please, man, I ain't got nowhere else to go. I need to warn my people before the Company kills us all."

"You can contact the Tong?" Mai asked. She stood up and took the boy's arm. "He's just a boy, Cain. I believe him to be telling the truth." She grabbed the boy's chin and turned his face so he looked into her eyes. "What's your name?"

"Batbayar Khan, but everyone calls me Bat."

Mai looked thoughtful. "That sounds Mongolian to me."

"It is. My father is, or he was," his voice cracked again. "Toghus Khan."

"I've heard of him," Cain said. "He used to run supplies in from Earth. His ship was the Wanderer."

"That's us," Bat's face lit up. "I need to get a message to them. They're orbiting Gliese right now." He paused. "The Company's going to destroy us. I gotta warn them. My father trusts me to get them a message."

"Well," Mai said. "You've come to the right place. All of us here have run from the Company at one time or another. Me and my daughter, Ju, came from the mines." She pointed at Ju and for the first time, Bat looked at the people assembled. He spotted Ju and Shayna and tried to smile.

"Where'd you get this weapon?" Cain asked.

"Took it off one of the CEO's guards." Bat's face brightened. As he examined them more closely a hesitant smile appeared on his tanned face. "The CEO's at the spaceport on the other side of the ridge. I think he knows you guys are here. The Tong sure did."

"We are aware of our danger," Cain said. "We're gathered here to figure out where to go. We know this place is burned."

Bat examined the room. "Looks like you folks been here a while. Where you plan to go?"

Cain shrugged. "I guess west. We heard there was a new spaceport going up on the other side of a mountain range."

"There's nothing but desert between here and that spaceport. I flew over it a bunch."

"You can pilot a spacecraft?" Shayna asked. She liked the look of this boy, especially if he had talents no one in the group possessed.

"Answer her question, Bat," Cain said. "Can you fly?"

"I should hope so," Bat said. "Spent most of my life in space. Not much to do up there when you're in hyper drive."

Cain tilted his head and examined the boy closely. Shayna could see the wheels of his mind turning. "What else can you do?"

"I, uh, I know some martial arts and I can fight."

"Okay then, Bat," Cain said. "Why don't you take the podium and tell us what you know." Cain gently urged Bat toward the front of the room. The kid didn't look at all enthusiastic, but he allowed Cain to escort him to the simple wooden lectern erected for Cain to speak from. He stood behind it for a moment, his dark-brown eyes taking in all of them, his hands gripping the edges of the lectern. Shayna thought he was a handsome boy with a well-defined jawline, firm chin and long black hair tied at his neck. He was muscular with lean hips and long legs. She glanced at Ju and saw the girl staring with open admiration at him.

"You folks are in trouble and so are my folks," Bat began. "The CEO isn't human. I saw him with my own eyes."

Shayna surged to her feet. "That's what Logan told me. I just got a message from him and he said the CEO is an alien."

"That's just nuts," Cain said. "As far as any of the Vagrants in the mines or from Earth know, humans had never encountered any aliens. The Company must have been hiding it for a long time." He put his hand on Bat's arm. "Are you sure?"

Bat shook his head. "Uh, yeah, saw them with my own eyes," he replied firmly. "The CEO had guards with him that looked human. I kicked one in the head and his head exploded green slime. They can hide their forms so they look just like humans, but they're not like us at all."

"Where do they come from?" Shayna asked. She was thinking about the message from Logan. He'd said something about alien technology in the ship they'd destroyed.

Bat shrugged. "I didn't even know they existed until just a while ago. I almost shi . . . sorry pooped myself when I was dragged into Big Ping's office. No Big Ping just this ugly alien sitting behind Ping's desk. He had four arms and kinda looked a little oriental. He had a thin mustache and slanted eyes. But his head was bigger, and round like a ball. They aren't real tall, just wide. The CEO is fat, like a Sumo wrestler; big belly, lots of chins."

Cain was still standing beside Bat. He lifted his hand to quiet the hub bub caused by Bat's information. "Why is the CEO here on Gliese?" Cain asked.

Bat shook his head. "Sorry, sir, I got no idea. It looked like he was personally overseeing the removal of my people. They brought in a lot of transports; lots of guards, building material and plenty of Guild ships. They have all this new equipment. Stuff I ain't never seen before. Ships I ain't never seen before. They're so modern, they make Tong ships look like hunks of junk."

Shayna stood up. "It's clear," she began. "Cain is right. We have to move." She turned to the people staring at her for direction. It was a little unnerving to see adults looking to her for guidance. "I think we better pack up and get out as soon as we can."

The colonists stood up and formed small family groups and groups of friends. They jabbered excitedly and it was clear many were terrified. Bat and Cain strode toward her. Cain introduced her to Bat. "This is Shayna. She can probably help you get a message out."

Chapter Three

Logan Hall wiped sweat out of his eyes. It was hot. The jungle was alive with bugs, snakes and strange creatures crawling and slithering through the muck underfoot. Knock gave him a shove. "You fall asleep, man? We gotta lot of ground to cover. If you could call this ground." He lifted his foot, the mud made a rude sucking sound, his boot popped out and he shook it. "Can you smell that? Dude, it's like the worst fart Hump ever let."

Logan nodded. "Smells like Tunnel Three under the Loop."

"That's because all the Mole People used the bathroom at the end of Tunnel Three," Knock said.

In front of Logan, Fenfang stopped swinging her machete and looked back. "This is crap. I mean it sucks, it blows and it's like, never ending."

They'd been slogging through the jungle for two hours. The sun was high above their heads sending steam off their sweaty bodies and off the wet leaves of the strange grass growing around them. It towered above their heads, the blades were sharp, and it was an evil, poisonous green. Logan had cuts from the grass all over his arms. The slices were already swelling and an angry red as thought the plants were indeed poisonous.

Behind him, the rest of his team slogged along. Mrs. Nagata was being shepherded by Jordie, their tech. Bobby, the pilot, carried a huge pack just like the one Logan and Knock carried. The packs contained all the food they could scrounge out of the lifeboats before they blew them, and containers of fresh water, also saved from the lifeboats. There was water everywhere around them, but none of it looked like anything the Vagrants would or should drink.

A scream from the back of the line barely registered. Logan was so tired. When he turned to look, he saw Raj holding a snake. The scream had come from Midori, a Vagrant from Bakersfield. Raj noticed Logan staring and grinned. "It is not a poisonous specimen. Regina grahamii, or otherwise known as Graham's Crayfish Snake."

"Just don't," Logan said.

"It could be quite tasty," Raj shot back. "You do know snakes are edible."

"Then you kill it and carry it, but don't wave it at Midori any more. Understand?"

Raj tossed the snake back into a pool of muddy water. "I was only trying to lighten the mood. Everyone is so depressed."

"Living is kinda hard right now, "Logan said. "I got enough on my plate without you scaring the chicks."

"Fang," Knock said. "Give me the machete. I'll take point. You can have a break."

She sighed with relief and they fist bumped when she handed off the machete. Logan offered her a canteen. She guzzled water and handed it back. "Were you able to figure out how far this jungle stretches?"

Logan had spent a few quick moments on the lifeboat IT searching for a way out of this jungle before they blew both the small flyers to pieces. "The jungle's not even on the maps. The map I saw showed a desert with no water at all."

Her laugh held no humor. "You sure we're in Texas?"

He rolled his eyes. "The locator on the lifeboat says we're somewhere near San Antonio. If I remember, the San Antonio River runs through the city."

"What city?" Jordie asked. "I ain't seen a fricking building, much less a city."

"Maybe the computer was wrong and we aren't even in Texas," Fang said.

"It gave me a location close to San Antonio on the west side. Next city is supposed to be Castroville. It said Lackland Air Force Base is about five miles to the south."

"Then let's go south," Fang said. "Maybe we can find some transportation, or the Loop, or some way to get back out west."

"Jordie," Logan called. "How do I tell which way is south?"

Jordie and his buddy Corey passed Fang on the narrow trail through the tall grass and stood next to Logan. Jordie shaded his eyes and examined the sky. "The sun came up over there and it's going that way." He pointed and then turned around. "South's that way."

Logan stared into the thick swampy jungle in the direction Jordie pointed. "That way?"

"That's south, man. What can I say?"

"Knock, hack us a path in that direction."

Knock rolled his eyes. "You're kidding, right?"

"I think we should head toward the Airforce Base. Jordie says it's that way."

"Dude, look at all that water."

"I see it. Look for a way around, but go in that direction."

Why did everyone question him? Was it because he was so young and they'd known him as a friend? He wished his dad was here. There would be no questions, no pranks, everyone would do as Dek ordered without any arguments.

Knock found a narrow game trail leading to the general direction of south and started slashing the thick vegetation blocking it. They slogged on for what seemed like hours. Logan finally stopped Knock on a small hummock surrounded by more water. A rattlesnake lay curled under a dying mesquite tree. At this point seeing a snake was a nonevent. Knock flicked it into the water and watched it swim away. Shirley Nagata sat under the dying tree right where the snake had been. She looked exhausted. They were all tired. Walking long distances through this muck, coupled with the heat, had them dragging.

"We can rest here for a while," Logan said. "There's room enough to sit. But we can't stay here. We have to push on."

He opened his pack and took out some energy bars. He cut them into thirds and gave everyone a third. There were twenty-two of them and a limited amount of food. He allowed everyone to have a few sips of water and then hustled them all to their feet. Grumbling and whining, he ignored. There were two children younger than Raj. He put Raj in charge of watching them as they descended the side of the hummock into knee-deep water. Logan took the machete and slashed thick palm fronds, dead thorny branches, and tall razor grass. Behind him, his people slogged along. They were still in water which was slowly, to Logan's dismay getting deeper as the rays of the sun began to filter through the vegetation to the west.

"Sun's going down, dude," Knock said. "What're we gonna do?"

"Take over," Logan said. "I'll scout ahead and see if there's a place to camp"

"Right on," Knock said as he took the machete.

Fenfang joined them. "I'll go with Logan. Keep an eye on Mrs. Nagata. She's really tired."

Logan and Fang hiked fast through the water and strange vegetation. They came to a tall pine tree. It was dead. Pine trees must not like two feet of water on their roots. It still had the broken stubs of cracked limbs. Logan thought it looked like a ladder. "I'm going up," he said to Fang.

She pushed him aside. "No, let me. I'm lighter and, well, more agile." She grinned.

Logan could hear the regular slash of Knock and the machete from far away. The sun had disappeared and shadows were long. He gave Fang a boost up to the first branch and watched her scramble to the top. He fairly danced with impatience as she rotated around the top of the tree looking in all directions. When she slid to the ground, he could barely wait to hear what she had to say. "Well? What'd you see? Come on, Fang. I'm dying here."

She grinned. "I saw lots of water, an ocean of jungle and...."

"What? And what?"

"There's a wall about half a mile away. A really big wall. It's causing all this water because it dammed up the river."

"A wall?" Logan said. "They built that?"

Fang closed her eyes. "Yes, a wall. The good news is they built a big berm next to the wall. It's dry. We can camp on it."

When Professor Depak Goswami opened his eyes, he thought he must be dead. Clouds of steamy white vapor surrounded his face. He quickly realized he could not move because his wrists and ankles were strapped into place. An alarm sounded. It was only a tiny beeping noise, but Goswami interpreted it as an alarm. Where was he? He vaguely remembered a hideous monster mutant burning him with a torch. He remembered talking to Logan Hall. Where was Logan? Was he still alive? Goswami remembered they'd been detained in San Francisco in the city jail.

The fog abruptly cleared. A man's face leaned close and a fat thumb lifted one of his eyelids. A doctor, Goswami decided, as the man shined a light into his pupil. "So, you're finally awake," the doctor said.

Goswami tried to answer. His throat was sore and scratchy. "Yes," he croaked.

The doctor touched the side of Goswami's face. "Your burns are healing nicely. You had a heart attack, Professor, but you are now completely recovered. Your burns have been healed and you are ready to become one of us."

The doctor rolled a table close to Goswami. He picked a jar off the table and tilted it back and forth. He then shook it. "Wake up little one," he said to the jar. "It's time to go to work."

The Professor realized he was lying in a medical healing bed. He'd heard of them but never seen one before. There was a plexiglass canopy over his head. When the doctor raised it, the highly-oxygenated gas filling it had dissipated. There was a needle in his arm giving him nutrients and fluid and possibly drugs. His head felt fuzzy. The restraints made no sense since he'd been drugged into unconsciousness. The effects still had his thought processes slow. He watched as the doctor peeled back a seal and opened the jar.

What he saw inside the jar cleared all the fog in his head. He struggled wildly against the restraints. The doctor used forceps to grasp a hideous creature inside the jar. The creature was a cross between a slug and a scorpion. Its tail held a stinger, but its body was grossly fat and lumpy. It had to be alien. It was a reddish color with yellow spots. Red and yellow usually denoted danger in the animal kingdom. The creature wiggled in the grasp of the forceps as the doctor dropped it on Goswami's chest.

Goswami's scream tore through his aching throat emerging as a croaking blast. The doctor put a restraining hand on his wrist. "The styngar worm will help you embrace our way of thinking, Professor. It only hurts for a moment. I've increased the pain medication in your IV so you should only feel a small stick."

The creature didn't crawl, it humped across Goswami's chest leaving a slug trail. Whatever the bug secreted must contain acid. The trail it left burned. Goswami could only watch in horror as it neared his throat. He strained his neck to watch its progress. It reached a spot on his chest, seemed happy there, lifted the tail and stabbed the stinger into Goswami. Excruciating pain lanced through Goswami's chest. Fire raced through his veins. Unable to do anything but scream, Goswami arched his back and surged against the restrains. When the searing poison reached his brain, he passed out.

Chapter Four

The rust-colored desert stretched out in front of the colonist for miles and miles. The strange purple moon of Gliese hovered above the horizon as they trudged ever westward. Shayna's back hurt, her feet hurt and she was always tired. Cain walked beside her carrying a massive pack. Everyone but her, and an old woman the people called Granny Hawkins, carried a pack. Even the youngest of them, Cressy, carried a pack filled with water in hopper stomachs.

Hoppers were indigenous creatures adapted to the dry conditions of the desert through natural selection and evolution. They hopped much like rabbits, were brown like everything else on Gliese, and had a second stomach just for holding water. When the hoppers found a drinking hole, they filled the second stomach with water. The colonists ate the creatures and used their tough hides to make clothing and shoes.

Hoppers were the most common animal on Gliese. They reminded the colonists of kangaroos, but they had six limbs instead of four and no pouch. Four of their legs propelled them forward in a springing jump, while the remaining set of legs had paws adapted to picking fruit from tree branches, or even holding small stones to crack nuts and the shells of sea creatures. They were omnivorous. They ate anything.

"How long is it going to take us to get to the mountains?" Shayna asked Cain.

"Well, we can't even see them yet, so I'm thinking at least two weeks."

"Do we have enough water to last that long?"

"Nope," Cain said. "I'm heading for an arm of the inland sea. I flew over this part of Gliese when I was working for the mining company. The sea juts inland ahead, maybe a day's walk from here. I'm thinking we'll camp there and rest for a couple of days, send out some hunters, stock up on grub and water, then move on."

Thomas Curran jogged toward them. Cain stopped the colonists by lifting his hand and shouting. "Hold up the march."

Curran was breathing hard. He'd been scouting the trail ahead. "There's a Company flyer on the ground about four klicks in front of us. I watched for a minute. Looks like a group of Company tourists hunting for gorp." Cain carried Dek's sniper rifle with its long-range, infrared scope. "I counted seven and the pilot. They were wearing these ridiculous outfits. Desert camo jackets, pants with cargo pockets, lots of expensive weapons and long-range viewers. They set up tents in the shadow of a small set of cliffs for the night. Big camp fire. You can see it for miles. Country starts getting hilly and rough up ahead. We need to take a more southerly course to avoid it. Definitely gorp country."

Gorp were gigantic lizards much like a dinosaur crossed with a crocodile. They could change color to suit their environment and liked to hunt in the fresh-water seas of Gliese.

Cain nodded. "How many were hunters and how many were servants?"

Tom grinned. "I know what yer thinkin', and it could be doable. There was a pilot. He was off to himself. Looked like a Company man, uniform and pilot jumpsuit. Then there were three tents. One looked like it was for eating and two for sleeping. The big shot of the group was an older man. Looked like he had three guests, one of them was young like a teenager."

"Were there Company guards?"

"Yup, I counted one probable guide. He was wearing camo, but it didn't come out of no hunting catalogue, and two Company guards. They were armed to the teeth, but I'm thinking they were mine guards just along for security. They looked like all the guards we knew; soft, fat, pale and used to living the good life, doped to their eyeballs on Sopore, in Company quarters."

Shayna looked around. The rust-colored earth was cracked and dry. Ahead of them, an old riverbed, long without water, offered some shelter. "Do you think we can find water if we dig in the dry riverbed?" She asked Cain.

Cain laughed. "Maybe if you dug for a hundred years. It does look like it might have a good place to camp. Let's stop and form up a raiding party. I'm thinking going after the hunters is worth a try. They'll have supplies we can really use."

"What about them telling the Company about us?" Shayna asked. "If you get caught, they can radio our location to the Company and we're all dead."

"Then we'll have to make sure that doesn't happen."

"How?" Shayna demanded. "Are you going to kill all of them?"

Cain put a hand on each of Shayna's shoulders and stared into her eyes. "Listen, this is war for us. We're fighting for our very survival. It's coming down to us or them. Who do you want to survive? How much do you want to get off this desert in one piece?"

Shayna touched the tiny bulge of her belly. A child grew in there. A child she desperately wanted to be born, to live, and to grow up strong and healthy. Logan's child. As she stared into Cain's clear, brown eyes, his steady gaze and his sincerity created a palpable aura around him. She sighed. "Do whatever it takes. Don't get caught and don't die. We need you."

They moved into the dry riverbed. After walking about a mile down it, they found a high bank with two strange tree-like growths on it. The growths looked dead, but when touched, it became clear they were very much alive. The soft covering of the trunks was made of tiny filaments. When Shayna ran her hand over them, they flowed to the side as one, and she saw their undersides were pink. Cain broke off a branch and water poured out. Amazed, he tasted it. "We can drink this," he said.

"You sure?" Shayna didn't think drinking the pinkish water was any kind of a good idea.

"I remember hearing about this plant. The miners called this plant the Kool-aide tree because the water is sweet and kind of fruity. I heard them describe it, but I've never seen one. If we pulled this up, the roots go down miles."

"Where's Granny Hawkins?" Shayna said. "Don't let anyone drink it until she says it's okay."

"Works for me," Cain said. "I'm getting this raid going. We have about four more hours until dawn."

The new guy, Bat, suddenly appeared at her shoulder. "You going on a raid?" He asked Cain.

Cain looked thoughtful. "Yeah."

"I'll go."

"I'm not sure that's a good idea," Cain said. "We hardly know you, and truthfully, you could be a plant. I mean we've all thought it. I'm just putting what we've been thinking into words."

Bat's earnest expression touched Shayna. He seemed so sincere and she believed his story. She laid a hand on Cain's thick forearm. "Let him go. I believe him."

Cain closed his eyes. "You think everybody is honest and telling the truth, Shayna. You look for the good in people. I see it every day. Let him prove himself first." He pushed Bat to the side. "You wanna do something? Make yourself useful here. Help set up camp and protect these people with your life. We need a strong person here with all these civilians."

"You can help me," Ju, Mai's daughter said to Bat. "I'm putting up the tents and making a fire."

Cain stopped her. "No fire. We're still too close to those hunters. Cold food only. Journey bread and jerked hopper meat."

Ju nodded. "Okay, no fires." She smiled at Bat and Shayna thought her smile was a blatant attempt to flirt with the young man. Bat returned the smile and followed Ju to the campsite while Cain went to organize his raiding party.

"We can't stay here long," Logan said to Knock. "This road on top of the berm gets some use. The Company probably sends a patrol down it every once in a while, and with our luck, that one time will be tomorrow."

"You're probably right," Fenfang said. She stood on the edge of the berm staring into the swamp. Behind her, a narrow gravel-covered road butted the huge concrete wall rising fifty feet into the bright, sunny Texas sky. The heat and humidity were stifling.

Their party sat against the wall where the structure cast some shade against the blistering sun. Some slept and some just sat staring into the jungle. All of them were tired, bug bitten, hot and filthy. There was maybe another two hours of sunlight left until darkness descended on them and with it clouds of mosquitoes.

"Get everyone up," Logan finally said. "I think we should risk walking the road. It's easy and I can see where weeds and vegetation from the swamp are encroaching on the road, so it can't be that well-traveled. Maybe we'll be safe, especially at night. Why would anyone drive out here at night? We don't even want to be here at night."

Knock swatted at a flying, buzzing insect. "You got that right. Let's get going now. We can make better time when we can see our feet."

"Dude," Logan said. "The dark is so thick out here you can't see your feet or what you're stepping on."

The dispirited group gathered for a moment in the middle of the road. Their heads drooped and their eyes had the wild feral look of starved dogs. "Let's get as far as we can tonight," Logan told them. "Maybe we'll get out of this swamp and find a way to get to a safe refuge."

"Where's it safe?" Jordie asked. "Where can we go?"

Logan shrugged. "I'm thinking Vegas. They're still a few Vagrants there."

"That's a million miles away," Midori said. "It might as well be on the moon. Let's try for Denver. I heard there's still a big colony of Vagrants under the airport. It's been there since the beginning of the century."

Logan nodded. "Sounds like an idea. Let's see what we can do."

They slogged along the gravel road until a blanket of darkness settled over them. The wall to their left had solar-powered lights every fifty feet. The lights were dim, some were broken or just burned out, but it helped guide them, and the light they emitted gave them a tiny ray of hope. They were all from the city. Jungle, swamp, bugs, these were all new to them and they were uncomfortable in a strange disturbing way. Logan had lived on Gliese in the colony. He, Fang, Knock, Raj, Lizabeth and Bobby were used to living a rougher life. They were the least affected. The rest of the group and the kids were not handling the situation well at all. There was a lot of moaning and groaning and complaining going on. Logan, raised by a military man, had no use for it. Knock was the voice of reason.

"Can't they see I'm doing the best I can?" Logan said to Knock as they humped along the road.

"Don't pay attention to them," Knock said. 'It's human nature to complain. You just don't see that because of your father."

Fenfang laughed. "Yeah, living with Dek was like being in the Army."

They walked for what seemed like hours with nothing changing but the sky. The stars and the sliver of moon were gone. Bolts of lightning shot across the sky as thunder rumbled. "We're going to have to stop and look for shelter," Logan said.

They were searching along the wall for a place to set up camp when Corey suddenly screamed. The boy grabbed his head and fell to the ground. Logan was beside him in seconds along with Corey's best friend Raj.

"What's wrong?" Raj asked as he tried to pull Corey's hands off his head.

Corey opened his eyes and wailed. "They're inside my mind. Make it stop."

Tears streamed down Corey's face. His eyes suddenly rolled back in his head and he began having a seizure. Logan put his knees on both sides of Corey's thrashing body and held him down. "Someone get me a stick."

Fang shoved her knife at him. "Use this"

The hilt of the knife was bone. Logan shoved it into Corey's mouth to keep him from biting through his tongue. White foam frothed on the boy's lips as he rolled his head wildly from side to side. Corey's wild thrashing went on for what seemed like forever to Logan, but was only about two minutes. He suddenly stopped and his eyes flew open.

"He's alive," Corey croaked. "I saw him and felt him. He's alive."

"Who?" Logan said. "Is it my dad? Who's alive?"

Logan helped Corey into a sitting position while Fang brushed bits of gravel and dirt off the boy's shirt and hair. "The Professor," Corey whispered. "The Professor is alive."

Chapter Five

Professor Goswami knew something was wrong with him. He felt out of control. His movements were jerky and mechanical. When he tried to order his body to stop walking, nothing happened. He kept walking. On either side of him, guards paced. The guards weren't human. Their heads were round. A stiff brush of black hair grew down the center of their pink heads. Their eyes were slanted and facial hair was trimmed into a drooping mustache on both sides of a small mouth. They had four arms and a round body. They seemed to only have two legs, but Goswami couldn't be sure. From his vantage point, all he could see was two short, fat little legs. Each guard was heavily armed with a thick-barreled, ugly weapon.

Goswami wanted to talk to them, but was unable to formulate words or control his speech. All that came out of his mouth was a steady dribble of saliva. He couldn't even swallow correctly.

They reached a door. Goswami stood quietly waiting as they opened it. He'd just walked down a long hallway from the medical suite where he'd been strapped to a bed. The place smelled institutional, not like a hospital, more like a school or a mental institution. A hint of some stringent cleaner containing ammonia, lingered in the hall.

The guards pushed him and he fell forward into a small office. A grotesque alien sat behind the desk. He was fatter than the two guards, but had the same shape and drooping mustache. He waved one of his top set of arms and Goswami noted delicate, long, multi-jointed fingers. The second set of arms had thick digits with sharp claws at the end.

"Come in and sit down, Professor," the alien said. "I be CEO of this Company you fighting for many years." The CEO laughed like he'd just told an hysterical joke. The two guards laughed as well. Their humor emerged as a blast of twittering.

"You now mine. I owns you thanks to the styngar worm. We have thems on our planet. They live in the jungles surrounding the equator. Very hot it is on our planet which is called Dogar. Much hotter than we like. Your planet is good, but getting too warm here like on Dogar. We move soon to new planet. Many to choose from. Kruellians like us spreading to all parts of the galaxy. Soon there will only be us and those we rule." He and the guards went off in more gusts of insane twittering.

Goswami tried to move his head to look at the guards, but he was denied even that small movement. Deep inside his chest, he felt the worm stir. He gagged but no words came out and he stopped fighting. The worm was wrapped around his spine, using his body for the will of its masters.

"Soon, styngar worm will have more control and you will move like normal person," the CEO said. "When ready, we will send you to meet your friends. They think we don't know where they are. They very sneaky, but we find soon. When we does this, you will lead them into trap we set for them, and off to the mines they go. Except their leader. Him's father killed Drayvon. Drayvon was very good leader for me here. Make it so I not have to work." The CEO used one of his clawed hands to smooth the brush of hair on his head. "I don't like to work. Much better to go to Vegas, enjoy large-breasted Earth women, and do nothings all day."

Goswami willed his eyes to close so he wouldn't have to see the bloated face in front of him. Nothing happened. He couldn't even shut his own eyes. They were going to make him infiltrate Logan's group and lead them to a place where they could be captured. Logan would be tortured and killed by this hideous alien and there was nothing he could do to stop or even hinder their plan. Logan trusted him and would listen to anything he said. His poor friends wouldn't know they were being duped by the CEO. If

Goswami could have taken his own life at that moment, he would have. Just thinking such a thought made the worm move.

When he suddenly spoke, he was horrified. "I will do anything you order, master." It was Goswami's voice, but the worm talking. Could things get any worse?

"Yes, styngar worm very obedient to us. You know why, Professor?"

Of course, Goswami couldn't answer, but the worm did. "Professor knows nothing. I have searched his mind. He was suspicious about the Company's collusion with aliens, but had no facts to base those suspicions upon."

The worm had been through his thoughts. Goswami's horror level rose even higher. The aliens would now know everything he had done in his entire life. It would know all of his contacts and all of the Vagrant hiding places he was privy to. This was a disaster of enormous proportions. Goswami wondered how the CEO controlled the disgusting creature. It seemed impossible.

A small box sat on the CEO's desk. It looked much like Helga's control box. When the CEO ran one of his articulated fingers across the top of the box, the creature inside of him quivered. "Yes, K'Vogen," Goswami heard himself say. "I will perform as you wish."

K'Vogen must be the CEO's name because the alien answered. "If you do not as we order, I will place you and each member of yous family in a pain enhancer for rest of your very long lifes." The corners of K'Vogen's round little mouth turned up in what Goswami assumed was a smile. "We monitor everything you does and keep close eyeballs on you. Guards, take this garbage person who is so useful to us back to his room until we's found the runaways."

"The Professor is alive?" Logan grabbed Corey by the front of his shirt and pulled him close. "You're sure of this?"

"I was inside of his head for a minute. He's very frightened." Corey wiped saliva off his chin. "What happened to me?"

"You had a seizure," Lizbeth their medic said. She held out a small white tablet. "I think you should take this. It will calm your nerves and perhaps keep you from having another."

Corey looked at the pill suspiciously. "What is it?"

"Phenobarbital," Lizbeth said. "It's all we have, but it should help. Have you had seizures before?"

Corey's face flushed a bright red. His freckles stood out clearly as the blush faded and Logan saw how pale he was. "Not so bad I can't remember what happened."

"Corey," Logan knelt in front of him on the rough gravel road. "Where is the Professor?"

Corey shrugged. "Looked like he was in some kind of hospital. I remember smelling antiseptic or some kind of cleaner like hospitals use."

Logan sat back on his heels. Knock and Fenfang hung over his shoulders. "Did you see any guards? Is he a prisoner?"

Corey's eyes closed and he started shaking. Lizbeth pushed Logan aside. "The questions are putting too much of a strain on his nervous system. If you keep it up, he'll have another seizure. Help me get him over by the wall where he can lie down."

They'd set up some tents against the wall to make lean-tos. The ominous rumbling of thunder and bolts of lightning stopped. A moisture-laden breeze ruffled the vegetation on the side of the road. The breeze did nothing to cool the air. It was hot and stank of rotting vegetation and death.

Logan took Knock and Fang aside. Raj joined them, sitting on the gravel with his legs crossed. "This is very strange news indeed," Raj said. "It is good news my uncle lives, but very hard to understand when Logan saw him die in San Francisco County Jail."

Professor Goswami had practically started the resistance with Logan's father, Deklan Hall. Goswami was a doctor and had saved hundreds of Vagrants, working out of his underground laboratory. Logan had been a runner for him most of his life. Racing through the tunnels and subway systems of New Washington to bring life-saving drugs to Professor Goswami. The old doctor had seemed to die after he was ruthlessly questioned by the maniac mutant, Drayvon, in the San Francisco county jail. Logan had seen him die. Or thought he did.

"I could have been mistaken," Logan said. "I was escaping. I'd just been tortured by a gigantic mutant lizard who thought burning people with a torch was fun. Professor Goswami was on a stretcher in the lobby. I saw a medical van pull in and take him away. He looked dead to me, but I guess I was wrong."

Fenfang patted his back. "Not your fault," she said.

"Dude," Knock said. "They got machines that can just about bring you back from the dead."

Bobby the pilot inserted himself into the group. "Saved me and I was pretty far gone. Put you in some kind of coffin-like machine, fill you full of knock-out drugs, and fix you right up."

"Then the Company has him," Logan said. "They're the only ones with that kind of equipment. Bobby's right. I saw a couple of those machines in the infirmary on the battleship. Lizbeth used the machines to save some of our people." Logan focused on Knock. "What's this mean for us right now?" Logan had to concentrate on their current situation. It was the only thing that mattered. The Professor might be alive, but all they had to verify this was Corey's vision, and he'd been in the middle of a seizure when he had it.

"It doesn't mean a frigging thing to us, Logan," Fang said. "It's just a distraction. Especially for you. What we need to do right now is get out of this jungle and find a way to get home to Gliese."

Knock put his arm around Fenfang and hugged her. "Babe, way to get right to the point."

She shrugged. "Well it's true. We can't help Professor Goswami. We don't even know where he's being held. I know how much you care about him, Logan, but that's the truth."

Logan nodded. "I get it. I wish we knew where he was, but knowing would only make it worse. I mean, if we knew where they were holding him, what could we do? We can't even get ourselves out of this stinking jungle."

Knock rocked back on his heels. "Listen Loge, everyone's beat. Let's just hole up here. Maybe the storm isn't going to hit us, but the weather feels really weird."

Fenfang had grown up on Gliese. She'd never experienced any weather on Earth. "I don't like the way the air feels," she said. "If we were on Gliese, I'd say we were in for a dust storm or a tornado."

Logan stood up and stared into the sky. It was too dark to see anything. A sudden arc of cloud to cloud lightening illuminated black clouds. They appeared to be boiling right above their heads. Another crack of lightening and the wind roared. Gravel from the road swirled around them driving them toward the wall. The people huddled against the wall hurried to catch precious supplies blowing everywhere.

Leaves, jungle debris and gravel pelted Logan as he ran for the wall. Corey sat huddled with his back to the wall holding his head. "Under us!" He suddenly yelled. "There's a tunnel under us. I can sense movement down there."

Corey began digging into the debris piled against the wall. He dug furiously, like a crazy dog hunting for a lost bone. Raj helped him and Jordie joined in. The top of a buried door appeared and Logan screamed to Knock. "Help dig."

Terrified of the storm, his people pushed close to the wall using their hands to move loosely packed earth and mud, rotting leaves and sticks aside as they dug. Knock appeared with a small camp shovel and hurled himself into the work. Fang used one of her biggest knives to loosen more dirt against the wall. As rain poured out of the sky, a line appeared in the side of the wall. It was the top of a gray, metal hatch.

"I got this," Knock said. "Back up."

Logan motioned for Corey and Raj to back away from the wall as Knock dug like a madman. In minutes, he had a three-foot deep hole. The wall had been there so long, jungle debris and dirt had covered up something all Vagrants understood. A maintenance hatch. When he and Knock had lived underground, hatches just like this one had been part of their roadways.

A circular indentation on the side of the metal door was very familiar. Logan grabbed his pack from Bobby, filed through it rapidly, and emerged with a Level Five key. He fit it into the indentation. The mechanism in the door squealed and creaked, but nothing happened.

The wind had built to a raging crescendo. Logan's small band of people crowded close to him. Knock crouched in front of the door staring at the key. Logan willed it to work. Bigger pieces of debris crashed into them and the wall. "Do something," Logan screamed over the wail of the wind and the boom of thunder.

Knock took the key out and blew into the indentation. He wiped it clean with the tail of his shirt and stuck the key in again. A green light appeared on the key. The door squealed and groaned. Knock tapped dirt out of the edges of the hatch as the screech of the metal became a low grind and the hatch slowly inched up. Knock used his shovel to push more debris away from the door.

When there was an opening two feet by two, Fenfang pushed Knock aside and wiggled through. She stuck her head out and held out her hand. "Light," she screamed. "Get me a light."

Jordie handed her a hand-held lantern. She disappeared only to stick her head out again. The opening had grown to three feet. She waved to them. "Come on. It's dry in here."

Logan waited until his people were inside then followed them into the welcome quiet leaving the raging storm outside.

Chapter Six

Cain Hollyroad and his second-in-command, Thomas Curran, led four more colony members to the top of a small rise. Because the new guy, Bat, said he'd been gorp hunting here with big-shots before, Cain had reluctantly listened to Shayna and allowed Bat to come on the raid. Bat was little more than a kid, he said he was eighteen, but Cain thought he looked more like sixteen, seventeen at the most. He barely had any facial hair.

They stopped just before the hill crested and hunkered down. Besides Thomas and Bat, Cain had brought Milo Deforest. Deforest was ex Special Forces Navy and he said he'd been an ordinance man. He'd been on the demolition crew in the mines, blowing new tunnels into the bedrock of Gliese, so Cain figured he knew his way around explosives.

When they edged up to the top of the hill and peered over, Cain saw the hunters were not in camp. Their helo was parked close to a small outcropping in the cliffs across from the raiding party's position. The small group of cliffs and hills sprouted out of the middle of a barren flat plain. The inland sea was close enough to see a golden shimmer rippling across the water as the sun rose over the horizon. Gorp liked to live near water because they were good swimmers and often hunted in the water. They preferred to make their homes in caves, so this location was perfect gorp country.

The pilot sat around a small fire drinking something hot. He cupped his hands as if for warmth around the drink and stared off into the distance at the rising sun. The rest of the party seemed gone, but Cain didn't trust that to be true. They had to have left at least one guard to ensure the safety of the helo. As he watched the pilot, a small movement the pilot made to smooth back a lock of hair that had fallen across his forehead stirred a memory. Was it possible he knew the pilot? The pilot put his cup on a rock, stood up and stretched. After the stretch, he pulled something metallic out of his pocket and put it to his lips. Vapor. The pilot was vaping who knew what in the small hand-held device. What had begun as a replacement for smoking tobacco, had morphed into a delivery device for all kinds of drugs, most specifically liquid Soap. Soap was a deadly combination of Sopore, opium, and or heroin. The more Cain watched the pilot, the surer he was of the man's identity.

"I know that guy," he whispered to Thomas. "Look at him. It's Small Paul McGuire."

The pilot was indeed short; an asset when you were a pilot. Thomas peered over the edge of the rise and dropped back to lie next to Cain. "Small Paul as I live and breathe and still huffing Soap."

"He was a prisoner. What's he doing ferrying bigshots around?"

Thomas tilted his head as though thinking deep thoughts. "You know, Bat says the Tong is out. The Company always used Tong to fly their helos, so does that mean this new Smugglers Guild is providing pilots? Wasn't Small Paul affiliated with the Mafia?"

"Bat," Cain beckoned to the young Asian. "Didn't the Tong used to fly all Company helos on Gliese?"

"Used to," Bat said. "Told you we're out. Company's using only Mafia and Guild guys for everything. I gotta get offworld and warn my family."

"Can you fly a helo?" Cain asked.

"Every day of the week," Bat answered.

They made a quick plan to go around the camp and come down the cliffs behind the helo. "You," Cain pointed at Bat, "warm up the bird while we take out the guard and Small Paul."

"What do you want me to do?" Ju asked. She'd insisted on coming and Cain felt more positive about her abilities under fire than he did of Bat's, so he'd included her. Seeing the situation, he was more positive than ever of Bat's story. The Tong was out of favor. The rest of his story could then be true which meant aliens ruled this world and Earth and maybe all the colonies. It was a shock and something he found very hard to believe.

"Go with him," he pointed to Bat. "Milo, go with them."

When they'd skirted the camp, and climbed the small hill behind the helo, they rested for a minute. Cain examined the hunters' camp through his field glasses. Below them the helo squatted like a giant bug. It had articulated landing legs that folded during takeoff, two rotors, a main rotor over the cockpit and a tail rotor. It had ample room for eight to ten people and plenty of cargo space. If he had this aircraft, it would hold half of the colony and would expedite their escape. Cain badly wanted it. They needed it. With this one aircraft, he could move the colony to a safe location and after that, the helo would give them a much-needed mobility they'd never had. It was a like a gift from God and so, so close. He had to make it happen.

The pilot was indeed Small Paul. And he was using his vaper so he was high. The guard was eating a bag of candy and drinking soda from a plastic dispenser cup. Even from this distance, Cain saw the guard was zoned on Sopore. Too much candy and soda filled with corn syrup and corn sweeteners was almost as bad as vaping Soap. Corn, genetically modified to produce the drug Sopore, was in everything. Most of the population of Earth was addicted to it. The drug caused lethargy, stole a person's ambition, and created a complacent population of worker bees addicted to the drug. Of course, the Company imported plenty of Sopore-rich food to keep the prison guards and legal mining colony residents comfortably numb.

Cain dropped the glasses and rolled onto his back. "This is what we're gonna do," he said and began outlining his plan.

They crept down the hill in two parties. Cain and Thomas slipped around the nose of the bird, while Bat, Deforest and Ju came in on the back side of the helo. Cain was inches from grabbing the guard by the throat when screaming erupted from beyond the camp at the base of the mountains. "What the . . .? The guard snapped around and loosened his weapon. Small Paul was slower. He exhaled a huge lungful of sweet-smelling smoke. "Huh?"

The over-weight, teenaged member of the hunting party, his natty hunting togs in shreds, ran toward them shrieking like a woman. "Holy Mother of . . ." Cain didn't finish. Behind the teen, the biggest, ugliest, gorp Cain had ever seen closed in for the kill, loping along on four of its appendages. Behind that gorp ran another, smaller one. The biggest one was nuclear red. Cain had never seen a red gorp. They were usually rust-colored like everything else on Gliese or purple-rust colored like the one chasing the red one.

The guard pointed his neurolizer at the big red gorp. Cain smacked it out of the guard's hand. "You'll only piss it off."

The guard seemed to register Cain's presence through his Sopore haze. "Who?"

Cain shoved him hard. "Run, asshole."

The guard nodded. "Right," and took off at an awkward gallop down the gorge toward the inland sea. Cain shoved Small Paul. "Better go with him."

"Cain? Cain Hollyroad?"

"Run, Paul, or you're dead."

"Got that right," Paul said and took off after the guard. Bat, Ju and Deforest popped out from behind the helo. Bat spotted the charging gorp and slid to a stop as the fat kid raced by. He took one look at the charging creatures and shoved Ju into the helo. Seconds later, Cain heard the engine stutter and start. Cain opened up on the red gorp with his hunting rifle. The high-velocity bullets merely bounced off the gorp's tough skin. "Shit." He pushed Thomas into the helo after Bat and Ju and then took off running.

He hoped the gorp would follow him. He was wrong. He heard a thunderous crash and dove for cover behind a mushroom tree. The red gorp was tearing off parts of the helo. It ripped the tail rotor off and used it to scratch its back as the smaller gorp tore off the helo door and tasted it. Well, using the helo was out.

He fired at the red gorp. Why was it that color? The red blended with some orange and yellow hues on the creature's stomach. Its round belly was swollen to what looked like the bursting point. The bullet ricocheted off the creature and struck a rock above the helo. Waste of time, but it did get the creature's attention. It opened its cavernous jaws and bellowed. Its long tongue rolled out and it sprayed poison all over the helo. Its four eyes were on stalks. Three of them rolled in Cain's direction while one remained focused on the helo. Cain leaped to his feet and screamed. "Over here," while he waved his arms and jumped up and down. "Come eat me." Cain hoped if the creature got close enough, one of the high-velocity bullets would penetrate its thick hide.

The red gorp seemed to consider, stopped for a second, and suddenly barfed up parts of the guide and the hunters. The smaller gorp immediately swallowed them as Bat, Ju and Deforest exited the helo through the rear door and ran toward Cain. The four of them watched in horror as the gorps entered the helo. Thomas Curran, Cain's partner, was still inside.

"Why's the gorp red?" Cain asked Bat. "I've never seen a red one."

"It's a breeding female," Bat whispered. "The little one's a male. The females get a little cranky when they're in that season and they turn red."

"I'll say," Cain said. "Why are we whispering?"

"Super good hearing," Bat hissed as the red one stuck its head out of the door in the side of the helo. "Oh crap. I think it heard us."

"Good," Cain said. "I want it closer so I can shoot it."

"Unless you're packing a cannon, bullets won't get through the red one's hide. Too big," Bat said. "Skin's way thick."

The purple one dropped the helo door and started sniffing around the red one's tail. She dropped her rotor and attacked the purple male. The two shrieked at each other as they circled. "She must not be ready," Cain said to Bat.

"Oh, she's ready," Bat replied. "If she wasn't, she'd just kill him. She probably will anyway after he's bred her."

"I once knew a woman like that," Cain said. The rear door of the helo formed a ramp. A motorized air sled suddenly shot out the back door of the helo and down the ramp. Both gorps looked up as Thomas Curran drove the speeding sled around the edge of the helo, turned sharply, spraying dust and gravel, and shot toward Cain and his small group. The gorps followed.

The quiet inside the wall was a shock after the howling wind and driving rain of the jungle. Once the entire party was inside. Logan shut the hatch with a clank. The only sound was their panting.

Knock and Fenfang sat next to Logan with their backs to the wall. The darkness wrapping around them was so thick Logan swore he could feel it on his skin. Fenfang lit her battery-powered torch and lifted it high. The blueish light illuminated a bunch of ragtag, scruffy, filthy, exhausted people huddling together inside the narrow confines of the wall. From the outside, the thickness of the wall couldn't be determined. In here, it was easy to see, the wall was about three-feet wide. The top was too far up for Fang's light to penetrate. It went on as far as they could see in both directions. It was a clear road for them to travel for as long as they wanted to follow. Logan could only assume the hatch they came through would be repeated further down the wall.

A sudden noise in the terrible quiet startled all of them. It was the sound of well-oiled wheels turning. Logan leaped to his feet. "Hand me the torch," he said to Fang. Logan fanned the beam of light over the floor of the wall. A thick layer of dust had two tracks dug into it. A wheeled carrier or vehicle of some kind traveled up and down this corridor all of the time and if Logan was right, it was close by and getting closer.

He looked up and down the long empty stretch in both directions and saw nothing. "Please to turn off the torch," Raj said.

Logan clicked it off. "There," Raj said.

Logan squinted his eyes and saw a tiny light closing in from the western section of the wall. "What is it?"

"Maintenance?" Fenfang said.

"Dude, not to worry, we're gonna find out in just a moment." Knock drew his weapon and crouched in the dust with it pointed at the approaching light.

The rolling noise grew closer and the light became larger until it was plain to see it was a headlamp on a motorized cart of some kind. The big question; was it manned?

When the cart was fifty feet away, Logan saw it contained a hooded person, crouched over the front. The cart slowed and stopped inches away from Knock. Knock stood up, kept his weapon pointed at the cart and walked around it to stand by the crouched figure. "Hello," it said and threw back its hood.

"Dude," Knock said. "Who are you?"

A small, hunch-backed, elderly man climbed off the cart. "I'm a watcher. We got one out here all the time hoping to find people like you. Don't happen much, but every once in a while, we come across runaways or lostees like you."

Logan stepped forward. He thrust out his hand. "My name's Logan, Logan Hall." Logan quickly assessed the cart. It was a maintenance sled with plenty of room on it for equipment and workers. Probably used during construction to haul both up and down the length of the wall.

"Hi, Logan, I'm Milton Cooper."

The rest of Logan's party began jabbering excitedly around Milton and his sled. "What group do you belong to?" Logan asked. "I mean, if you don't mind sayin'."

Milton stared intently into Logan's eyes. Logan felt for a moment like they were the only two people on Earth. "I'm gonna trust you. At least for now. Could change on a dime. Been known to be wrong, but I heard of you stealin' the battleship. We all heard of you going to the moon and rescuing folks. I'm part of a group known simply as The Resistance. We plan to take our planet back and get rid of the alien filth runnin' things."

"There's a revolutionary force?" Logan was stunned.

"Damn straight and we're global. Did you think you were the only one pissed off about Sopore and what's happening to our world? Kruellians got it took over and they're 40lanning' to destroy our world just like they do every world they control. We got plans. Big plans. Now load yer folks up and let's skedaddle. Every blue moon the Company sends a cleaner through here and it destroys everything it finds."

Logan waved his people onto the maintenance sled. It was tight, but everyone found a spot. He sat next to Milton. "Where's your headquarters?"

"Never you mind. I don't trust *any* of you that much."

Chapter Seven

Professor Goswami sat still as death in a straight-backed chair inside a large windowless office. The office could be anywhere, in a building or deep underground. There was no way to tell. The only things differentiating the office from any other military office were the photos of blond and Asian women decorating the walls. All the women had very large breasts. Goswami shook his head. Apparently, the aliens felt an attraction to the female humans. He remembered the posters on the wall in another office. The one where he'd met the CEO, K'Vogen. He'd assumed the CEO was just using a human's office and thus the posters. Maybe this was now the case. Maybe this alien was just borrowing the office. It would be very strange indeed if these aliens desired human women.

The grotesque alien sitting behind the desk appeared to be speaking into his hand. From where Goswami sat, he thought he saw a glimmer of a face inside the alien's palm.

The alien had four hands. Two of those hands had finely articulated fingers with two opposable thumbs. The other set of hands were weapons with four nasty clawed digits, each talon curved and filed sharp. Goswami had to assume a kind of communication device was actually implanted into the alien's hand, either embedded, or perhaps surgically inserted into the palm of one of his articulated hands.

As long as Goswami was quiet, his thoughts were his own. Whenever decisions had to be made, his passenger would make them, and Goswami had no choice but to obey. He'd tried every kind of resistance. When he refused to perform a task his passenger wanted, pain would explode in his neck right at his brainstem. The hideous bug the aliens had inserted into him was wrapped around his spine somewhere close to his neck. It could send excruciating pain up, to his head, or down to his lower body. Goswami had been experimenting to see how long he could take the pain, how long he could resist. The longest he'd been able to stand the pain, so far, had been sixteen seconds. He'd passed out after his last bout of resistance. The bug had been very upset.

The alien behind the desk snapped his palm shut cutting off his com unit. His smile revealed two rows of pointed teeth inside a small, wet mouth with thin rubbery lips. He twirled the end of his drooping black mustache. "We have news of your peoples, Professor," the alien said. "My name is Vaerfeky. I come from a vastly superior world. We travel in space many for many of our generations. You peoples new to the galaxy. We notice you have nice world here with many interesting organisms. We taking it. You will helps us." He giggled. "Of coursing, you no choice have."

Goswami felt the bug inside him squirm. The alien got up and walked behind Goswami. When the Professor tried to turn around to follow his movements, Vaerfeky pushed him back into his seat. He used a hand-held device to shine a purple light on Goswami's neck. The light was cool on his skin. Vaerfeky leaned close to look at the spot on Goswami's skin lit by the purple light. "Aaah yes, the styngar worm has a good hold on your greater occipital nerve."

Vaerfeky leaned around Goswami to stare into his eyes. Goswami noted without blinking that Vaerfeky's slanted eyes were not brown but a murky gray-brown like dirty dishwater. "Styngar worm make your life hell, huh? But you does our bidding, so no matter to us."

Goswami didn't feel like answering the alien, but the worm forced an unwilling mumble out of his mouth. "We are ready to do your bidding, great master."

"Good, because I have location of you friends and soon you will lead them to us."

Goswami willed his eyes closed to block out the vision of the gloating Vaerfeky. He succeeded and rejoiced inside. One small victory over the worm's control. He felt the immediate stab of pain in the back of his head, but ignored it and held his eyes closed in silent rebellion for a count of seventy. More than one minute. When he opened his eyes again, he was dizzy from the pain, but with a feeling of renewed hope. Hope that all was not lost and he might be able to outwit the worm when the critical moment arrived. And it would arrive. Goswami had no doubt of that.

When Thomas pulled up beside the hunting party in the air sled, everyone piled on. The sled floated on a cushion of air. When they'd loaded onto it, Curran hit the hand throttles and sped away from the charging gorp. He circled around and landed close to the tents. "Might as well get everything we can," he said. "Hunters ain't coming back."

Bat glanced over at the helo's broken hulk. The body parts barfed up by the female gorp were gone, eaten by the male, but he could still see them in his mind. The image had not faded. "What about the kid and the two others?"

"Not our problem," Cain said. "Kid's a big boy and he has Small Paul and the guard to take care of him."

Bat shrugged. "I guess."

Hurry and load these supplies," Thomas said. "Red gorp just spotted us."

They all worked feverishly, tossing cases of food and bottled water onto the sled. Bat looked down the gorge and saw the two gorp closing in. "We better hustle," he said. "Mrs. Nasty and her hubby-of-the-moment are almost here."

They leaped on the sled and Thomas hit the throttles. The sled took off just as the two gorp arrived and began tearing into the tents squealing and squawking. Tent poles flew as the two gigantic creatures ripped the nylon tents apart and tossed the few supplies left behind into the air.

"Well, that was interesting," Bat said to Ju. He was on the back of the sled beside her, holding a box of protein bars in his lap. She held another box filled with caf packs and real tea.

"First time I ever saw a live gorp," she said. "I've helped clean hides after a hunt, but I never saw one alive."

"They taste pretty good if you can get them cleaned before the poison taints the meat," he told her. "I've seen a lot of picture books. They look like a cross between a huge bird and a dinosaur. If the dinosaur had eyes on stalks and six legs which they didn't."

Ju giggled. "I haven't read many books and I haven't been anywhere but Gliese. Have you traveled much?"

Bat threw back his shoulders, aware of pride in his family history. "I been all over the known galaxy. Been to a bunch of different planets in a bunch of different solar systems. I've seen creatures way weirder than gorp. We had a digital library on my father's ship. I read almost all of the books."

Ju lifted adoring eyes to his face. "That sounds like a wonderful life."

Bat nodded. "It was cool, but now it's over. Somehow, I gotta get a message to my family. If they don't already know, the Company is throwing them away like an empty soda can. They're in terrible danger."

"Maybe Cain will let you take this sled back to the hunter's camp and use the com equipment on the helo," Ju said. "You might be able to get them a message." She looked thoughtful. "Maybe they could come get us."

"Too many of you," Bat said. "Our ships are small and some are really old. My dad just refitted his with the new Stanhope drive." Bat sniffed. "But he's dead and the ship's probably been stolen by the Guild."

"I'm sorry about your father," Ju said. "I never knew mine. Mom was transported with us when we were little. The only father

I ever knew was Logan's dad, Dek, and he wasn't exactly warm and fuzzy. He was a strong influence on us. Especially on Fenfang. I miss her and Logan. I wish they would come back."

"Has anyone heard from them?"

"Just the message Shayna got right before we had to move. All it said was they had escaped and were hiding in a jungle Logan thought was Texas. Nothing else. He said Dek was dead and Shayna's mom was with him but her dad was dead, too. So many people have died. I hate the Company."

When they found the rest of the party, Bat saw Shayna had set up a hidden camp under the embankment shading the dry riverbed. It was almost impossible to see. They quickly unloaded the sled and stashed their stolen supplies out of sight.

Cain grabbed Bat's shoulder. "I know you want to contact your people."

Bat nodded. "Yeah, I need to warn them. If it's not already too late."

"Take this sled back to the helo and leave it there. I'd love to have it, but there's a tracker on it and the Company will find us."

"Can't you disable it?"

Cain shrugged. "I might be able to, but it would take time and time is something we don't have. The Company's gonna come looking for that hunting party soon. I want this sled right where it should be."

Bat nodded. "I'll take it back for sure. Can I use the helo's com to contact my people?"

Cain grinned. "That was my plan. If they can't send us help, maybe they can send us some supplies. We're never gonna make it across the big desert without more supplies."

"Okay, can I take Ju with me?"

"Sure, and go soon. Sun will be up in two hours. You need to be out of there by then."

Ju was excited about going with him. Bat fiddled with the hand throttles for a minute, got the hang of them and they shot down the dry river bed. It only took them thirty minutes to get back to the camp. Bat slowed the sled. "See anything?" He asked Ju.

She had the field glasses up and was scanning the camp and the destroyed helo. "No gorp," she whispered.

"What about the fat kid and the guards?"

"They could be hiding inside the helo, but I don't see them anywhere."

Bat guided the sled around to the back of the helo, staying out of sight as much as possible. The sled was painted rust-colored camo to blend in with the Gliese background. It had been designed to haul supplies for hunters in the Gliese outback and was hard to see for that reason. The sled was also silent, intentionally so. The power came from a big solar battery. Bat glanced at the power indicator as he steered behind the helo and saw it would need charging soon.

"See anyone?" he whispered.

Ju still had the glasses up. She dropped them and scanned the helo. "Nope, not so far."

Bat stopped the sled in the dark shadows behind the helo. The purple moon hung low on the horizon. When it set, darkness would be complete until the sun came up.

Bat climbed off the sled and motioned for Ju to stay on it. The helo seemed empty and quiet. The gorp had torn out some of the insides of the aircraft. Wires dangled from a control panel hanging off the edge of the rear door. He slid close to the helo and laid his ear against the metal side. It was quiet. Taking a deep breath, he entered the wrecked aircraft. It was dark as space inside. He pulled a small flashlight out of his cargo pocket and clicked it on. There was a lot of damage. Bat hoped the gorp hadn't destroyed the com units. He took one step down to enter the cockpit. The main controls were destroyed. The wires looked chewed on and the smell of burning electrical equipment hung in the air. A black spot on the control panel still smoldered.

The com center for the helo was a recessed space in the small hallway between the step down and the two seats for the pilots. It was a big bird and it had a huge com center. Maybe because it was recessed and separate from the controls, the gorps had missed it. And then maybe the control panel hadn't tasted that great. One or two bites and they realize it wasn't food. The fire probably encouraged their distaste.

Bat went to work on the com. He sat on the rolling stool set in front of the console. A tiny keyboard rolled out when he punched a button. He knew his relatives monitored a certain band for messages from other Tong members. He figured out how to set the signal for that band and began typing on the small keyboard like a maniac. It didn't take long for him to get an answer. It came through on a holo screen that appeared when the message blinked in.

His people were on Gliese's purple moon. They were hiding on the dark side. They'd seen a lot of activity, new ships landing on the old spaceport in Gliese City, and many landing in the spaceport where Bat's father's ship was docked. All of the ships had been either Company or Guild ships, many sparkling in their newness and very high-tech. He quickly understood he was talking to his uncle, Sammy Lee. He told Sammy about his father. Sammy said they already knew Toghus Khan was dead. The Company had broadcast video of his hanging. Sammy said he was very sorry for Bat, but glad he'd survived.

"We have many ships here," Sammy said. "They're coming in from all over the galaxy. Tong is out. Guild is in. We must hide."

"I know," bat answered. "Can you pick me and a few friends up?"

"We have a shuttle we stole from the Guild at their base on Detheon in the Trappist system. We snatched it right before the Company went nuclear on us. How many friends you talking 'bout?"

"Forty or so," Bat typed.

"Where you get forty friends?"

"Colony here on Gliese. You know, people who escaped the mines and the folks rescued from the moon by that guy Logan."

"Okay," Sammy replied. "The shuttle should hold them. We had intel from some embedded people in the Company, so we knew this was coming. The surprise was the timing. We didn't expect it to happen so soon, but we were preparing. Our plan is to run to Waterworld on Europa. We stole a freighter from the new port the Company is building on the southern continent. It's in fair shape and big enough to get us to the fringes of the galaxy if that's where we have to go to be safe."

"When can you get us?" Bat shot back.

"Need your coordinates. We have you located. Is this your pickup point?"

Bat rotated his neck and thought. This helo could be a bad spot for them. The Company would send people to search for the hunters. The question was how soon. He nodded his head even though no one was there to see him. "Yes. Give me twelve hours." Bat figured in twelve hours, it would be dark again. If the Company sent any people here to search, they could be gone by then. They certainly wouldn't hang out here in the dark.

Sammy's answer was brief. "Be ready. We have room for sixty-three."

That was more than enough room for the entire colony. Bat's chest swelled with pride. He was going to be able to save all of them. He was shocked when he stepped out of the helo into the weak light of a Gliese dawn to see the fat kid from the hunting party sitting on the sled with Ju. His clothes were in shreds and he was bleeding from dozens of small cuts. His face was swollen to twice its normal size, his eyes almost invisible. He held up his hand in a feeble wave and Bat noticed his fingers were as fat as sausages.

“Who are you? Where’d you come from?” Bat demanded. He shot Ju a questioning look and she lifted one eyebrow. He thought she was adorable and smart.

“My name’s Mark Moretti. I was in the hunting party. Gorps ate ‘em all. There was screaming and blood and I ran and ran.” He burst into hysterical sobs. “My family will pay you to take me home,” he wailed.

Bat laughed. “What’d you tell him, Ju?”

“I laughed at him, too.”

Bat looked the overweight teen over carefully. His hunting togs, so carefully chosen and ridiculously expensive, hung in ragged strips from his body. Bat could see his under shorts were covered by hearts and barely fit. His belly drooped over them and Bat had to look away. Too much dude flesh was hanging out everywhere. The kid’s brown hair was long and at one time had been carefully styled. He had an earring made from a bluish gem Bat had never seen before high on the top of his left ear. His eyes might have been blue, but they were hard to see set under a heavy brow and thick brown eyebrows carefully plucked into steep arches giving him a startled look.

“Listen, Mark, sorry you had such a rough time. I think you must have run into some thorn trees. They’re poisonous. Looks like a lot of your scratches are swelling. We don’t have any anti venom for that and we have no transport except this sled. The Company will be here hunting for your party. Probably soon. I can’t allow you to be found. Sorry, man, but we can’t leave you here. You’ve seen us.”

Mark began sobbing. “Don’t kill me. Please.”

Bat sighed and closed his eyes. “Not planning to. You have to come with us and that means walking.”

“Why can’t I just wait here? I won’t tell them about you. I promise.”

Bat opened a tool chest under the control panel of the sled and pulled out a long length of nylon cord. "Told you, man, you'll rat us out. I can see it in your eyes."

"No, no I swear I won't."

"Ju," Bat said. "Tie his hands and then rope them to his neck and leave enough for a leash."

Ju rolled her eyes. "I have to touch him?"

"Well, I ain't," Bat said. "At least you're a chick. I don't touch almost-naked dudes. Ever."

Mark's panic was obvious. He turned and looked ready to bolt. Bat pulled his blaster and poked Mark in the back. "Don't make me use this. I will fry you if you run."

Mark groaned and allowed Ju to pull his hands behind him. Unfortunately, his bulk prevented his wrists from getting close enough for her to tie together. She rolled her eyes again and tied his hands in front of his jiggling belly. Tears ran out of Mark's swollen eyes and down his flabby cheeks. "You're gonna kill me. I know it."

"Dude," Bat's voice was filled with irritation. This kid was so much more trouble than he was worth, but killing him was not in Bat's makeup. "If I was going to kill you, you'd be dead by now. Why would I drag you with me? Certainly, ain't for giggles. Man, look at you. Stop blubbering. You're an embarrassment to your sex."

Ju ran the cord from Mark's tied hands, up his chest, around his neck twice where she looped it and made a leash out of the six feet leftover. She handed Bat the end.

"Why we have to walk?" Mark sobbed. "My feet are killing me."

Mark's one remaining boot had holes. "What'd you do with your boots?"

"When the two gorp caught Dwight, our guide and my pop, they ate them." He moaned and gulped. "It was so gross. Blood was everywhere. I barfed my guts out, but I ran into a rocky gorge. I kept tripping and falling and the thorn trees were everywhere. I caught my foot between two rocks. I had to leave my boot behind, and then there was this hole, I stepped in it and something attacked my foot. It ate my boot." Mark dissolved into more sobbing and a fresh flood of tears.

"We have to leave the sled here," Bat said. "So, your choices are; one, I kill you now, or two, you walk. Choose."

"Walking sounds great," Mark said. "I'll walk. I'm glad to walk. I love walking. Walking totally works for me. Let's go. I'll show you how much I like walking. I can walk fast, too. I'm a terrific walker. Walking is good for me. Everyone says so. I love walking. I can walk for miles. You'll see."

Bat sighed again. "Can you shut up?" He glanced at Ju who was fighting back laughter. Her control finally burst and she snorted. "It's not funny, Ju," Bat said with a grin. "He's a pain in the ass. I can't imagine what Cain's going to say."

"Can you do anything, Mark?" Ju asked kindly.

"I play a lot of games," he answered. "I'm a terrific gamer. I play all the time. You should see my scores. I'm better than almost anybody."

Ju sighed. "Gaming isn't a skill, Mark. Do you have like any *real* skills?"

Mark brightened. "When all my friends are offline, I hack into their computers." His face reddened. "I guess I shouldn't a done that, but it was so easy. I can hack into almost any system. I'm home alone a lot. Nothing else to do. Pop worked all the time. Mom likes Soap so she sleeps a lot." Mark sobbed. "Now he's dead. Oh god, Mom's gonna kill me."

Ju patted his back awkwardly. "Try not to worry so much. I'm sure your mom will be fine."

Bat snorted and Ju shot him a dirty look. "Try to be nice, Bat, Mark just lost his father. You have that in common. Were you able to get in touch with your family?"

Bat nodded and tilted his head to indicate he didn't want to talk in front of the prisoner. She stepped closer and whispered right into his ear. Her warm breath on his neck was disturbing, but disturbing in a good way. He stared into her eyes, leaned close and whispered, his lips touching her perfect shell-like ear. She shivered. Bat saw goose-flesh ripple down her long, slender neck. "Pick up for all of us in twelve hours."

"Oh," she breathed and placed her hand in his free one.

"Guys," Mark said. "How far do we have to go?"

"Shut up," Ju and Bat said in unison.

Chapter Eight

As Professor Goswami sat quietly in the alien leader's office, he examined the posters hung on the walls. Many of the women resembled Knock's holo-maid Helga. He seemed to prefer blond, Scandinavian-types with huge mammary glands. The oriental women had smaller breasts, but looked like warriors. They brandished swords and had been photographed in fighting poses.

Vaerfeky was holding a meeting between two other aliens and five humans. One of the humans Goswami recognized as a famous Army general, General Kisliak. "Why Area 51?" Kisliak asked.

The gathered aliens spoke among themselves in hushed tones about a bunker filled with a secret weapon. This bunker was supposed to be in Area 51. Goswami had heard of this secret base hidden in the Southern Nevada desert. The Company had used it to build black weapons and there was a hidden airstrip and a huge installation under Groom Lake. It was also supposed to hold artifacts relating to aliens. Goswami thought that was pretty funny considering who was now sitting at the desk in front of him.

"We liked site," Vaerfeky said to Kisliak. "Humans already there working on some pretty sophisticated weapons, so we just made bigger the operation and moved into the base our antimatter cannon. Works good for us."

One of the humans raised his hand hesitantly.

"What you do that for?" Vaerfeky snapped.

"Uh, I have a question."

"Speak it," Vaerfeky growled.

"What does an antimatter cannon do?"

"We prepare," Vaerfeky smiled. "Soon humans will fight us back. Always this happens. Can't be stopped. Stupid races don't understand our power. How much we know. Kruellians very old race. We've destroyed more worlds than you puny humans know exist. Black matter is harnessed, antimatter you understand antimatter?"

Kisliak nodded and Goswami stared at Vaerfeky. This weapon sounded horrific. The alien spoke of it with obvious pride. For a moment, Goswami wondered why he was even here in this room. They must feel the worm had such total control of him, he was like furniture. He'd been included in several other strange meetings, mostly ignored, but occasionally trotted out as Vaerfeky's pet human. When Goswami had a rebellious thought, the styngar worm wrapped around his spine squeezed. Each time it exerted its control of him, Goswami fought back. Sometimes he even won.

Vaerfeky seemed to read Goswami's mind. Either that or perhaps the styngar worm had a way to communicate with the aliens. His beady, black, slanted eyes focused on Goswami like tiny lasers. "You," Vaerfeky snapped. "Stand up and bark like a dog."

Goswami struggled with the worm's control, but lost. He stood up and began barking.

Vaerfeky and the other aliens chortled with glee. "Not big dog. Bark like little Chihuahua."

Goswami yapped like a tiny dog.

"Drop to the floor and bite General Kisliak's ankles."

Goswami actually groaned as he exerted agonizing effort fighting to not fall to his hands and knees. The worm squeezed. Stabbing pain in the region of his spine right below his neck hit him like a hot poker. To stop the pain, he dropped to the floor and immediately attacked the General's ankles. He grabbed a piece of the General's starched, knife-edged, khakis in his teeth and shook his head. All of the aliens and one human laughed like maniacs. Goswami's head felt like it would explode as he fought to spit the fabric out of his mouth.

"Now expel gas out of your butthole in loud explosion," Vaerfeky's order was issued through a storm of giggles.

Goswami's face redden, but he farted long and loudly.

"Enough," Vaerfeky ordered. "Resume sitting in your appointed seat."

Goswami clambered to his feet, face beet red, and sat down.

Vaerfeky continued bragging about his weapon as though nothing untoward had occurred. "We steal weapon from Rigellians," Vaerfeky said in a supercilious tone. "Them older race than us, but very weak. Look like lizard things with only two arms. They think peace is the best thing. Stupid lizards were using black matter generator to terraform worlds. Didn't know it could be used as weapon." Vaerfeky laughed uproariously. "We killed most of them, but they hide on bases we can't find." Vaerfeky growled. "We still hunts them. One day we wipe them out of universe and take their treasures which they hide from us. Black Matter Cannons are so powerful they can destroy your moon. Very, very dangerous. If they are not cared for properly, they can self-destruct this entire planet. So, this is why we have them in the very safe Area 51. On old military base and all around is desert and a big lake. Safest place on this planet for our weapon."

The five humans were united in looking horrified. Vaerfeky pointed at Kisliak. He was wearing a military uniform with a lot of medals. "You be in charge of this base and the weapon. If anything happens to base, you make sure it not happen to cannons. Take these other human creatures with you and gather as many as you need from the ranks. I will send one of my people and this dog," he pointed at Goswami, "to watch over."

The leader of the humans spoke again. "Is the weapon operational?" His voice was more like a squeaky croak than a regular human voice and Goswami wondered if he also had a styngar worm riding his spine.

"Not yet. Is still parts coming on ships from Thyria. We have anti-matter accelerator there to manufacture the black particles.

We harvest raw anti-mater from nearby black hole." He giggled. "Learned all this from the Rigellians. Thyria was their main world."

"You," Vaerfeky pointed at Goswami. "You will go with these humans and report to me directly." He handed Goswami a wrist com. The worm inside him stirred. "Yes, master," Goswami replied in a reedy voice. "I will do as ordered."

"Of course, you will do this. Have no choice in matter." Vaerfeky laughed again. "Humans are so weak." He waved his four arms and spit flew as he laughed. "Kruellians will soon rule entire universe while all races in the universe grovel in the dirt and do as we order."

Milton drove the maintenance cart loaded with Logan's people down the narrow tunnel inside the wall separating the US from the world, but mostly Mexico, even though Mexico no longer existed as a country. The world had become one giant entity ruled by the Company. Nations had ceased to exist under Company rule. Genetically altered corn was raised everywhere to keep the population sedated and most of the poor and uneducated from all the bigger countries had been transported to mining worlds where they lived short lives working like animals in Company-controlled mines. Need for replacements was endless. Earth was running short of cattle for their mining operation. The Company ruling class had come from the top one percent of rich humans, the billionaires who cared nothing for anyone but themselves and making more and more money.

As mile after mile of ground was covered, Logan wondered where Milton was taking them. Milton turned the maintenance cart into a side tunnel that began to angle down, deeper into the earth where Milton stopped the cart. Logan looked around finding they were in a large open cavern with water at one end. Milton climbed off the cart and indicated this was the end of the line.

"You folks get out here. There's water and some food in crates over there. Most of it's Sopore-free, but some ain't. I'd eat sparingly cause food with no Sopore is at a premium. They've even figured out how to get it into the water. That there spring over there is good drinking water and it's free of any Sopore."

Logan helped Shayna's mother off the cart and then approached Milton. "Is this your headquarters?"

Milton laughed. "No, it ain't. Think I'm stupid enough to bring a bunch of strangers into our nest? I don't think so. I'm gonna go tell Zacharia about you and he'll decide what to do. I'm just one of his lieutenants. I patrol the wall. We got us a whole army all over the world, and even though I heard of Logan Hall and his dad, don't mean you're him. Got to do some checking."

Logan glanced around the spacious cavern. At least they weren't in a bug and snake infested jungle anymore and it wasn't raining. His people were all exhausted. Their situation was still precarious, but definitely better. "So, you're leaving us here?"

"For the moment. I'll be bringing someone back with me to look you over and talk to all your people. We gotta be careful. I know you can understand that."

Logan nodded. "Okay. For the moment, we'll sit tight, but if you're gone too long, we'll be gone, too. I have to take care of these folks. They're my responsibility. You understand that?"

Milton nodded. "Rest easy, son, I'll be back shortly. Zacharia's gonna want to meet Logan Hall. If that's who you really are. Your name is like a rallying cry in some circles. You're the only person who ever went to the moon and successfully escaped with prisoners. That speaks for your courage and it has given us all hope. When one person can stand against the Company and succeed, there is hope for us all. Like I said. You're famous."

Milton climbed onto his maintenance cart, turned it back into the tunnel leading to the wall system and disappeared. "What do you think? Loge? I mean, do you think he's for real, or should we bug out?" Knock asked.

Logan didn't know what they should do. He wanted to trust Milton, but he'd learned the hard way not to trust anyone. He looked over the tired, dispirited group of people he'd brought out of the jungle into this cavern and closed his eyes. "Everyone is so tired. Let's rest and eat something. After that, if Milton ain't back, we'll bug out."

Fenfang put her hand on Logan's arm. "I know being the leader is hard on you. We're here for you, Logan." She looked at Knock. "We got your back."

"Am I making the right decision?" He asked her.

"Dude, these people are beat," Knock said. "We don't even know where we are. That ride through the wall covered miles. I'll take first watch. Let's go through those crates, find something we can eat, and rest. I'm pretty sure you're making the right call. After we're rested, I think we should send out a scouting party. We need to know where we're at."

"The kids are tired and everyone here is about on their last legs," Fang said.

"Would it be acceptable for us to go through the crates?" Raj spoke from behind Logan. "Everyone is thinking about eating. They are starving."

Logan waved his hand toward the crates. "Tell everyone to eat as much as they can and then sleep," he told Raj.

"It is good to hear you make such a choice, Logan," Raj said. "I don't think anyone can go much farther without rest."

Logan and Knock tore into the cardboard boxes and crates of food. The crates contained fruit, some spoiled, but most of it edible. He passed out apples and oranges. The boxes held cans of beans and soy-based protein in soy gravy. Disgusting food, laced with Sopore, but it was protein. There were large cans of dry biscuits. These were filled with Sopore. Logan pushed his people to eat all of it. The Sopore would wear off and as long as they ate no more, they wouldn't be addicted.

Filled with food, partially sedated by the drug in it, the people spread their blanket rolls out and fell into a deep sleep. Logan, Knock and Fenfang consumed no Sopore. They ate dried fruit, apples, stared longingly at the biscuits, but ate none. Fang and Knock took first watch and Logan laid down beside Corey and Raj and fell instantly into sleep.

When he woke up, Knock was gone. Fenfang was sitting on a crate with Knock's neurolizer on her knees. Logan stretched and stood up. Every bone in his body ached from sleeping on the rock floor and from sleeping so hard. After he got a drink of water and used the makeshift latrine set up in one corner, he sat next to Fang. "Where's Knock?"

"He took a nap, changed his shirt, and went to explore. He hates not knowing where we are. He found a tunnel he thinks might lead out of here behind the spring and took off."

Logan nodded. "He's grown up so much since I knew him back when we were kids in the tunnels under New Washington. I never thought it would happen."

"What?" Knock's voice came from behind him. Logan whirled around and smiled. "You thought I'd never grow up?" Knock said. "Hey, dude, I ain't Peter Pan."

Logan laughed. Knock could always make him smile. "Did you find out where we are?"

Knock grabbed an apple and flopped down on another crate. "Yup and you ain't gonna believe it. We ain't in Texas anymore. We're in Colorado, dude. Colorado Springs to be exact. There's a Loop station about fifty feet up that tunnel over there. It goes to the Denver Airport."

Logan nodded. "I've heard stories about people living under the airport. Stories from when I was a little kid before the Company ruled everything. Supposedly, when they built it, they screwed up five buildings. Underground buildings which were never demolished. I heard there's an enormous underground system of bunkers and fallout shelters for world leaders. It's all rumors, but maybe some of it's true."

Fang selected an apple from a crate sitting next to her and bit into it. She chewed thoughtfully for a minute. "You know," she said. "That must be where this Zacharia dude's headquarters are. That's why Milton dropped us here. Especially if the Loop goes right to the airport."

"It does," Knock said. "It's running, too. I didn't see any passengers waiting for it, but I felt the power in the lines."

Logan stood up and stretched again. The aftereffects of sleeping on the floor were wearing off. He felt rested and ready to take on anything. "We need to get out of here," he told Knock. "I don't think we should wait for Milton. Where does the Loop go in the other direction?"

"West," Knock said. "Through the Rockies and Utah heading for Vegas."

"Are there still Vagrants in Vegas?"

Knock shrugged. "I thought most of them bugged out when the Professor came through. They had all that radiation sickness and a bunch croaked. Aren't some of our folks here from Vegas?"

Logan touched Fang on the shoulder. "Ask around. Maybe we should go that way."

"Dude," Knock said. "We can't ride the Loop. We got no credit discs, none of us have chips, we'd have to walk all the way. It's like a thousand miles."

Logan glared at his friend. Knock was wearing his Zombieland T-shirt. The one with the list of rules. "Can't you see I'm trying to figure out what's best for us?" Logan erupted.

"He's afraid he's making the wrong decision," Fang said gently. "Look, Logan, you have to trust somebody. I mean, we need help. We have women and children here, and old people. If Milton is full of crap, then we're screwed because he's our only option. Just accept it and stop driving yourself nuts questioning every decision you make."

Knock pointed to his T-shirt, looked down and indicated rule number sixteen. “When opportunity knocks.” He grinned. “Or maybe this one. “Rule number twenty-two; When in doubt know your way out. As long as we know where we are, we can always run.”

Logan grabbed his head and squeezed. “You’re right. I’m driving myself crazy worrying about every little thing. We can’t walk all the way to Vegas. And I remember Professor Goswami saying he treated a bunch of Vegas Vagrants for radiation sickness. I’m just thinkin’ it’s scary trusting someone we barely know. What if these people turn us over to the Company? I bet there’s a big reward.”

“Take a chance on Milton,” Knock said. “I feel like he’s on the level. Don’t you?”

Logan sighed and flopped onto the crate again. “I guess so. I’ve been running so long, running seems like the only option.”

“If there is a huge world-wide resistance like Milton said, this is where we need to be.” Knock grabbed Logan’s shoulder. “They need you, dude. People will rally around your name. You escaped from the moon with a star ship. You’re a hero.”

“I don’t feel very heroic,” Logan muttered. “I feel scared.”

“Rule seventeen,” Knock said. “Don’t be a hero, but he crossed that off and changed it. Remember? Changed it to be a hero.”

Chapter Nine

The ship sent by Bat's relatives was exactly like a Company shuttle. The Company kept starships, space craft that could travel to distant galaxies and far away planets, in orbit and shuttled big shots and new conscripts for the mines to the planet in them. When it landed, the colonists rushed for it. Bat loaded them into the bus-like aircraft and slammed the door behind them. "Go!" He shouted to the pilot.

The pilot ignited the thrusters and those not in seats were thrown to the floor. Shayna was one of the lucky ones. She even had her crash harness buckled. Bat, Ju, and the rich kid, Mark, were knocked to the floor, but Bat leaped up almost immediately and fought the thrust to help everyone get in a seat and buckled down. The gravs were intense. Shayna felt like the child in her belly was being forced against her backbone. She held onto it with both hands. Mai threw an arm around her shoulders and held them. Shayna's look of gratitude brought a smile to Mai's face. "We so lucky get off Gliese in one piece."

Shayna couldn't speak. Her lips were drawn back and soon even Mai was forced to hold onto the arm rests. The huge thrust only lasted five minutes. When it stopped, the uncomfortable lurch of her stomach told Shayna they were out of the planet's gravitational field. There were tiny windows in the shuttle. Shayna saw the rusty planet of Gliese growing smaller and the big purple moon getting bigger.

The shuttle slowed as they neared the moon. It went from light into darkness suddenly as they headed for the dark side. The shuttle descended quickly, cruising slowly above a dusty plain as it approached a cluster of parked starships. The shuttle didn't stop. It slowly flew into the open bay doors of an enormous starship. When the doors clanked shut, the shuttle stopped. Bat leaped to his feet and hustled everyone out of their seats. "Hurry," he said to Shayna. "The ship is taking off in seconds. The Company has found us and are sending some of the Guild ships to destroy everything. They want us all dead."

They ran out of the shuttle into an open hanger area with several small fighter ships and two more shuttles. Bat led them to an elevator. Shayna waited until Mark caught up. For the life of her, she couldn't understand why this useless, overweight, spoiled kid was being dragged along with them. Bat must have a softer heart than she'd supposed because he was the one who'd insisted they drag him along. "We can't very well leave him here," Bat had explained. "For starts, he'll probably die. And then if he gets discovered and saved, he's going to tell them everything he can think of about us. We have to take him. Or we have to kill him. He's just a kid. I couldn't."

Cain had wanted to off the kid. "He's heavy, he'll literally weigh us down," Cain had explained. "Who knows what kind of hardships we'll have to endure to escape and to live. He's not used to doing without like we are. It would be kinder to put him down than to let him suffer." Shayna had almost voted with Cain to do just that, put him down, kill him and leave him on Gliese, but he was a kid, so she'd voted to save him.

When everyone had gone before her, including Mark, and climbed into the lift with Ju and Bat, Shayna reluctantly stepped inside. The familiar weightless feeling made her close her eyes. Try as she might, she could not get over being terrified of elevators. The ship shuddered and Shayna stumbled. Ju caught her elbow and steadied her. "We're taking off," Bat said.

Once off the elevator they were in a corridor covered with peeling green paint, rusty spots and a floor of metal rods. It was hard to walk. Doors led off the corridor. They looked more like hatches on a ship. This starship was old and had apparently been built during the first years of space travel. "How old is this rust bucket?" Mark asked.

"You don't wanna know," Bat said. "And I resent it being called a rust bucket. It's saving your fat, useless life. Don't push me. I can still give your gigantic ass to Cain."

Mark's horrified expression spoke volumes. "You wouldn't. That guy's a freaking monster. He was gonna kill me. He said he wanted to put me down like I was a sick dog. He's got no heart. He's old, and mean, and cruel. Please don't let him get me." Mark began sobbing. "Don't let him put me down. I'll do anything. I'll work. I'll walk as far as you want. I'll clean and mop and sweep and wash dishes. I'll do anything. I'm a terrific worker and I can endure plenty of hardship. I'm so sorry I called the ship a rust bucket. It's obviously a wonderful starship that's taking us to safety."

Bat held his hand in front of Mark's yapping mouth. "Stop," Bat commanded. "Can you be quiet?" He turned to Ju. "He needs an off button."

Ju laughed and touched Bat's hand. "I'll help him learn to be quiet."

He ran one finger along her jawline and smiled as he opened one of the hatches. It led to a common room. There was a holo screen on one wall, couches, and a caf machine and a food preparation area. The holo screen showed space and the outer skin of the ship. The doors of the hanger bay opened and two fighters flew out. The ship shuddered and groaned. More fighters appeared from the other side of the ship, formed into two groups and shot off. "I guess we're under attack," Bat said. "I'm gonna go see what I can do."

Ju grabbed his arm. "You're not going to fly one of those things, are you?"

"If they need a pilot I sure will," he said with a cocky grin. "Don't wanna miss out on the action."

When Bat was gone, Ju grabbed Shayna. “I can’t stand the thought of him out there fighting the Company. How do you handle Logan being gone all the time and so far away on Earth?”

Shayna’s smile was wistful. Ju was only sixteen. Bat must be her first crush and she had it bad. “I think about good things like my baby and try not to worry,” she said. “It’s wonderful when I hear from him, but when I don’t, I pretend he’s taking a trip for fun and is having a good time. If I worried about what he’s really doing, or even knew, I’d probably go nuts.”

Ju flopped on one of the molded foam couches and stared at the holo screen. A sudden phalanx of Company fighters, obvious by their sleek, shiny blue-gray metal skin and their double cockpits Two pilots for each one sitting side by side. There were six of them and one suddenly exploded. Flaming parts hurtled toward the cameras sending them their holo images. The scene on the holo screen flickered, blinked out, and then reappeared with striations across it. Ju gasped as two Tong fighters shot by the cameras firing laser cannons at the retreating Company fighters. Most of the Tong fighters were black with four cannons mounted on slender wings. The propulsion system took up most of the aircraft, a giant tube emitting heat and flames in the rear of the fighter.

“See,” Shayna said. “Tong fighters are faster.”

Mark’s face was the color of chalk. “We’re all gonna die,” he moaned. “Where’s the facility?”

“What?” Shayna said.

“Bathroom, john, head, toilet, you know, the facility.”

“There’s a small door over there.” She pointed. Mark walked to it, opened it and stared for ten seconds before turning around. “It’s too small for me,” he moaned. “How can I sit on the seat? Look, there’s no space.”

Shayna peaked inside. It was small. She fought the urge to laugh out loud. “You’re just gonna have to make it work, Mark. This is a starship, it’s old, and it never was a luxury liner.”

He stuffed his bulk through the small door. Shayna had to look. Ju joined her and they exchanged eye rolls. Mark was stuck between the waste disposal seat, or toilet, and the hand-washing station with no way to turn around. He'd have to climb onto the seat and step over it. She shut the door. "Let him figure it out," she said to Ju who was fighting back a fit of giggles.

"We shouldn't laugh at him," Shayna admonished Ju. "He's led a different life than us. He's probably addicted to Sopore. We'll have to help him with that. And then starships aren't made for large people." They went back to the holo screen and watched as more Tong fighters streaked by chasing one lone Company fighter.

"I'm so impressed," Ju said. "The Tong has better, faster fighters than the Company. How did they manage that?"

Bat burst into the common room and grinned. "We got great mechanics. They souped up the old Company rigs we mostly stole, patched the broken ones, and copied and installed this engine we found on Cleron 8C. We found the strangest alien ships there stashed inside a mountain. The planet's dead. Burnt to a crisp in some long-forgotten space war, but there was this bunker hidden inside a slagged mountain. Most of the mountain was melted, but a huge chunk had broken off and left a cave and an entrance into the bunker.

"The Company gave us the planet because there was nothing on it. Nothing. Most of the metal and anything worth money had been incinerated or melted like that mountain. The planet is close to the shipping lanes, so we built a spaceport and a small base to maintain it. The guys stuck there get bored when nothing's happening so they explore and found these ships. Company knows nothing about them. It's our business, not theirs. They didn't want Cleron, so we got it. There's rumors ancient artifacts of crazy advanced civilizations are all over the universe. So, we found some."

Ju had leaped to her feet when she heard Bat's voice. She whirled around and Shayna saw her admiration for the young man clearly blazing from her eyes and was embarrassed for her. Time to have a serious chat with the girl. She shouldn't be throwing herself at Bat like this. Who knew what the boy was hiding under his handsome exterior. They'd just met him.

Bat seemed to be oblivious. Shayna closed her eyes. Men could be such blockheads.

Chapter Ten

When Milton returned, he brought a bigger vehicle and two people. A large black man with gray dreadlocks climbed out slowly followed by an older man with a shaved head, a long gray beard, and a sword strapped to his back. They all wore body armor, some of which looked old or homemade. Milton and the three of them walked over to Logan and his assembled companions.

"So, you're the famous Logan Hall," the tall black man said.

Logan nodded. "Don't know about famous, but, yeah, I'm Logan."

The black guy stared at Logan. "Can you prove it?"

Logan shrugged. "I've never had to." He turned to Knock and Fenfang. "Hey guys. Who am I?"

Knock shook his head and sported a cocky grin. "You're Logan Hall. Together, we rode the Lift, broke a bunch of detainees out of prison on the moon, and stole a starship."

"Fang nodded. "He's Logan Hall."

"Sorry, the black man said. "Can't just take you and your friends' word about who you are. Logan Hall is famous. He's an icon. His name is synonymous with the rebellion. Our resistance is based on his work."

Logan shook his head. "All of these people." He waved his hand to indicate everyone who traveled with him. "Will verify my identity."

"They could be trying to infiltrate our group. We have to be very careful who we let in. The Company's got spies all over the place. Someone tries to infiltrate our group all the time. We kill 'em."

"Seriously?" Logan's eyes narrowed. "You kill infiltrators? Are you sure they're infiltrating? What if they're just like us and looking for a safe place?" This was a unique experience for Logan. His identity had never been doubted. He didn't carry an ID card, had no chip, nothing to prove who he was. "How do you propose to verify my identity?" He asked the leader.

"Trial by combat. If you agree, we can go back to our headquarters. Since you're claiming to be the leader, and Logan Hall, you fight." He glared at Fenfang. "Not her. She looks like a serious badass. If you win, we'll accept you at your word."

Logan was in a tight place. He had no choice but to agree. If he didn't, these people might murder him and his companions. He was the leader. It was his job to take this responsibility on himself. "Okay, I'll fight. Who do you want me to fight?"

"Not here," the leader said. "You and your friends come back to our compound and that's where you find out who or what you have to fight."

"Whatever," Logan snarled. This guy was a pompous jerk, but if it meant his people would be safe, he would do what was necessary. "Promise me you'll take care of my people if I lose."

The leader nodded and held out his hand. Logan reluctantly shook it. "I'm Zacharia." He said and waved his hand to indicate the rest of the people with him. "I'm the leader of the Resistance. We've been preparing for this day for decades. We believe God is on our side and will punish all who do not believe. We plan to take back our planet and then move on to take the universe away from the Kruellians."

Logan glanced at Knock. Knock shrugged and rolled his eyes. This guy had a god complex, thought he was going to kill all the aliens. "Kruellians? Those the aliens?"

"It's what they call themselves."

"Sounds about right," Knock said.

"You got some big goals," Logan said. "But I don't see how you're gonna accomplish them."

Zacharia shrugged. "If you defeat your opponent, I'll be glad to include you in our plans. If you really are Logan Hall, having you on board will help us recruit. Logan Hall has become more famous than you can imagine. When he, or you, rescued those people on the moon, stole a Company starship and took it to Gliese, you achieved a degree of fame we haven't seen on Earth for a generation. Then Logan Hall improved on that reputation by stealing the Company's newest, most technologically modern battleship. Everyone's heard of Logan Hall. If it's really you, the Company has a huge reward on your head. Did you know?"

"Hadn't heard. And I didn't take the battleship. My father did."

"Oh, Deklan Hall is part of your notoriety. We all know he died killing the tyrannical mutant Drayvon. The fact he was Logan Hall's father just adds to Logan's importance. We need Logan Hall. If you prove yourself to be the real Logan Hall, you're gonna be the magnet that draws more people to our purpose. We'll improve and elaborate and spread your story until every child wants to grow up to be just like you, and every man wants to be as brave and smart as you. Your name will be a rallying cry for the resistance."

Logan snorted and smacked Knock on the back. "Are you listening to this? They're nuts. I can't be that famous."

"Dude," Knock said. "If they wanna make you into some kind of folk hero, let 'em."

Fenfang pushed his shoulder. "I think you're brave, but what you really are is a good leader. People trust you. You inspire them to excel and to push forward even when they don't want to. Just like your father." Fang brushed a tear out of her eye. "Dek was an amazing man and he was a good father to me and Ju. I'll miss him forever."

Knock gave Fang a quick hug as Zacharia beckoned for them to board the strange vehicle he and his men had arrived in. Logan followed behind him and sat on the bed. The vehicle was another maintenance sled designed to travel inside the wall. It was considerably larger than the one Milton had brought them in. There was more than enough room in the flat bed behind the two seats for all of Logan's company of Vagrants. "Sit here," Zacharia said to Logan as he indicated the empty seat next to him. "Tell me where all these people came from."

Logan shook his head. "If you don't mind, I'll sit with my own people." This Zacharia character was a jerk. Logan didn't trust him as far as he could throw him. No way he was sitting next to him.

Zacharia frowned as Milton took the seat next to him. "I think he really is Logan Hall," Milton's voice carried enough for Logan to hear him, but whatever Zacharia answered, he missed. Zacharia steered the maintenance sled in a circle and pointed it back the way he'd come. They entered a maintenance tunnel next to the Loop. Sensitive to the energy produced by the Loop rails, Logan could easily feel it on the other side of the wall on his left.

"You haven't told me yet," Zacharia said. "Where did all these people come from?" He spoke over his shoulder. Driving the sled through the narrow tunnel didn't require a lot of focus.

"They're Vagrants. They came from all over. Most were living in Las Vegas, some came from as far away as New Washington with Professor Goswami."

When he mentioned the Professor, Zacharia turned his head and stared at him. "The Professor is rumored to be alive and in the hands of the enemy."

Logan cocked his head and tried to appear surprised. It was best not to reveal Corey had already seen the Professor in a vision and they all knew he was alive. "Uh, I saw him die. He was tortured and burned by Drayvon. His heart failed and he collapsed in the same cell they were holding me."

Zacharia shrugged. "Well, it's just a rumor. Someone who'd been captured and held in a hospital in San Francisco said he was reputed to be there. The guy never actually saw Goswami, so, as I said, it's a rumor."

The sled entered a side tunnel after four hours of chugging along beside the Loop. Logan thought the sled traveled at about sixty kilometers an hour, but he couldn't be sure. It seemed fast and everyone hung on tightly.

The side tunnel they entered was dark. The only light came from the narrow beam of the sled's headlamp. It illuminated sand-colored rock walls. There was more sand drifting on the floor of the tunnel. "We must be under desert," Knock said. Logan shook his head. "I think we've been going up for miles. The tunnel has been angling slightly upward the entire time we've been in it. I have no idea what direction we've been going, but I think we're in the Rockies."

When the sled entered an open cavern, and stopped, Zacharia jumped off. "Before we take you into our headquarters, it's my job to tell all of you our rules."

Logan's people stirred and slowly climbed off the sled. They were stiff, hungry, the kids strangely quiet, and many had to go to the bathroom. "Before you give us your rules and regulations, these people need something to eat and a bathroom," Logan said.

Zacharia narrowed his eyes. "I'm in charge here."

Logan sighed. This guy's ego was enormous. "No kidding."

"Dude," Knock said to Zacharia. "You might be in charge, but I still gotta pee, and so does everyone else."

Zacharia waved his arm indicating a dark corner of the spacious cavern. "There's a privy over in that corner."

Fang smiled at Zacharia as she strutted by. "Was that so hard?"

When he lunged for her, she ripped her katana off her back, crouched, ready to eviscerate him. "Come on," she snarled. "Try me."

He held his hands out, palms up and flat. "No offense."

Knock put his arm around Fang's shoulders. "Looked pretty freaking offensive to me."

Logan stepped between Zacharia and Fang. "That's enough. Knock, help get these people something to eat out of the stuff we brought."

"Dude needs someone to show him he ain't god," Knock snarled as Zacharia slowly backed away.

"I imagine Fang will handle that if he tries to grab her again," Logan said through clenched teeth. He really didn't like this Zacharia guy. He already regretted saying he'd join Zacharia's resistance, but at this point, what other option did they have? He'd committed them. The end result would be on his shoulders.

Chapter Eleven

The journey to the Tong's Waterworld took a month on the ancient freighter. Shayna fretted every minute. There was no way to communicate with Logan. They had no idea what was happening on Earth.

The view on the holo screen in the passenger's lounge showed an enormous red-gold planet Shayna recognized as Jupiter in Earth's solar system. The Tong's Waterworld was on Europa, a moon orbiting Jupiter. Jupiter had a lot of moons, as she recalled, and Europa was one of the largest. When she'd learned about it in school, the Company had decided not to explore it because it was supposed to be covered with a thick layer of ice crusted with centuries of salt. Under the ice was a very salty sea with no monetary value the Company could see or imagine.

Their ship closed in on Jupiter, slowed and took up position near a planet-like body, whitish, and crisscrossed with rust-colored lines. It was huge on the holo screen. Bat and Ju sat down on the cushioned bench next to her. They watched a geyser of water vapor shoot high into the atmosphere. Bat pointed. "Our base is partially on and under the ice crust. The water under the ice is warm, believe it or not, heated by a strong tidal flow caused by Waterworld's close proximity to Jupiter. That's what causes the geysers. Warm water bursting through the ice. Cool, huh? Only happens on this side because one side of Europa always faces the sun, and one side always faces Jupiter."

Shayna shook her head. "Not cool, more like crazy. Do you guys have a way to talk to Earth here?"

"Of course, we do," Bat said. "We're in Earth's solar system."

"Does the Company know you guys are here?"

"Not so far," he said. "Come on. I heard they're loading the shuttles taking us planet-side."

Shayna's growing belly made getting up and down different, more awkward. Bat stuck out his hand and pulled her to her feet. 'How far along are you?"

"Three months. I was hoping Logan would be with me when our child is born."

Ju hugged her. "He'll make it. You'll see."

The ride to the planet was fast. Shayna sat close to a window so she could see Europa. The shuttle shot through a sky-scraper-sized plume of water. As the shuttle closed in on the icy surface, Shayna saw the red streaks were wide fissures in the ice. Bat leaned over her to look. "The red is from minerals in the salt," he said as he pointed. "See that cave. That's the entrance to Waterworld."

The cave was inside one of the huge crevasses. The shuttle slowed and entered the cut through the ice. It looked narrow from far up, but was at least a mile wide. The shuttle shot down the ice canyon which grew steadily wider. Under them blue water slopped against the walls of the crevasse which were made of ice. When the water hit the walls, it froze instantly making a crust that looked like flakes of crumbly ice.

An enormous cavern loomed ahead. When the shuttle was close, it slowed even more and turned into the opening. Once under the ice crust, the world became a glittering blue. They were in a huge air bubble formed under the ice. Beneath them, the water and layers of ice were covered with platforms. The shuttle settled on one and stopped.

Bat jumped up. "My Aunt Seraphina lives here. She was one of the original Tong colonists. This base is huge. Wait till you see it." He grabbed Ju's hand. "Come on."

Ju smiled at him, but shook her head. "I'll stay with Shayna and Mom. They'll need me."

Bat frowned. "I was hoping to show you around."

"Maybe later," Ju said. "After we're all settled in."

Shayna examined Ju. Was the girl falling out of her infatuation? She couldn't tell. Ju's face showed almost no emotion. It was calm, as always. Bat squeezed Ju's hand. "But I want you to meet my aunt."

"I will when Mom and Shayna and all of these people are settled."

Cain stepped up and helped Shayna off the shuttle onto the platform. The surface was hard rubber. It was so thick and heavy even the constant movement of the water under the ever-changing layers of ice could not move it. It seemed as steady as dry land. "Weird place, huh?" Cain said.

"I doubt if the Company could even imagine it's here," Shayna said.

"The base runs under ten of those giant cracks in the ice. One is large enough for ships to land. I heard they harness the tides for power."

"What kind of material did they use for that platform?" Cain asked. "Ships burn hot when they take off."

There is solid land under the northern edge of our base. It's only an island," Bat said," and a small one, but it makes it so we can land ships."

They trailed in a line across the rubber platform. It ended at a prefab building created from a shiny material Shayna had never seen. The structure was on legs and made of stippled, bluish metal with a row of windows across the middle. There was a transparent dome on the top of the building which was shaped like a star with four points. The dome had a solid roof made of more of the bluish metal. The metal, light blue and dull, made seeing it from far away very difficult on this ice planet. A ramp led to the entrance. The door slid up and when six of them were in the small space on the other side of the door, it closed and another door opened. This was an airlock. "Why the airlock?" Shayna asked Bat.

"There's oxygen on the planet. You can live for a while out there, but eventually your body doesn't get enough, and you start slowly suffocating from lack of oxygen."

"Oh," Shayna said. "That's not good."

"We oxygenate the atmosphere in here and we've been looking into manufacturing more in Europa's atmosphere. We know about terraforming planets. The Company has that technology. Only the Tong used to know. Now I guess the Guild knows. Thing is, they're not using it to terraform. They made a weapon out of the technology with the help of ancients we believe are long gone, a wiped out, dead race. The aliens who run the Company have a lot of radical technology. They didn't invent it; they found it."

As Shayna entered the base, she turned and stared at Bat. "They have a weapon? What kind of weapon? What's it do?"

Bat shrugged. "Only a few of Tong leaders even know about it. I know because my father was part of the leadership." He sighed. "That's why they killed him."

"Tell me what kind of weapon it is." Shayna's anxiety for Logan felt like it was reaching critical levels. If the Company had some kind of secret terrible weapon, there was no doubt in Shayna's mind that Logan would try to destroy it.

"I heard it's a dark matter weapon. Something they stole from the ancients just like the drive we use on our fighters. They're not smart enough to invent their own junk."

"Dark matter?" Shayna asked. "What's dark matter?"

"You know, anti-matter. Something that's capable of destroying an entire planet with one shot."

"Oh, my god," Shayna moaned. "Logan is there."

"Don't worry, Shayna. I'm sure it's well-hidden somewhere no one can find."

The interior of the base was painted white and blue. Shayna tried to repress her terror. There was nothing she could do about Logan. He was on his own just as she was. The general effect of the color scheme was that of being under water. They weren't but it seemed like they were. "Are we floating on water?" She asked Bat.

He nodded. "The only part of this base on solid ground is that landing platform, and our space port."

He turned back and forth down many narrow corridors finally arriving at a passage lined with doors. "Your people can stay in these dorms. We set them up for our own people. More are on their way, from what I heard, but not here yet. When they get here, we're gonna be crammed into smaller spaces."

Shayna, Ju, Mai and two women with kids entered one room. Shayna claimed a bunk under Ju's. The room was lined with bunks that were four high. There was a small shelf on the wall of each bunk for personal items and no more room anywhere. The row of windows let in little light. Shayna glanced out and all she saw was ice. The wall of the crevasse was six feet from the window. This dorm room must be at the end of one of the star-shaped building's arms.

Shayna took one look around, tossed her belongings onto the bunk and left the room. Ju trailed behind her. "Where you going?" Ju asked.

"I need to get into the communications room, talk to a leader, or someone in charge," Shayna said. "I have to find Logan. I need to know where he is right now. I have this bad feeling he's in trouble and I can't shake it."

"Let's find Bat," Ju said. "I know he'll help us."

They had to leave their building to get to the men's quarters. They found Cain on his way and he stopped them. "Where do you want to go?" He asked Shayna.

"I need to find a communication station or department so I can tell Logan where I am and get news from Earth."

"We have to go outside," he said. "Come on, I'll show you where they keep the cold weather suits."

He led them down another one of the star arms to an airlock. Beside the lock was a storage locker filled with state-of-the-art cold weather suits. "Take one and keep it with you. You never know when you'll end up needing it."

Shayna and Ju struggled into one, zipped it, then snapped the outside closures. The suits weren't as bulky as Shayna thought they would be. Once all three of them were suited up, Cain handed them face masks and close-fitting black caps fitted with headphones, then led them out through the airlock and alongside another one of the strange buildings. "Men's quarters," he said and grinned. "You really don't wanna go in there."

Shayna was not amused. She was two seconds from a full freak out. "I need to talk to a leader or someone who can help me contact Logan," she said.

"Have you seen Bat?" Ju asked him.

'He took off right after he showed us to our rooms. Got no idea where he went."

Tears welled in Shayna's eyes and her chest ached. They were on a strange planet, inside a weird base floating on a constantly moving sea. At times, she felt the vibrations of the water beneath her feet. She had no idea where the command center could be located. She didn't know where anything was. Cain saw her distress and wrapped a strong arm around her shoulders. "Come on, we'll explore."

"Thank you," she breathed with sincere gratitude. Cain was strong, Dek had trusted him and so did she.

"We need to know the layout of this place anyway. I'm just as concerned about Logan and the group on Earth as you, so let's go."

He carried his rifle with him. No one had taken their weapons which was about the only thing making Shayna not lose her mind. Being forced to trust people she'd never met, criminals in the bargain, was a bad idea and she knew it. Ju tagged along behind as they walked along a well-defined pathway around the arms of the men's building. They met no one, which was not encouraging.

"Where are all the people?" Ju asked.

When they were on the other side of the men's quarters, they stood on the edge of a large open area. The air was freezing cold but the strange platform beneath their feet was warm. Above them, weak light shone through the ice bubble. The bubble was closer to their heads than it had been and Shayna could see where it ended. The Tong had made an arched gate through the side of the bubble. Shayna shivered and hugged herself. Cain grabbed her arm and pulled her into a squat. "If you huddle down here, you'll be warmer."

It was true. Close to the rubber platform, it was warmer. The water under it must heat it. The thick rubber under their feet extended into the open arena which was filled with men and women doing martial arts forms. Shayna recognized the forms from watching Ju's sister Fenfang practicing with Logan's father, Dek. They moved in unison, striking, kicking, yelling at each move. They were all dressed in quilted, black pajama-like garments, wore strange masks on their faces, and had kitanas on their backs. They stopped doing physical movements and pulled their swords, then the drills moved into using swords. "Look, there's Bat," Ju said.

"There's at least two hundred soldiers out there practicing," Cain said. "That's the beginnings of an army."

"Do our masks provide oxygen?" Shayna asked.

"How long can you stay out in this atmosphere without supplementing oxygen?" Ju asked.

"I can't say," Cain said. "But we need to know if we're going to work with these folks."

They watched until the practice session stopped and the martial artists headed for them. Bat spotted Shayna and Ju and ran to them. "What are you guys doing out here?"

"Hunting for you," Ju said with a shy smile.

"Not really hunting for you as much as we're looking for the com center," Shayna said. "Have you guys got a way to communicate with Earth?"

Bat nodded. "We do, but now is not the time."

"Then when is the time?" Shayna snarled. "I need to know what's going on with my husband. I haven't heard from him in two months. I'm worried sick."

"I'll take you to see Muunokhoi," Bat said. "He's the leader of our family now that my father is dead."

"That would be a good place to start, I guess," Shayna said.

"The hierarchy here, on Waterworld, is really stringent. Our society is very correct. You follow the chain of command or you're marched outside and left there."

"Executed?" Shayna couldn't believe it.

"We have to maintain discipline in some way. The Mongolian culture, which is my heritage and my family's heritage, has always been a harsh one."

"Are all of the people on this base Mongolian?" Ju asked.

"No, of course not. We are a diverse population made up of Chinese, Japanese, Koreans, Malaysian, Vietnamese, many oriental cultures under one roof, grouped together now to defeat the Company. Revenge will be ours."

"How can you fight the Company?" Shayna asked. "They're ruled by aliens with technology far in advance of ours."

"We will never bow to them again. We seek revenge and we shall have it. They violated every agreement we lived under for many years and their treachery has been noted." Bat's face reflected sincerity and an intensity Shayna found oddly comforting. He went on. "And we've been taking notes. We're not stupid. We know everything they know, though our ability to use the knowledge is limited. Our leaders have plans to get better."

Bat took them into another of the star-shaped buildings. It was bigger than the women's and men's quarters. They flipped up their masks as they walked through the building. Shayna thought this building passed outside of the ice bubble and they were now either under the open sky of Europa or in another bubble.

This building was more open. More light shined through the strip of windows in this building than the windows in the women's quarters. People were eating, talking in common rooms and many of them sat at tables cleaning weapons. Every one of them, men and women, wore the quilted black uniform. Shayna noticed on the shoulder of each uniform was a patch. There were many different patches.

At the end of one of the star-shaped building's arms, Bat stopped with one hand on the lever that opened the hatch-like door. "We go through another open, outdoor space, and then into the command center. Say nothing to anyone you see. Keep your heads down and look neither right nor left." He grabbed Cain's weapon. "This would be considered an insult and you would be punished."

He opened the hatch and they exited through another airlock. Once outside Shayna looked around in awe. This must be the island. Hundreds of fighters, small ships and even bigger spaceships crowded together in an obvious spaceport. Bat led them across a rise. Under their feet, reddish gravel crunched. The ice bubble was no longer over their heads. Instead, a man-made dome covered the spaceport. It was freezing cold. A terrible wind blew across the spaceport. Icy fingers of air ate into Shayna's exposed skin. Without the warm water under their feet, it seemed a hundred degrees colder.

Bat hustled them across the open space. Shayna and Ju ran. The cold felt deadly and no doubt it was. The building housing the command center was another huge star-shaped structure covered in the same strange bluish metal. The building, like all the others was on legs. A ramp led to another airlock.

"There are many buildings on the other side of this one," Bat said. "They house the machinery that we need to run the base, supplies, and weapons. You have no need to ever go beyond this building, and if you do, you will be stopped and detained. Rules on Waterworld are strictly enforced."

Once inside the building, Shayna breathed a sigh of relief. Warmth. Bat walked down a short hallway, opened another hatch and led them into a room filled with holo screens, consoles, desks, computer terminals and people manning these stations. A huge holo screen on the wall showed the solar system, some of the galaxy beyond and small dots moving across the screen. Shayna figured the moving dots were ships. Some of the dots were blue, some green, some yellow, some red. Probably the colors indicated the origins of the ships and their owners.

A tall, lanky man with no hair, incredibly colored and detailed tattoos on his arms and neck, and suspicious, narrowed oriental eyes climbed out of his chair and strode toward them. "Who are these people?"

He spoke in Mandarin; a language Shayna had learned the basics of from Logan who spoke it fluently.

Bat bowed low. "Honored Muunokhoi, these are the leaders of the people I brought with me from Gliese."

Shayna found herself being examined critically by those narrowed eyes. "Two half-Asian girls and a white man? Where did they come from?"

"Honorable sir," Shayna said in the best Mandarin accent she could manage. "We are all running from the Company. Do you need to know more than that?"

"You speak our language?"

Shayna smiled stiffly. "Yes, honorable, sir, but poorly."

His smile never reached those narrowed eyes. "What is it you wish?"

"Do you speak English, sir?" She asked.

"I do."

Shayna sighed. "Thank goodness, I can barely follow you in Mandarin. I need to contact my husband on Earth. Do you have a way of doing that?"

"Do you have a location for him or an email address he checks or can check that's encrypted and safe?"

"Yes," she said.

"You do?" Cain demanded.

"I have an email address he gave me. Whether he can check it or not, I don't know, but the address is totally safe. It goes to an email only Logan can access. He just has to be able to check it."

Muunokhoi pointed to Bat. "Take her to a com station."

"Before I do that, sir, have you any news from Earth?"

"It's chaos down there. The Kruellians control everything. They're rounding up people and sending them to the mines. Even people with chips aren't safe. It's as though they plan to eradicate all human life."

"What about the Guild?" Bat asked. "The Company is using them now instead of us."

"They think they're safe," Muunokhoi said. "In the end, the aliens will turn on them as well. It is up to us to find a way to destroy the alien invaders before they destroy us."

Chapter Twelve

When Logan and his group arrived at the sanctuary promised by Zacharia, his people were on their last legs. They hadn't had enough to eat or enough rest for a long time. Zacharia led them through a hatch cut into solid rock. It opened on a tiled room with a door on the other side. There were benches against the walls. His people dropped their packs and fell onto them.

Knock stood at his elbow with Fenfang. They presented a united front to Zacharia and Milton. Logan wasn't feeling friendly or in the mood for any more crap. He'd fight whoever these people said he had to fight and then they'd have to accept him as Logan Hall. It felt stupid that he had to prove who he was, and fighting seemed a dumb way to do it. If he wasn't Logan, but a great fighter, they'd have to believe a lie. Their logic was bizarre.

"When you pass through this door, you will be in our stronghold. This is a privilege. Do not speak to anyone you see. Until we establish your leader's identity through the ritual fight, you are untouchable. Punishment for any infraction is death."

Logan shook his head. "Look, Zach, my people are tired and hungry. We've been running from the Company since we blew up that battleship you heard about. Yeah, that was us. Your rules are strange and unbelievably cruel. Cut us some slack . . ."

Zacharia interrupted and cut him off. "My name is Zacharia. It's never been Zach. Do not call me that ever!" Zacharia screamed into Logan's face, his visage a contorted mask of insane rage, spit flying and forming a white crust at the sides of his fleshy lips.

"My people predicted this day would come. We prepared for it." He grabbed the front of Logan's shirt and drew him so close Logan could count Zacharia's eyelashes and smell his awful breath. "Just because you say you fought the Company does not make it true. We've been fighting them for fifty years. You will obey our laws. Your people will attend daily church services and worship as we do. There are no other options save death."

The door leading out of the room slammed open. A cadre of oddly dressed men pushed into the room. Each wore a scarf wrapped around their face hiding their features. Zacharia backed up and pointed to one of the masked newcomers. "Take these neophytes to their quarters. Make sure they do not speak to any of our people thusly polluting them with heresy."

Zacharia let go of Logan's shirt. "This one you will put in the box. He will fight the rats tonight."

Fang drew her sword. "We stay together, or we'll leave the way we came," she snarled.

One of the masked cadre fired a neurolizer at Fang. She dropped her sword and fell to the floor twitching.

"Anyone else?" One of the masked fighters asked. No one moved.

Knock knelt over Fang as she convulsed in one spasm after another. He pulled her trembling body into his arms and tried to comfort her. His narrowed angry eyes glared at Zacharia. "You'll pay for this."

"No, I won't," Zacharia sneered. "You and all of your people exist only at my benevolence. Obey me or suffer the consequences. I am in control!"

Raj knelt next to Knock and helped him hold Fang. "Do not fight them," Raj hissed. "They are the power now. We must obey."

Knock's only response was to continue to glare at Zacharia.

One of the masked men cuffed Logan's hands behind his back. Logan had to watch helplessly as his people were hustled out the door. He had no idea where they were, or where these religious zealots were taking them. He felt completely helpless. His heart ached. He was a bad leader. He couldn't seem to do the simplest thing right or make a correct decision. He should never have agreed to ally himself and his people to these religious whack-jobs.

They dragged Logan out the door into a corridor painted asylum green. The tile on the floor was a darker shade of the same color. Logan examined the place as he was dragged down the hallway. A gray metal door stopped them. One of the masked men used a key to open it and waited until all of them were through before locking it behind them.

There were no windows giving Logan the feeling they were underground. They went by metal doors with wire covered windows and through another locked door. At the end of this corridor was a short metal door. He was dragged to it while the leader used another key to open it. “Get in,” key guy said.

Logan protested with all of his strength. He fought hard, received a punch in the eye and a bloody nose for his efforts. A big black man, scarf slipping off his bald head, square forehead, flat nose, slanted eyes, manhandled Logan into a crouch and shoved him into the hole with his boot. When he was inside the door slammed and Logan heard the key turn in the lock.

He was in a dark room. No light at all. Only Logan’s cat-like eyesight, developed from living underground for ten years, allowed him to make out his surroundings. He was in a square box, six by six, made of concrete with the metal door. It was less than three feet high. He could sit up if he bent his head. There was no bed, no blanket, no food or water and no toilet. It was damp and cold. In a few minutes, Logan was shivering. Blood dripped out of his nose. He felt it with two fingers. At least it wasn’t broken.

Knock followed Fenfang but he kept glancing over his shoulder to see where they were taking Logan. He saw them drag Logan into the corridor and then hustle him in the opposite direction. When Logan and his guards disappeared through a metal door, he turned and looked straight ahead, his mind spinning. This entire adventure was going from bad to worse in seconds. Being separated from Logan felt bad, really bad.

The crazies, as he was calling them, led them through a locked metal door and into a large open area. It was tiled like everything here and there were murals on the walls. Murals of a huge soldier wearing a gas mask and abandoned children. One mural showed the same soldier rising out of a swirling gray cloud. The murals were dust-covered and old, but chilling.

They walked through the open area into another building. This one was more cheerful though still painted the green of hospitals and insane asylums. There were more murals. These were of happy children and animals in pairs. The creepiest part was all of the animals had duct tape covering their heads and faces so only their bodies were visible.

A short corridor opened into a cafeteria-like space. Long tables were sparsely populated with men eating. The stainless-steel counters were full of pans of food. The leader, Zacharia stopped them. "My men will now take all of your weapons."

Knock protested. "We can't go unarmed. The entire world above ground is out to get us."

Knock realized the scarves wrapped around the faces of Zacharia's men covered the fact, they were indeed all heavily-bearded men. How strange. The men circulated through Knock's people and quickly took all of their weapons, patting each of them down to make sure they were unarmed. This felt terrible. When they took Knock's neurolizer, a weapon he'd taken from the Company battleship, he felt naked. Fang refused to give up her katana. She drew it, planted her feet and stood snarling in the middle of a pack of men each one aiming a weapon at her. Knock stepped forward and gently put his hands on her arms. "Let them have it, Fang. You can't fight this army alone."

"Dek gave me that sword. He made this scabbard I wear on my back to hold it out of gorp hide. This katana has more meaning to me than anything else I own."

Zacharia stepped close. "What are you waiting for?" He snarled at his men. "This is just a breeder. And look at her. Tight pants, her hair uncovered, she's a harlot. You can be sure of that. Take her sword."

"She looks pretty dangerous," one of them said.

Knock pried Fang's hands off the sword and handed it to Zacharia. "This sword was given to Fenfang by Deklan Hall himself. See you keep it safe. Fenfang here is Dek's stepdaughter."

The man held his head high and stared at Fenfang as though she were a piece of meat. "We'll see about that."

When the katana was out of her hands, the men moved forward and one grabbed Fang. When he lifted his hand to backhand her, she dropped low, swept his feet out from under him and was on his chest with her elbow in his throat before he could realize he was in danger. She glared at the men surrounding her. "I am no ordinary female. As you can see, I'm trained to kill." She lifted one hand holding out three straight fingers. "I could take this man's life with one blow. I could put my fingers through his chest and stop his heart, or his throat and break his neck. Just because you took my sword does not mean I am unarmed."

She leaped off the man's chest, but kept her low stance, stiff knife hands in blocking position. The men who were about to search her for other weapons slowly backed away. "Leave her alone," Zacharia said. "We will find out shortly whether she is really Deklan Hall's stepdaughter." He waved his hand to indicate all of Knock's people. "Eat. After you will be escorted to chapel services and then your leader, the one who claims he is Logan Hall, will fight the rats."

"That sounds great," Fang mumbled to Knock. "Rats are those hideous rodents with red eyes and sharp teeth, right?"

"Not to worry," Knock said. "Logan and I have killed hundreds of rats. They don't scare me and they won't scare Logan." He pushed Fang behind him and faced Zacharia. “Dude,” Knock said. “Is there Sopore in this grub?’

Zacharia shook his head. “No, we’ve been preparing for this time for many years. Our leader and the man who created our sect, Charles Meade, predicted these times. He said God would have a mighty army in his end of times. We are that army. End Timers such as we are, saved money and stored away supplies for the end of times. We believe this is what we were called upon by God to do, and thus we have survived.”

“Awesome, man,” Knock said. He turned to his people. “Go ahead and chow down. Zacharia here, says there’s no dope in the food.”

Raj shouldered his way through the group heading for the chow line. He grabbed Knock’s shoulder and whispered. “Where did they take Logan?”

“Don’t know, but he’s pretty familiar with rats so I ain’t worrying.”

“Corey says these people want us dead.”

“How does Corey know this?” Knock knew he’d felt something off about these people.

“He can read minds, remember. Or at least he can read intentions. If Logan doesn’t defeat the rats, they will kill all of us. They’ve been down here for forty years and they’re very paranoid of any strangers. They believe in kill first ask questions later.”

Knock nodded. “That’s the feeling I get, too. We need an alternate plan in case Logan fails us. I can’t imagine it happening. I mean Logan is awesome and we’re not bad ourselves, but still.”

Raj nodded. “There is a way to the surface over there.” He pointed with his chin. “Do not look or pay too much attention. Corey says it is well hidden but leads up and into the old Denver airport which is now abandoned. From what he can read, Denver is pretty well abandoned as well.”

“Think we can find some kind of communications center in here?”

"They have no communication with the outside world that Corey can discover. Their minds are strangely shielded, as though they have experience with people who have Corey's talent. They forage for food using the tunnels beside the Loop. They have a very militaristic system, but they treat women as sub humans. Women stay apart, wear long concealing clothing and raise children, cook, and only perform jobs they consider fit for women. All men and boys over the age of fifteen train and fight."

Knock wandered toward the food trailed by Fang who was looking at the End Timers like they were cockroaches. She bent low and whispered to Raj. "They really treat women like that? What's wrong with them?"

Raj shrugged. "I do not know. I believe it has something to do with their religion."

"Well they're missing out on the awesomeness of chick fighters," she said.

Chapter Thirteen

Logan sat with his legs crossed and waited. The door opened and a plate of food was shoved through. After the door clanged shut, Logan ignored the tray. Any food could be tainted with Sopore or even poisoned to take away any advantage he might have in this upcoming battle. As he waited he thought about Shayna. He had no idea what was happening on Gliese. He should never have left her alone. In retrospect, it was a terrible decision. He couldn't figure out what he'd been thinking. He ruthlessly shoved those thoughts aside and concentrated on his focus. He had a feeling the rats he was to fight would be more than ordinary rats and he wished to be prepared.

After what seemed to Logan like forever, the door was opened and he was called out. He ducked to exit the box and stood up with ease. His body was a well-oiled machine. He was young and he was fit. Three men with scarves wrapped around their faces waited for him to exit the box. Each was well-armed holding battle rifles, dual weapons with blasters on the top, shotguns on the bottom. One stepped forward and indicated Logan should walk ahead of them by flicking his rifle.

Logan walked by them with his head held high. They walked down the corridor and through two locked metal doors leading to a junction with four corridors heading off in four directions. The man behind him shoved him toward the corridor on the left. He turned and walked down it. It ended as all the hallways in this warren ended, in a locked metal door. The leader opened it with an old-fashioned key on a large ring of more keys attached to a chain clipped to his belt.

The door opened on a spacious room with a low ceiling. The room was tiled and the walls covered with strange murals of children and terrifying armed men wearing gas masks. A ring had been roped off in the center of the room and benches set up around it. Logan was reminded of another arena in a Tong-controlled New Washington town. Genetically enhanced chickens and strange alien birds fought in the arena while men watched and bet on them. Logan's heart pounded. What if these rats were genetically altered? Were they going to give him a weapon or send him into the arena with only his bare hands?

He marched past the benches. They were filled with men. Were there no women down here? A small section of the benches was cordoned off. The male members of his party sat on those benches. Where was Fang? Where were Mai and all the other women and children? There was an empty roped off section close to the ring. Maybe the women would sit there.

He didn't have time to wonder. He was shoved under what he'd thought was rope, but was actually thick wire cable, and into the arena. Once he stood in its center, he saw a chute of metal panels leading off the arena to a door. Zacharia ducked under the wire and faced Logan. He held his hands up as if invoking some spirit and started praying. The words were unintelligible, complete gibberish. When he was done invoking whatever god they believed in, he grabbed Logan by the shoulders. "If you are indeed, Logan Hall, you will defeat the rats and your victory will be celebrated among the people."

"Do I get a weapon?" Logan demanded. This entire situation, while being beyond weird, was starting to feel downright dangerous.

"If you are Logan Hall, you won't need a weapon. And beware of the wire. Once the animals are in the ring, it's electrified."

"I'm not a god. I'm just a man. I don't know what you got coming at me down that chute, but I'd like a weapon."

Zacharia didn't answer just ducked out of the arena. "Take this." Logan heard a hissed voice and jumped to look around. The women of these strange people had arrived. They sat in the enclosed area he'd noticed upon entering. They wore head coverings, long sack-like garments that covered them from shoulders to feet, and veils which covered their features and hair. Logan recognized the hissing whisper. It was Fang. He backed slowly toward her. She had a knife in her hand. She must have been allowed to keep her weapons. Or at least these people hadn't searched her thoroughly. Fang was always well-equipped with sharp toys she hid all over her person. He reached behind stealthily, took the knife from her hand, and palmed it. She was gone with a swish of her long garment.

With the small Gerber Ghoststrike in his hand, Logan felt a lot better. He'd never seen this particular knife on Fenfang. She must have kept it well hidden. He planted his feet in the middle of the arena and waited.

A gong sounded and the door leading to the chute slowly rose. Three huge shadows raced into the chute toward the arena and Logan. Whatever they were, they weren't normal rats. They were as big as collies. The three rats exploded into the ring, spotted their prey, and launched themselves at Logan. He fell back under their combined weight, stabbed one in the eye and slashed another in the side. Blood spurted from the one he'd stabbed in the eye. It fell dead. The slashed one backed away with its friend and circled Logan, watching him, stalking his every move.

Logan turned, keeping his face toward them. They really were rats. For a moment, he'd doubted that. They had oversized front teeth and the eyes that followed him were red. They were hairless, their skin black. Their long hairless tails swished like a cat's tail when it was angry. Someone had fed these animals GMO-laced food and growth hormones. These were not rats he'd ever seen before. Not only were they enormous, they'd mutated. Their front claws were abnormally long and looked unnaturally sharp. They were smart and seemed shocked to discover he was armed. Maybe they'd had an easy time in previous battles inside this arena. They chattered to each other as though conversing. It creeped Logan out. Were they planning their attack?

The one with the slash in its side limped slightly, and blood dripped out of its wound onto the ring's tile floor. Logan tried to stay calm and come up with a plan, but the rats moved first. The one with the limp suddenly didn't limp anymore. It was a fake out. It leaped at Logan while the other ran behind him and savagely sank those long front teeth into his calf. Logan caught the one on his chest and fell back, his leg weakened by the bite. He landed on his left shoulder pinning the one rat under him as he tried to roll quickly onto his knees to leap to his feet.

He wasn't fast enough and both rats were on top of him. Logan knew this was the end. One of the rats lunged for his face while the other went for his belly. He fought hard, slashing with the knife and cutting deep into the rat on his face, but the rat's skin was tough as gorp hide and his blade so short. Fiery stabbing pain shot into his gut as the rat clawed into his belly. A sudden shout and the rat clawing his gut was torn away and thrown to the floor. Knock had jumped in to save him.

Logan wanted to shout thanks, but had too much on his hands dealing with the teeth and talon-like claws of the rat on top of him. Claws raked his chest. The rat sank his teeth in Logan's cheek as Logan finally found a vulnerable spot in the rat's tough hide. He stabbed into its throat. Thick gouts of blood and gore spewed across his face. Even as it expired, the rat snapped furiously at Logan's neck. With a loud gasp, Logan flipped the rat off him and onto the floor. He leaped to his feet and launched himself onto the back of the huge rat that had Knock pinned under it.

Knock had no weapon. He was helpless. Logan ripped the rat's head up and stabbed his short-bladed knife into its throat. Its death rattle was music to Logan's ears. He tossed the twitching corpse to the floor and bent over Knock. His friend's right eye was gone. Logan pulled his friend tight against him. "Why'd you do it, man? Why?"

"Dude," Knock whispered. "I couldn't let you die. Shayna'd never speak to me again and Fang, well she thinks I'm a hero."

Logan lifted his head. "We need a medic here. Get a doctor."

"Doesn't hurt all that bad," Knock said. He reached up and touched Logan's face. "Gonna have scars, dude. Chicks dig scars."

Zacharia ducked under the wire. Logan stood up prepared to have Zacharia angry because Knock had interfered in their staged battle. Zacharia grabbed his shoulders. "You are a true leader. This was the test. Your man was willing to sacrifice himself to save you. That is the sign of true leadership. You are Logan Hall." He grabbed Logan's hand and lifted it above his head. "And Charles Meade said, 'God is going to have a mighty army in his End Time.' We have Logan Hall to draw recruits from all over the world."

The people in the auditorium leapt to their feet and cheered. Logan thought this entire scene was nuts, but went along, waving at the cheering masses. When the noise died down, he pointed to Knock. "I think we both need a doctor."

Zacharia was instantly solicitous. "So sorry, we will attend to both of you immediately."

Zacharia led them out of the auditorium area. Two men helped Knock. Logan's stomach wound was superficial. The rat had clawed up his abdomen. It bled sluggishly, but mostly Logan figured it just needed antiseptic. Rat claws couldn't be clean. He followed the men carrying Knock through more of the ubiquitous locked doors into a hallway resounding with the laughter of children. This must be where Zacharia's people lived.

The room they hauled Knock into looked like a dispensary. A white-coated man stepped forward and helped the men lay Knock on a table. Logan hovered over his buddy. "You gonna make it?" He asked Knock with a crooked grin."

"Too mean to die. It's just my eye, dude. How's it look?"

Logan didn't want to tell Knock but felt obligated to be truthful. "Lost your eye, man. I think the rat ate it."

"Oh crap. Fang is never gonna look at me again. Where is she anyway?"

"She slipped me a knife. That's the only reason I'm here. She's hanging with the other women. These people are pretty Gothic in their attitudes toward women. She was wearing a black dress that looked like a sack and a veil when she slid the knife into my hands. All the women are separated from the men. Aside from that one little group watching our fight, I haven't seen a one."

Knock grimaced. "I don't like her being so far away from me. I want her here, by me, where I know she's safe."

Logan knew his friend was in pain. He'd never heard that peevish note in Knock's voice. The doctor bent over Knock and began cleaning the blood and gore off his face. He looked up and his eyes met Logan's. "If you take a seat over there, my assistant will see to your wounds."

Knock grabbed his arm. "Find Fang and tell her I'm okay and I love her."

"I will," Logan said before he allowed the doctor's assistant to drag him to a chair. The assistant cut Logan's shirt off and fingered the ragged edges of the wound on his abdomen. Logan bit his lip. It hurt.

"Just some shallow gashes," the assistant doctor said. He dabbed some alcohol on them and used butterfly bandages to close them. By the time he was finished with the wounds on Logan's body, dressed the one on his face and provided Logan with one of the ubiquitous black shirts, Logan's patience was about gone. Zacharia stuck his head in the door to check on them. Logan pushed the assistant doctor's hand away and jumped up. "Hey, Zacharia, do you have a way to communicate with the outside world?"

It seemed to Logan he spent an inordinate amount of time hunting for ways to communicate. He wanted to find out what was going on with Shayna on Gliese in the worst way. He had a drop box on an email site and was hoping to get some mail from her.

Zacharia smiled. It was weird. Logan had never seen him smile. The gray beard and mustache parted and there was the smile with teeth and lips and everything. "I was just going to take you to our com center. Now that we know you're really Logan Hall, we want you to send out a broadcast to all Vagrant and End Timer holds, uniting them to fight the Company and the alien invaders."

Logan followed Zacharia through more doors. He was getting a good idea of the layout of this place. He figured there were five buildings all linked by doors. It was a huge underground complex. "How long have you and your people been down here?" He asked Zacharia.

"Since 2010, us End Timers started seeing the need to find a safe hide-away way before that. We saved money. We organized When I heard about this place under the Denver Airport, well it seemed perfect."

"How many fighting men do you have?"

Zacharia stopped walking and stared at Logan. "None of your business. When you need to know, then you'll know."

Logan stopped himself from rolling his eyes. It did no good to aggravate this guy. He was touchy, overly sensitive about way too many things, and Logan thought he was a giant jerk, full of his own self-importance, and then there was the crack-head religious thing to round out the picture of a total whack job. His people did need Zacharia right now. Logan thought aligning his people with the End Timers was a good idea at the moment, but the first chance he got to move onto something better, they were out of here.

Zacharia stopped at another metal door. It was equipped with a retinal scanner. Zacharia lifted a plastic case and stuck his eye against a rubber ocular scanner. A green laser-like light ran down his eye and the door beeped open. The End Timers might be religious zealots, but their level of security was top shelf. As he walked through the door he asked Zacharia about it. "Did you guys install the retinal scanner?"

Zacharia shook his head. "No, all that stuff was already here. We just reprogrammed it."

The room they entered contained what Logan immediately noted was the most high-tech communication equipment he'd seen since he was on the alien ship. Four consoles were manned by men wearing black pants and black shirts. They all wore beards and their hair was long and tied up in ponytails or buns. All were young. None of them looked to be above thirty.

Zacharia led Logan to an empty console. He turned to one of the young men. "Mordecai, show Logan Hall here how to connect to the main server and the web. He needs an account affiliated with us. I want a video made of him talking we can send all over the world to rally Vagrants and End Timers to our cause."

"Can I check my personal email account from here?" Logan asked. "I'm worried about my wife. I left her back on Gliese."

Zacharia grinned and slapped him on the back. "Congratulations. Married yourself a breeder. Best thing we can do is breed up a new generation to fight the Company."

"The access?" Logan asked politely. He knew exactly how Shayna would feel if she were ever to be called a breeder.

"Sure. Mordecai, hook Logan up so he can see if his wife is okay."

Mordecai was a tall, skeletally thin man, with stooped shoulders. He wore bottle-thick glasses perched on the bridge of a hooked nose. His hair was brown but his beard was red. His skin was so pale, Logan doubted if he'd ever been out of this bunker. He said nothing, just hung over Logan's shoulder, ran his hand over the desk which immediately lit up. When he touched a button, a screen rose out of the console. He touched a lit spot and a virtual keyboard appeared on the top of the console. "You're on," he said. "Just type your email address into that box and the server will find it for you."

Logan tried not to show amazement on his face. He'd never seen equipment like this. He did as Mordecai told him and his drop box appeared. He typed in his password and his account opened. There were five letters from Shayna. He opened the most recent one. He'd go back to the others in a minute.

"Dearest Logan," it began. He read it thinking each word in her voice. "I'm so worried about you and I miss you so much. Everything here is fine. There's a doctor and the Tong has been very hospitable. Cain, Mai and Ju are doing well. I'm sure Ju is in love with Bat. My only worry is about you. Please write as soon as you can." She signed out with her love and Logan opened the previous notes one at a time. In her first note he discovered where she was and what had happened. He also discovered she was pregnant. Stunned, he closed the letters, changed his password and shut the computer down.

Shayna was pregnant. He was going to be a dad. The news filled him with wonder and additional terror for her safety. She was hiding out with the Tong. That could not be good. The Tong had been their enemy for a hundred years. He'd almost died at the hands of Tong thugs when he tried to book passage off Earth to the moon. Shayna was pregnant. He kept thinking that over and over. Pregnant. He was going to be a father if they lived, and at the moment, there were no assurances for either of them.

Just thinking about her flight from Gliese terrified him. He closed his eyes and dropped his head into his hands. He knew it. He never should have left her. He should be there with her. He wanted to be with her, see her, hold her, rub her growing belly. He was missing the most incredible thing that had ever happened to him. It sucked.

He ran out of the communications room and headed back to the infirmary with his mind squirming in circles. He found Knock sitting up on the side of the bed with a gauze pad taped over his missing eye. Knock was a little groggy. When Logan touched his arm, he jumped. "Jeeze, dude, you freaked me out."

"Sorry," Logan whispered, "but I got some strange news. A lot of strange news."

Knock rubbed his swollen face all around the gauze pad. "This thing is killing me. Spill."

Logan hardly knew how to tell his friend. He was stunned and terrified at the same time, and even really excited as well.

"Dude, you look like you're freaking out. What happened? Is Shayna okay?"

Fang entered the infirmary and sat on the gurney next to Knock. She held his hand. "You okay?"

"I'm gonna be fine, just ain't got one eye is all. Now Logan here, looks like he's about to have a coronary."

"I noticed. I thought he was just hurting from the fight and worried about you."

"Nope, he just got a message from Shayna."

"Is Ju okay? What about my mom?"

"They're fine, or I think they are. I got a bunch of messages from Shayna and she said they were okay."

Fang smiled. "That's great. So, what'd she say to turn you whiter than these sheets?"

Logan put one hand on each of Knock's shoulders, glanced at Fenfang, and stared into Knock's one eye. "Shayna is pregnant."

Knock's mouth fell open. "Say what? You're yanking my chain, ain't you?"

Fang leaped off the gurney and hugged Logan. "Yow! I'm hurt, remember?" He said through clenched teeth.

She grinned. "Sorry, but that's amazing news. She'll make a perfect mother." She looked thoughtful. "And you'll be a good dad just like your father."

Logan touched Knock's shoulder. "She's really pregnant, dude. I'm gonna be a father."

Chapter Fourteen

Professor Goswami walked softly through a tunnel system beneath Area 51. He'd found this hidden passage during the time he was given to sleep. The creature inside him believed him asleep, so needing rest the creature slept. Goswami was blissfully free to do as he liked for seven hours. The only drawback was he never got enough sleep and was eternally tired.

The tunnels he explored were high tech, the walls smooth, made of a material he'd never seen. He was looking for the alien weapon. He'd been looking for six straight sleep cycles. From what he read in the mind of the creature wrapped around his spine, it was accessible through these tunnels. The aliens didn't realize what the bug inside him knew, Goswami also knew.

He reached a wide door made from an alien metal he had never seen before. It was iridescent, like an oil slick on a puddle, and it glowed. The door had a red no-access sign painted across its iridescent surface and a small window. The universal sign for danger was under the window. This had to be where the weapon was kept. Goswami tried to see through the window but there was an odd pink material covering it on the inside. He tried to raise the bar and open the door. No deal, it was locked. He spotted a small box on the right side of the door. When he lifted the door of the box, he recognized a retinal scanner. To get to this new weapon, a registered user had to place his eye against the rubber frame and get his eyeball scanned.

Goswami sighed and dropped the cover of the ocular scanner. He was never getting inside. How he wished he had Knock and Logan. They would figure out a way.

Having found the weapon, he turned around and made his way back to his tiny room. He would sleep and try very hard not to think of his discovery. Masking his thoughts had become almost second nature. He feared the bug would discover his secret.

Shayna sat in the comfortable communal area of the Tong base, Waterworld, watching an old movie on the holo screen. All the movies were Chinese and all the actors spoke Mandarin. Shayna's ability to understand the language had improved dramatically since she'd arrived on Europa. Mark Moretti, the kid they'd brought with them from Gliese, sat on one of the formed foam couches with his chin on his hand. He was very unhappy. Rations on the Tong base were spare. There were no sweets and no fried food. What there was a lot of was rice, but even the rice was strictly rationed.

She glanced at the door as Cain walked in. Cain embraced the Tong whole heartedly. He was a warrior and this was a warrior society. They'd accepted him as well. Cain was involved in their plans to take Earth away from the aliens and privy to many secrets. He spent most of his time with Bat's uncle, Sammy Lee, the leader, Muunokhoi everyone called Manu, and Bat.

"Shayna," Cain said. "We received a message from Logan. It's weird. He's broadcasting on Fox news, but it seems to be an imbedded broadcast hidden inside Fox's regular news feed."

Shayna leaped up as fast as she could. "Can I read it now?"

Cain grinned. "They sent me to get you. They seemed pretty impressed when I told them you were his wife. There might be a more private messages in your drop box. I thought you should check it. If Logan has access to com equipment, he'll send you a letter. You know he will."

Shayna turned to Mark. "I'm going to the com center. Maybe you should come with us. You can stop at the gym and work out." They'd been encouraging the kid to exercise. He'd lost some weight, but his skin was so loose only exercise would tighten it, and he needed to up his level of fitness. He grew winded walking up a flight of stairs.

The kid shook his head. "Don't feel like exercising. I'm hungry."

"There are two more hours until another meal, Mark," Shayna said. She really wanted to help the kid. He was lonely, had a huge crush on Ju, and he was suffering. "You need to move, exercise," she said kindly. "It will take your mind off your troubles. I know. After I check my email, I'll join you."

Ju walked into the room and grabbed Mark's hand. "Come on, I'll go with you."

Mark's whole demeanor changed. He smiled and ponderously rose from the couch. "Okay, Ju, that'll be fun."

Shayna narrowed her eyes. Mark's crush on Ju might eventually prove dangerous for the kid. Bat was head over heels in love with Ju and wouldn't take poachers, on what he considered his property, well at all. In the end, it was on Ju. She could put an end to Mark's crush if she wanted to. At the moment, Shayna thought Ju liked Mark as a friend. It might develop into something larger. Bat was so involved in fighting and flying and his responsibilities to the Tong, he didn't have the time to devote to Ju, Mark had. Shayna watched as Ju held Mark's hand while they walked down the corridors of Waterworld. There was no telling what would happen. Ju was very young.

They had to go outside to access the command center. Mark had no cold weather suit so they ran. He was too large to fit into one. If there ever was an emergency, Mark was going to freeze to death. When they entered through the airlock, Ju went with Mark into the gym which was in one of the star-points, while Shayna continued down the hallway to the com center.

Her heart raced with anticipation. The thought of hearing from Logan had her giddy with excitement. If he'd written her, then he'd probably received her letter as well and now knew they were going to be parents.

Cain took her into a small room with several stations. All but one were manned by hard-eyed Tong fighters. Each wore the black uniform and a black headband.

Cain pointed to the empty station. If you tap on the keyboard, Logan's message to the world will come on and play. I think there's an embedded message. You will probably know better than I how to get it open.

Holding her breath, Shayna fell into the rolling chair and tapped the enter key. Logan's dear face appeared. He called on all Vagrants on all planets, especially Earth, to join together, rise up, and throw the alien lords off their planets. He explained in detail how the aliens had taken over Earth and now ran the Company. He told them who he was and how he'd fought the Company and won. He encouraged them to do the same.

When Logan finished, a bearded black man appeared and vouched for Logan. He said his name was Zacharia and he planned to coordinate an attack on Company strongholds through the embedded signal. He told all Vagrants to stay watchful. He said he would be back to give them further news and orders. Then he signed out.

Shayna absorbed all of this for a second before she went back through the message searching for the hidden icon that would open and give her a private message. She found it two minutes in. It was hard to see. An asterisk hiding inside of Logan's hair. His dirty-blond hair had grown long. His face was unshaven and he was growing a mustache and goatee. His face was tanned and his eyes bright. She clicked on the asterisk and waited.

A message box opened asking for a password. She typed it in and there was another box asking for a second password. When she'd passed all the security, Logan's video message to her started.

"I'm not going to comment on where you are," he said. "I'm terrified this message will someday be discovered and outing you to the Company would be the worst thing ever. I love you and can't believe you got off our planet and made it to a place of refuge. I can't believe we're gonna have a baby, a child to care for. I'm so sorry you're doing it alone. I should be there." He rubbed dirty hands across his bright-blue eyes to wipe away tears. She immediately burst into sobs and had to force control over her emotions so she could watch him talk.

"I'm currently with a group of people I can tell you are completely nuts, batshit crazy, religious whack jobs. Everyone that was with me made it here. We're safe. For the moment. First chance I get, we're losing these people and heading out on our own. The Professor is alive somewhere, according to Corey. I believe the kid. He knows stuff you can't challenge. He's got an amazing gift.

"I need to find the Professor. I trust him and believe me I don't trust many people right now. Just Knock and Fang and some of our people like Corey, Raj and Bobby. In the meantime, I'll help this group coordinate their forces. If they can, fine. If they can't, I have my own ideas about how to take out the Company. Send me a message when you can. There's a rumor the aliens have some kind of super weapon. These people used to call themselves the End Timers. They have their ways of knowing stuff. I believe them about the weapon. If you've heard about it or know where it's located, let me know. Take care of yourself, babe. Love you more than life itself. Kiss your belly. It's got our baby growing inside of it and he's our future. I want to be with you more than anything else, but, well you know I have some stuff I gotta deal with first." He blew her a kiss and the screen went dark.

Shayna wiped her eyes and snorted. What if their child was a girl? She rubbed her belly and spoke to it. "I think you're a little girl. You'll be beautiful because your daddy is."

She composed a long letter for him. She was worried the message would fall into the wrong hands. What if the Company or one of those alien things discovered their secret way of communicating? It could happen and if it did, she could be in serious trouble. They would know where she was, and they would know about the Tong base on Europa. Had she made a huge mistake by putting that information in an email? She prayed she hadn't but it was too late for recriminations. The deed had been done. She could only hope Logan had the sense to delete them, but then nothing on the web was ever really gone. If a really good IT expert wanted to find her letters and his video messages, he could.

The letter she wrote to him was carefully worded. It was a little late to be thinking about hiding information inside of their letters. She warned Logan about her fears and told him to delete everything and change his drop box. She gave him the address of a new box she created, told him she was working on finding out where the weapon was located. She told him the Tong wanted to know so they could destroy it. "I'm safe here for the moment," she wrote. "I have Cain and Bat to watch my back and this new guy we picked up on Gliese. He says he can get into any system. He might be our new Eddie. I sure miss Eddie. He was a genius. Don't worry about me and our child. This base has lots of doctors and I'm getting good care. Tell Fenfang her sister and mom are here with us and fine. All the Vagrants on Gliese made it off the planet with us thanks to the Tong." She signed it with her love and sent the message.

It was good to hear from him and good to know he was hunting for the alien weapon. Logan and Knock were a powerful team. She heaved herself out of the chair and left the com room.

Cain waited anxiously for news. She filled him in as he walked her back to her quarters. "The Tong is doing their best to locate that weapon," he said. "They've known about it for a while, according to Bat, who says it's supposedly guarded by the new Guild, the one that got the Tong kicked to the curb. When they discover the weapon's location, they plan to attack and try to destroy it. If the weapon is destroyed, we can take our planet back. The Tong has figured out most of the aliens are concentrated close to that weapon. Their numbers are spread thinly across the galaxies. Earth is just one planet they control. They haven't spread globally on Earth beyond a few key spots, but they use the Company's control over the people and their greed to run everything. The Tong thinks the aliens are vulnerable at this moment, but might fortify their garrisons on Earth if they think they're threatened. They also believe the weapon is not operational as yet. They're terrified of what it can do when it does come on line. Europa might be within range. So far, the aliens and the Company have no idea the base is here. I know if they knew, they'd attack. This base poses the biggest human threat to the aliens."

"What we need is someone who can hack into their system and discover where the weapon is located," Shayna said.

Cain snorted. "As far as I know, there's no one on this base with that kind of skill."

Bat was waiting in the corridor. He heard what Cain said and nodded. "Most everyone here is a fighter. We got pilots, we got skilled combat troops and we got a few IT people, but none of the Tong members on this base are able to hack into anything. We never had the need. We made our living hauling freight for the Company. We felt like we were safe. Boy, were we wrong."

Shayna looked thoughtful. "You know, there is one person here who says they have that skill."

Bat's eyes flew open. "Who?"

"Mark, the kid we saved from getting scarfed up by a gorp. Remember, he said he was a gamer and in his spare time, he liked to hack into his friends' systems. He also said he could hack into anything."

Bat scoffed. "You know he has to be exaggerating. I doubt if he could hack into my mother's personal computer. And she never sets up a password."

Ju shrugged. "At least ask him to try."

Cain shook his head. “He’ll probably contact the Company when we aren’t looking and rat us out.”

Ju batted her eyes and smiled. “Not if I’m there watching him. He likes me.”

Chapter Fifteen

Logan grabbed Knock's arm and dragged him into a quiet room. "We gotta get out of here," Logan said. "These people are never gonna leave the safety of these bunkers and attack the Company, I don't care what they say. And the rest of the world isn't gonna come here to help them just because I'm here. They're full of it. I'm not that big a deal. My name is not a rallying cry. So, that leaves us to take care of business. We've been on this path all of our lives. Things are no different for us than they were when we were kids. The Company is the enemy we must destroy, even if it means we sacrifice ourselves. And besides, I've got an idea. I think I might have a plan."

Knock rolled his eyes. "These people are certifiable, man. I mean, they are completely off their rockers."

Logan nodded. "Just what I'm thinkin'. Can we get everyone out of here or should we leave the women and children behind? They'll be safe here as long as they don't let the craziness get to them."

"I don't know, dude. That service we were forced to attend had everything but snakes. I swear, I was waitin' for that Zacharia crackhead to pull a poisonous reptile out of the altar and kiss it."

Logan sighed and nodded. "When he started spouting gibberish like he was possessed, I wanted to run."

Knock looked thoughtful. "But even though the level of crazy here is pretty high, I think we should leave all the women and kids here except Fang. I mean, Shayna's mom is exhausted, and the little kids need to stay where it's safe. The End Timers might be religious nut jobs, but they're alive and surviving when most of the world is either dead or transported to some mining planet to work like slaves until they die."

"I get you," Logan said. "They seem pretty safe in these bunkers. It works for me that they keep the women and kids separate. I know it's not something we're used to, but times are hard. Isolating them is one way to keep them safe. Let's take Jordie, Bobby, Raj and Corey. We can use their talents if we need tech help or we need that voodoo stuff Corey does. I'll leave a note for Zacharia and tell him we're going hunting for the aliens and ask him to take care of our women folk. I think he will. He might be pissed because we're running off on our own, but I think he'll roll with it. Don't you?"

"I honestly don't know," Knock said. "One minute he talks like a normal person and then the next like he's gone off the deep end and is pure cray."

"Think leaving him the message is a good idea?"

"Yeah, we don't want him cranked at the women and kids. Make sure you put in we'll be back as soon as we find out something."

"I will," Logan said. "I hope Shayna got my message. I need to find a way to access my box pretty soon. I gotta pay attention. She's in a crazy place. I can't believe she left Gliese."

Fang slipped her face close to Logan's. "I can't believe my mother and Ju are on Europa. What was Cain thinking when he took them off Gliese?"

"Chill, Fang," Logan said. "It sounded to me like there was no choice. At least they're all safe and they're together. They can look after each other."

Fang snorted. "Europa is a zillion miles from the sun. It's a ball of ice with almost no oxygen. How is that supposed to be safe?"

"Shayna said the Tong's base is solid and we have to trust it to be true." He put his arm around her. "We got our mission. Shayna and Cain have theirs. If I'm okay with my pregnant wife being there, you shouldn't worry about your sister and your mom."

Knock slipped close, putting his face right next to theirs. "I know how Loge feels about Shayna, Fang. If he's cool with it, you should be, too."

"Next chance I get, Ill check for news from them," Logan promised.

"You better," Fang snarled. "I still can't believe the Company dumped the Tong. What's the universe coming to? The Tong and the Company been together since the beginning of space exploration."

"It is pretty weird," Logan said.

"I think it's all about the cheddar," Knock said. "Somehow, this new Guild is putting more money into the Company's pockets than the Tong was. It's always about money with the Company."

"You got that right," Logan said.

"Where do you think we should go?" Knock asked.

"Let's head for Vegas. We really need to find Professor Goswami. If Corey can get a reading from him, maybe we can find him that way. Vegas is closer to San Francisco which is where he was when Corey picked up on him before."

"Dude," Knock said with a smile. "I'm with you."

The seven of them crept out of the bunker under Denver's airport late that night. Each carried a large pack and a weapon. Knock had discovered where the End Timers stored their munitions and broke into it. He'd also broken into Zacharia's rooms during one of their endless church services and stolen seven chips out of a wall safe and a handful of credit discs. The safe had been locked with a Level Five key which Logan just happened to have.

"You look like a crazy pirate," Fang said to Knock as she ruffled his hair. "Your hair's wild and you got that mad-dog look in your one eye."

Knock's lost eye socket was covered by a rakish black patch Shayna's mother had made for him. His vision would never be great again, but he could see.

He kissed Fang quickly to hide his embarrassment. "As long as you don't mind it," he mumbled.

They made it out of the End Timer's bunker and into the Loop tunnels. Once in the tunnels, they humped it to a station platform and climbed onto it. "Do you think the End Timers will punish our people when Zacharia discovers the missing chips?" Logan asked Knock.

Knock shrugged. They had boxes of them. I'm thinkin' they dug them out of a lot of dead people which kind of made me a little queasy. I'm not sure what those people are really after, but I think they done some bad, uh, stuff, in the past. Now the credit discs they might notice are gone. They had a small pile of them. I took about half. I'm hoping if they kept them locked up, there's still credit on them."

"Yeah, me, too," Logan said. "Boxes of chips? Really?"

"Looked like a couple hundred."

Logan pulled his chip out of his pocket. It was gold metal and shaped like a capsule. They were inserted under the skin at the back of the neck just below the hairline of all legitimate citizens when they were born. The doctors used a large-bore syringe specially made to insert the chips. "How long do you think we'll have to wait for the Loop?"

"I hope not too long. The End Timers aren't all that bright, but they ain't stupid neither. They'll figure out we're gone and come after us."

Logan shrugged. "Maybe they won't. We're leaving the women and kids here. That makes them hostages of a sort."

They piled their packs against the tiled walls and sat down, leaning against them. Logan squatted in front of Corey. "Can you read the Professor?" Corey had sandy hair and freckles. He looked about ten but assured everyone he was thirteen. His skinny frame housed a mutated intellect. He could read minds and sometimes tell the future. His milky-white eyes had pale green pupils. He sometimes seemed to look at things no one else could see.

Corey closed his eyes. "I'm getting a faint signal from him. I must have made a strong connection to him during the short time I knew him."

"It's because of me," Raj said. "I am his nephew."

Corey tilted his head. "Yeah, I guess that could be it. Give me your hand."

Raj put his brown hand in Corey's. Corey closed his eyes and squinted. Wrinkles appeared on his forehead. Suddenly Corey screamed and grabbed the back of his neck. "It hurts. It hurts. Stop torturing me."

Corey's eyes flew open. Tears filled the milky orbs. "The Professor ain't that far away. I'm reading him pretty clear, but his mind is partially walled off. He's definitely not as far away as San Francisco. I think he's being tortured by some weird kind of alien creature. I couldn't see it, but I got this crazy feeling like it's inside of him. He has a lot of pain at the top of his spine."

Logan sat back against his pack and thought. "Maybe they inserted a chip and that's causing the pain."

Corey shrugged. "You're probably right. I thought I felt an alien presence inside him, but it could be anything. Maybe the aliens holding him are projecting onto him. Sometimes I read several different people at a time."

"Where could they be keeping the Professor and why are they keeping him?" Raj asked. "He is my uncle and I am most sincerely attached to him, you know."

The rails began whining. Logan leaped to his feet and grabbed his pack. "Loop's up. Let's go."

The high-speed train zipped into the station out of the clear tube in which it ran. The tube, made of a high-tech clear material, is what gave the Loop its characteristic humming whine. There were no people at the station but them. When the train doors opened, Logan and his people ran into the middle car. They fell into empty seats, the doors slid shut without a sound, and the train shot off.

The Professor was awakened out of a sound sleep by one of his alien guards. "You must come with me," the alien said. Goswami had concluded all the aliens were males. He had yet to see any he felt he could label a female. The creature inside his head nudged him so he leaped to his feet and followed.

The guard led him to Vaerfeky's office. The alien leader sat behind his desk drinking something hot out of a tall cup. He used a straw made of blue plastic. Slurping sounds issued from his tiny mouth. Goswami stood in front of the desk and waited while Vaerfeky finished drinking. When he was done, he used one of his upper arms to wipe his rubbery lips. "You," he pointed at Goswami. "It is time for your usefulness to begin."

The creature inside Goswami urged him to speak. "Yes, master."

The edges of Vaerfeky's mouth turned up in what Goswami assumed was a smile. "I have news of Logan Hall, the human who stole one of our battleships and also attacked the prison on your moon. He is very dangerous. Other humans are gathering to rise up against us. They are being encouraged to do so by this Logan person." Vaerfeky waved his hand across the wall, a holo screen came on and there was Logan speaking.

Goswami didn't know whether to be elated or terrified. Logan was certainly inciting Vagrants around the world to rise up and take their planet away from the aliens. His story had become legend, his name a rallying cry. Goswami watched Logan speaking to the world and wondered how that had happened.

"You see," Vaerfeky snarled. "He be telling the humans to fight against us. He has much power and influence because of all the bad things he has done to us. He must be killed and you will either do this thing for me or you will lure him here where he can be disposed of."

Goswami felt the creature inside him stir. “Where can we find him great master?” Goswami asked.

Vaerfeky nodded. “Yes, find this slimy worm conspiracy person. We know he is on the Loop right now. Cameras recorded him and some persons of his friends probably. Thinking we are he is traveling toward your town in the desert, Las Vegas. You going there be to waiting for him and bring him to me here. Before we kill his living body slowly and painfully, we will use him to turn this stupid resisting thing to being gone forever. Resisting to us is not possible and we will show all human organisms how powerful are we. Now go.”

Goswami was ushered out of Vaerfeky’s office. He was taken to the entrance of the underground bunker beneath Area 51 and shoved into a pickup truck with a human guard driving. Goswami buckled his seatbelt as the guard slammed the truck into gear and took off down the dusty road leading off the base. His mind was whirling. The creature riding his spine had backed off and Goswami could barely feel it. The horror of what he’d been ordered to do filled him. He must find a way to disobey Vaerfeky and the creature inside of him. He could not lure Logan to his death. It was unthinkable.

Chapter Sixteen

The ride to Vegas was only an hour. No people, legal citizens or otherwise boarded the train. It stopped twice at small towns, but there was no one waiting. "Think anyone is left in Vegas?" Logan asked Knock as they sat staring at the walls of the Loop tunnel flashing past.

"You know, it's just the kind of city that will always have people hiding in the shadows. I'm betting there's Vagrants there, living in the underground parking garages, or the Loop tunnels."

Logan nodded. "My thoughts exactly."

Bobby spoke up. "It's Vegas. I'm sure the Company keeps Vegas alive. It's been a sin city for decades with gambling and, uh, women you can buy all legal and everything. I'm betting the casinos are now owned by the Company and filled with legal citizens sent there as a reward."

When Bobby said reward, it came out as ree-ward. Logan nodded. You could be right. Even the aliens might want to come to Vegas. You never know."

The Loop pulled into the Vegas terminal and stopped. The doors opened with a whoosh and Logan and his group exited the train fast. The sign over the station said this was the Las Vegas airport stop. Even though this was for the airport, and should be packed with people, there were none. Logan glanced at his watch. It was late, almost three in the morning. Still, in the past, Vegas was alive all night. However, the Loop rarely stopped anywhere longer than four to six minutes. It was designed to get people to their destinations on time, completely run by computers, with no exceptions for the vagaries of humans.

Logan hustled them off the train, waited until the doors slammed and it shot off down the tube, and then dove into the tunnel. They jogged down the Loop track until Logan spotted a maintenance room. He used his Level Five key to open it and they ran inside closing the door behind them.

Logan tossed his pack down. "Corey, try to feel the Professor," he said as they moved among the shelves and piles of equipment on the concrete floor. "We're under the airport," he said to Knock. "We should be close to everything."

Corey sat against his pack and closed his eyes. Raj sat next to him. In less than a minute, Corey's eyes flew open. "He's here, Logan. He's in Vegas. There are people here, too. In the hotels, lots of them. I felt a small group of Vagrants with the Professor. They're living in the bottom level of the Cosmopolitan Hotel."

"Where's that?" Logan asked.

"Uh," Corey shrugged. "Don't know. Should I?"

Logan rolled his eyes. "Can you read anything in any of their minds that might help us locate it?"

Corey went back into his trance. When his eyes opened again, he smiled. "Most of the major hotels are still operating. I guess there's plenty of guests and big shots coming to Vegas for the gambling and the, uh, the girls." Corey blushed to the roots of his hair. "Some of the Vagrants living under the Cosmopolitan work at the Mirage and even Circus Circus." He blushed again and stammered. "Most of the girl, I mean female Vagrants, work in the, uh . . . the show-girl industry. The ones that don't work, do the scrounging thing like all of us do."

Logan tried to control his patience. It was wearing thin. "So, where is the Cosmopolitan?"

Corey smiled and stood up. "I got this. It's on the main strip right near the City Center. There's a bunch of hotels right there; the Monte Carlo, Planet Hollywood, Veer Towers, there's a bunch all together. From what I'm reading, pickings are good, and there's not much Enforcer activity. The Enforcers think most of the Vagrants are gone, and even though they know some are still living under the city, they need them as workers so they leave them alone. Company's finding out you can't get rid of everyone. They need peons to farm and make their food and clean up after them. And women are becoming an important commodity." He paused. "At least pretty, young women are important."

Logan nodded. "They would be," he said with a sneer. "Even with hologram maids like Helga and Inga, real women will still be needed." He sat down next to his pack. "I'm having a hard time believing no Enforcer activity, though. Boy, that's weird."

"More than weird," Knock said. "I ain't never heard of no Enforcers, but what Corey said makes sense. There are legitimate citizens in the city, but they aren't gonna pick fruit or wash dishes. That leaves our people. Company's finally figuring that out. Amazing."

Logan looked around at his small group. "You guys got enough energy left to go find these Vagrants? The Professor could be with them."

Corey nodded. "I think he is. I can't say for sure, but he feels close to them. Kind of like he's there with them but not. I can't explain." He paused for a moment then added. "And he's really unhappy."

Logan just shook his head. "Are any of us happy?"

Raj touched Logan's elbow. "Please, let us hurry," he said. "My uncle, I have not seen him in such a long time."

They reentered the Loop tube and climbed onto the airport platform. Logan felt uncomfortable going up to the street level. He had to comfort himself with Corey's report about Enforcers and the fact it was late at night. When they exited the Loop complex, hot air hit them. It was like a fist to the face. Global warming must be accelerating.

"Dude," Knock said. "It's like a hundred degrees up here. Can't imagine what it's like when the sun's freaking out."

Logan ran his arm across his sweating forehead. "You know it must be an inferno."

They turned right and walked down the famous Las Vegas strip. Neon lights still blazed, flashed, and startled them with crazy imagery and color.

"Lights are on," Fang said. "I thought it would be dark like on Gliese. I've never imagined anything like this existed."

Knock pointed to his Zombieland shirt and frowned. "Rule twenty-one; Avoid strip clubs. This place feels weird."

Logan nodded. "Don't worry, Knock, we'll stay out of the clubs. And you're right. Place feels like it's on some other planet."

The neon, the street lights, they were blinding. Knock turned in a slow circle staring at all the magnificence. "Why do they bother with the lights? All the people are doped to their eyeballs on Sopore and they're asleep by now."

"I bet the lights are all set on some kind of timer," Bobby said. "The Company probably sends its people here as a reward and they wouldn't want them to be disappointed." He waved his hand to indicate the lights. "I mean, if you're in Vegas, you should get the whole package, right?" And as if on cue, every neon and streetlight blinked out leaving them in stygian darkness.

Logan glanced at his wrist com. Three a.m. exactly. "Bobby's right. I bet the lights just went out for most of the city."

They followed Corey down the deserted street. Logan passed a sign. They were on the corner of Las Vegas Boulevard and Tropicana. To the right was the MGM Grand, to the left New York New York. The neon lights were out on both huge hotels, but inside Logan saw basic lighting was still on in the lobbies and some of the windows on the rooms above were lit.

"How much farther?" He asked Corey.

Corey pointed down the canyon of huge casinos. "Your Professor is somewhere in the next block beneath that tall building with the pointy top. He's below us with a group of Vagrants. Most are awake. This is the hour many go to the street level to scrounge for food."

Corey's voice died away as they walked. A sudden shadow flickered next to Logan in the dry and dying shrubbery edging the wide boulevard. When he turned to squint into the darkness, he thought he saw another shadow move. Across the street set at an angle, was a familiar skyline, New York. When Logan saw the Empire State Building, he gasped. "Look, Knock."

"Dude, I know. Creepy or what? They even have old Lady Liberty."

"I think we're surrounded by Vagrants," Logan said. "I keep seeing shadows."

They walked under a pedestrian bridge crossing from the MGM Grand to New York New York and the shadows began to close in. Corey stopped. "They're here," he whispered.

In seconds, they were surrounded by a group of people dressed in dark clothing. Most wore hoods. Crazy eyes stared at Logan and his people out of the hoods. "Who are you?" One stepped forward. When the person pushed back the hood of a black sweatshirt, Logan saw the shadowed figure was a woman, a very beautiful woman. She was tall with a perfect nose, flawless, peachy skin, a wide lush mouth, and long blond hair. Her eyes were a weird light blue and stared at Logan without a trace of fear.

Fang stepped close to Logan and whispered. "Remember, you're married."

Logan pushed her away. "We're looking for Professor Goswami," he said to the drop-dead gorgeous woman. "I'm Logan Hall." Logan grabbed Raj's arm and pulled him forward. "This is Raj Kumaran, the Professor's nephew."

The woman turned her arresting gaze on Raj. She bent a little, she had to be well over six-feet tall, and peered at Raj in the gloomy darkness of the Vegas street. "You look like him," she said. "I'm Kylie Crystal. I used to be a showgirl. Now I'm a Vagrant. Welcome to Vegas." She eyed Logan. "So, you're the great Logan Hall I've heard so much about. You have a serious reputation almost everywhere. The Professor can't stop singing your praises. We all saw your broadcast. Pretty bizarre, but very dope. I mean it was epic."

Logan shook her hand. It was a lovely hand with long fingers and perfectly manicured nails. "Uh," he stammered. "Nice to meet you. Uh, ummm, this is Knock, Fenfang, Corey over there, Bobby's our pilot and Jordie. Jordie's our tech. He shouldn't be here. He was conscripted when we escaped Gliese. He was on the Company ship we stole, and Corey over there can read minds, and Fang is an expert with a sword, and Knock, he's my best friend. I've known him since we lived under New Washington and..."

Knock punched him in the ribs and whispered. "You're babbling, dude. It's embarrassing."

Logan's face flamed. Kylie smiled and flipped long bangs out of her eyes. "Come with me. Professor Goswami has been waiting for you to show up."

Suddenly, the sky to the north of the city lit up with an electric blue glow. The glow swelled. It contained sizzling sparks of darker blue light that shimmered as the glow grew until it illuminated the city around them in harsh, clear blue light shot through with the crazy sparks of energy. "Duck!" Kylie screamed.

Logan and his group instinctively fell to the ground with their hands over their heads. A powerful wind sucked loose gravel, sticks, pieces of paper, empty cups and garbage into the glow which had begun to spiral like a tornado. Kylie's group followed then to the ground as the earth shook and a beam of white light shot out of the blue glow and swirling trash. It penetrated the sky and shot high out of Earth's atmosphere into the heavens. The ground kept vibrating. A full five minutes after Logan had first spotted the glow, the earth stopped shaking. He slowly rose to his knees, dusted gravel and sand off his shirt, and stared down the boulevard. The top of the Empire State Building was hanging. It had cracked and fallen. "It's going to go," he shouted.

The top of the building was close. If it fell they might be splattered by pieces of mortar, concrete and glass. It would surely crash into the Statue of Liberty at its base and bring down the network of roller coaster rails crisscrossing in front of it.

"Run," Kylie screamed.

Her people leapt to their feet and bolted down the boulevard toward the tall building Logan now knew was the Cosmopolitan. A resounding groan was followed by a horrible thunderous crash. Logan glanced behind, saw the Statue of Liberty teetering on its base. It looked like it would end up falling toward the street and them. The coaster rails were tangled around the statue's green neck and raised arm. "Faster!" he shouted.

Kylie led them at a dead run across the boulevard. They leaped the shriveled, dying shrubs in the median and raced across the lanes to the other side of the street, pounded toward the MGM Grand sign, and threw themselves behind it. As they huddled on the far side of the huge MGM sign, now dark, the Statue of Liberty fell toward them. It was like slow motion. It weaved for a moment, rails from the roller coaster hanging around the statue's neck, then fell toward the boulevard. It crushed the MGM Grand's gold lion statue, barely visible in the dark and only a few feet away and shattered into hundreds of pieces. When the dust died, a weird silence fell over the city.

"What in the hell was that?" Logan demanded from Kylie.

Kylie stood up and patted herself down to remove the concrete dust speckling her dark hoodie. "I think, but I can't say for sure, that was a weapon test. Professor Goswami has told us the aliens have a complex north of us housing a super, planet-destroying weapon."

Logan tilted his head. "You say it's north of here? Does he know exactly where it is?"

She shrugged as the rest of their two groups struggled to their feet looking dazed. "You'll have to ask him."

The group with Kylie circled Logan's people as if corralling them, and Kylie started down the boulevard. The trees and shrubs of Vegas had long died. Without the lights and no water in any fountains, it was like a concrete canyon. No cars on the street, no pedestrians, just buildings and glass towers, huge billboards, and dark signs all right up against each other in a never-ending flow. The entire city sweltered, even in the dark. It had to be a hundred degrees with no water anywhere.

Kylie led them to a narrow walkway between a tall building with a few lights flickering in high windows, and what seemed an exact replica of the Eiffel Tower. She found a dark ramp leading down and turned into it. It was the entrance to the underground parking garages beneath the Cosmopolitan.

Logan's group hurried to keep up as Kylie jogged down the ramp onto the first level. The temperature dropped dramatically as they went underground. Kylie hurried through the first level of parking and continued down the ramp. There were odd murals on the walls. Some black and white murals were just writing in an ancient and weird style. A few of the murals were in color. There were crazy faces looking like goddesses from ancient times and one was a huge eye with radiating lines and writing that said, "Believe what you are told."

Logan stopped and pointed. "That looks like something the Company woulda put down here."

Kylie indicated they should hurry. "The murals are famous and have been down here forever. Keep your head down. There're cameras all around us. Few are monitored any more, but they're here. Never dawdle in this garage. Keep close to the walls."

Immediately, Logan's people flattened themselves against the walls. Knock and Logan looked in all directions. Logan spotted at least five cameras and several ears. The ears were on, blinking green. Bobby was alert, but Fenfang and Jordie, having lived most of their lives on spaceships or another planet looked confused. "What cameras?" Fang whispered to Knock.

Knock pointed to tiny plastic lumps in the corners with telescoping lenses.

They hurried further into the bowels of the earth ending up four levels below the city in the subterranean workings of the hotel. Kylie led them down concrete corridors into what had to be an old laundry room. She went past enormous washers and dryers to a tall metal set of shelving holding laundry products and folded towels and sheets. She rolled it aside revealing an exit, then opened the door and beckoned for Logan and his group to follow. Logan stayed close behind her as they entered the mechanical plant of the hotel. Topside it was almost a hundred degrees. The plant hummed as it manufactured air conditioning for the huge hotel. They exited the mechanical plant into another corridor. Kylie opened a metal door and led them into a room filled with the biggest hot water heater Logan had ever seen. The atmosphere was suffocating in the room; hot and damp.

The tanks of water were heated with gas. A slight odor of natural gas lingered. There was a poofing noise as the gas jets under the tanks ignited and the odor went away. The water heater must be on all the time.

Kylie glanced behind at them, dove under a network of gas lines, and into a narrow crawl space. She pulled herself along using her elbows, rolled to the left, and stood up. Logan followed and found himself in a dark, unfinished chamber. She led them through this chamber into a much larger one. Along the walls there were lit lanterns and cubicles built out of cardboard and hanging sheets. The Professor stepped out of one and stared at Logan as though he couldn't believe what he saw. Raj emerged into the chamber, spotted his uncle and ran forward. "Uncle Depak. I thought I'd never see you again."

They embraced for a second before the Professor set him gently aside and walked toward Logan. In the flickering light of a nearby lantern, Logan saw the Professor's face. He seemed conflicted and so much older. His faced was lined with wrinkles and deep creases. His skin was darker, but not browner, more like a dark gray. He looked unhealthy. Goswami smiled for a second, looked desperate and terrified for another second, and then smiled again. "Logan," he said. "You're here."

Logan grabbed the Professor in a bear hug. "I'm so glad to find you alive, man. Last time I saw you, you looked like crap. I thought you died."

The Professor patted Logan on the back. "I almost did, dear boy. I almost did." And then he said something Logan thought was pretty weird. "It would have been so much better if I had."

Chapter Seventeen

Mark Moretti was hungry. He was always hungry. His hunger had begun when he was a small child and his parents parked him with one nanny after another. They were rich and busy. He overdosed on Sopore twice before he was twelve. He liked cake, pie, cookies, ice cream and soda, all heavily infused with Sopore. By the time his parents ordered the new nanny to watch his diet, he was already caught in the deadly cycle of lazy, plus fat, equals lazier and fatter. His only friend was the computer. He spent most of the day trying to get sweets out of his new babysitter, who was really more of a tutor, and learning how to hack into systems. It was fun and his only outlet, and he was good at it.

As he sat on a rolling stool, most of the office-type chairs in Waterworld were too small to contain his bulk, he entered the code he thought would take him through a backdoor into Sequoia, a supercomputer in Livermore, California at the Lawrence Livermore Laboratory just east of Silicon Valley. The computer had been on the top-ten list of super computers for fifty years. It had over thirty million processor cores and an unthinkable number of megaflops per watt. Mark had hacked Sequoia three years ago when he was using his own equipment at home in California. The computer felt different now. He couldn't put his finger on the change, it just felt odd. Some of the questions it asked and paths he tried to follow were, well they were alien. Had the aliens taken control of it and were they using it for their own purposes? Mark thought so.

Because he was thinking the aliens were controlling Sequoia, he cut out of the connection and tried a different supercomputer. This one was run by the Chinese. The Tong owned it, but the Tong was out, the Guild in. So, who was running the Milky Way?

Milky Way was the translation of the Chinese name for the computer, Tianhe-8. He went through channels he'd used before, plugged in his password software and started it, and waited. He realized almost immediately Milky Way was no longer being operated by humans. Strange symbols appeared on his screen and an ominous feeling filled Mark. They knew he was trying to get in. Terror gave his fat fingers speed. He exited the system, shut down the computer station he was using and rolled away from it. If the aliens controlled all of Earth's super computers, they were screwed. He heaved himself to his feet and went looking for Shayna and Ju.

He found them in the control room. Shayna's face glowed partly from her pregnancy and partly because she looked so excited. She sat at a computer station with Ju hanging over her shoulder. Ever watchful, Bat hovered next to Ju. Mark sighed. Ju would never look at him or prefer him to the handsome and dynamic Mongolian. Bat was everything Mark was not. Just look at him. Mark knew he didn't stand a chance with Ju. Mark had been in the gym with Ju faithfully for two weeks and had lost some weight and gained some muscle, but he would never be a darkly handsome warrior with a trim athletic body and magnetic personality. He was always going to be the chubby, boring, computer geek, Mark Moretti. He might as well accept it. Ju would never look twice at him if he couldn't hack into big systems, and now he'd failed at that. He had to tell Shayna and the humiliating part was Bat was standing right there to hear all about his defeat along with Cain Hollyroad, the leader of the Gliese Vagrants.

He shifted uneasily from one foot to the other. His clothes bagged on him. He wore the same uniform Bat wore, black pajama-like pants and over tunic. His was just twenty sizes larger and didn't possess the gold emblem of a Tong warrior over the left breast. He finally had to interrupt Shayna's concentration. When Mark glanced at her holographic screen, he saw she was opening her message program. "Shayna," he hesitated.

She looked up at him and smiled. Ju backed away from Shayna and pushed Mark forward. "Have you made any progress?" Shayna asked.

"That's why I'm, uh, here," he stammered. "I'm pretty sure all the super computers on Earth are now controlled by aliens. I think the Milky Way, that's the one the Tong runs, knew I was there. I backed out pretty fast. Sequoia, that's the one in California felt weird, too. I been in that one before and it was different. It felt off."

Shayna patted his arm. "Don't worry. I think I have a message from Logan. He might have discovered the location of the alien weapon."

Mark tried not to groan. He wanted to be the hero.

Shayna opened her message. It was from Logan. As she read, her face grew hotter and hotter. All he talked about was the group he'd found in Las Vegas and the incredibly beautiful women that seemed to be in charge of it.

"Dearest Shayna," the letter began. "I'm safe and I've found the Professor. He's living with a group of showgirls. They're these super-hot women the Company has kept on even when they sent away almost everyone else. The girls are here to entertain Company officials in shows and as waitresses and stuff like that. I know this sounds weird, but the leader, this chick named Kylie Crystal, she's like six feet tall, has the best body I've ever seen on a real woman, not like a hologram maid, a real woman with long blond hair, says the aliens like women with, uh, with large breasts. Can you believe it? Anyway, I thought it was pretty weird, but Kylie says it's true. These Vegas girls are not only hot, they're smart, too. The leader, this Kylie chick, can fight like Fang and she sings at clubs on the strip for Company big shots. All the girls here with this group are smokin' hot. No wonder the Company kept them on."

After reading that over her shoulder, Bat snorted. "What a moron. He should know better than to tell you stuff like that."

Shayna rounded on Bat. "You be quiet. Logan can tell me anything."

Bat rolled his eyes. "Sure, that's why your face is the color of a fire extinguisher."

Shayna grabbed her cheeks. They felt hot. She was angry, and hurt, but Logan's words showed how artless and innocent he was. If he'd concealed these details about the Vegas group, and she found out about them, that would be bad. She stifled the urge to shriek at Bat, and said calmly. "I trust Logan. He'd never hurt me."

She went back to reading her letter.

"There are some dudes here, too, people that wait tables, clean hotel rooms, cook in the casinos and they're some dealers. There are no old people or children in this group which makes it even stranger. Some of the people are wanted by the law. The ones who don't work, they scrounge. You know the deal there. Vegas is different, but it's still Vegas. All the lights shut down at three in the morning and the streets are empty. The Professor is freaking me out a little. He seems different, preoccupied, not at all like his old self. When you ask him a question, he goes away for a minute. Not his body, it's like his mind just shuts down and then a few seconds later, he comes back and answers the question or resumes talking. I'm worried about him, but I still trust him. No matter what's happened to him, he'd never hurt me. I just know that and hold onto it so I don't completely freak out."

"Did you read that?" Shayna asked Cain.

Cain had scanned ahead rapidly. He pointed further down in Logan's note. "See where it says here the alien super weapon is north of Vegas. Logan's description of the weapon test is terrifying. It sounds like anti matter, black hole technology. I heard the Company was working on that, but now, I'm thinkin' it was always the aliens that had it. Not the Company. But then it looks like the Company is run by the aliens and has been for a long time. They seem pretty settled in."

"Logan says he's using equipment scrounged by this group of Vagrants to contact me. They get access to things no other group can because of the women." Shayna's voice dripped with venom when she said women. Ju patted her shoulder. "Don't worry about Logan, dear. He would never be unfaithful."

Shayna burst into tears, stood up, and fell into Ju's arms. The younger girl stroked her back and hair as Shayna sobbed into her shoulder. "I know. But I'm not there and we're so far away from each other." She sniffed and wiped her nose on her sleeve. She wore one of the ubiquitous black pajama suits just like everyone else. Her belly was a sizable bulge and the pants were enormous and bagged around her ankles in puddles. "If he saw how fat and ugly I've become he would hate me."

Ju glanced over Shayna's shoulder. "Not true. You're glowing. Pregnancy has made you even lovelier."

Cain leaned down and finished reading the letter from Logan. "He says the Professor knows where the alien base is located. He's going to take Logan and Knock to it tomorrow."

Shayna nodded. "I read that. I hope he doesn't do anything crazy or stupid."

Cain grinned. "He's with Knock and Fang, so crazy will no doubt be part of anything they do. Ditto stupid."

Shayna groaned. "You're not making me feel any better. I was thinking the same thing. If anyone can get Logan into deep trouble, it's Knock."

Ju nodded. "And Fang is no better. She was always getting into trouble when we were kids."

Shayna rolled her eyes. "Thanks, just what I needed to hear."

Kylie drew Logan into her private room. It was a tented enclosure with a narrow cot, a small table and two chairs. A hand-crafted quilt lay crumpled on top of the cot. Logan sat in one of the chairs as Kylie plopped two mugs on the table and he examined his hostess. Today, she wore a tight leather skirt, thigh-high boots and a leather bomber jacket over a blue T-shirt that said, "Good girls go to heaven, bad girls go to Vegas." Her hair was pulled into a knot on top of her head. A gold ring detailed her sculpted right nostril. "Coffee," she said. "No cream or sweetener, just pure java."

"Mmmm," Logan said as he picked up his mug and sniffed the delicious aroma. "It's been a long time since I had the real thing."

"We get some pretty good stuff down here. The Company goes all out for the people they send here. It's a reward so they make it a good one, and we benefit as a result. Still have to screen everything for Sopore, but that goes without saying."

It was noon. Most of the residents of the underground city had been asleep. The heat from five stories above had reached them. It wasn't a hundred, but the temperature was rising. "It even gets warm down here," Logan said as he sipped the scalding liquid. It was rich, aromatic and bitter. He savored each tiny sip. "I can't believe it."

"The equatorial regions of Earth are virtually uninhabitable," she said. "Most of the remaining population has gravitated to the far north and far south. We're hanging on here by a thread. I've heard there is some plan in the works to build a dome over Vegas or maybe to attempt some kind of terraforming."

"They can do that now?" Logan was stunned. Terraforming technology would enable them to settle on any planet close enough to the sun to be warm, as long as it had water. Water was always the key issue.

"They're close. We hear a lot because of our position with the Company. Some of our girls, uh, spend private time, you understand what I'm saying by private time, with high up Company officials. The aliens are also interested in Earth women, but in what I have to say is a weird and strange obsession. They find breasts fascinating. I've been told their women don't possess them."

"Breasts? What the heck?"

Kylie shrugged. "I know. Go figure. It has, however, given us some golden opportunities I'm not ashamed to say we've taken every advantage of."

Logan nodded. "I can see how it would." He forced himself to look only at her face. "I know what you're talking about. Men blab when they're in bed with a woman. Do the aliens have their own women on Earth? I mean did they bring them along?"

"There's a huge mother ship on the other side of the moon. We've heard the alien leaders get leave and go spend time up there for recreational purposes. A few have wives, but rumors say they're not monogamous. They can have more than one woman, one chief wife, but lots of concubines. So, they feel perfectly fine about fiddling around with Earth women on the side. Logan, some of the stuff I hear about is pretty freaky."

"I don't wanna know," Logan said. "I don't even wanna imagine. You said there's a mother ship on the other side of the moon? Now that's something I'm interested in." He needed to get that info to Shayna right away. He'd already written to her and hated to ask for more time on the group's com equipment. He decided to wait until later when maybe, he'd have more info to send her. "Have you heard anything else?"

Kylie smiled. "I get most of my information from the humans working with the aliens and the majority of the humans visiting here are either drunk, doped to the eyeballs on Sopore, or both. They like recreational drugs which we supply, and then they spill what they know, but that's not much. They say the aliens are afraid us humans will rise up and threaten them. They've started to have a little more respect for us as a species. Especially after you and your friends captured the battleship and killed the mutated nightmare, Dr. Dray."

"Do they have plans to control us?"

Kylie nodded. "They do. We're not sure what, but we're pretty sure it has to do with that weapon."

"The weapon sounds scary," Logan said. "But is it mobile or stuck here on Earth?"

"It's mobile," Professor Goswami said from behind Logan. They sat in Kylie's small tented compartment so when Goswami spoke, Logan was startled. Where had he come from? Was he snooping? But the Professor seemed more normal today. His smile was so familiar. Logan unwound and relaxed.

"Where's Shayna?" The Professor asked.

Logan told him without even thinking about his response. "She's on Europa with the Tong."

The Professor's eyes lit up. "Europa? The Tong has a base there? That moon is supposed to be a frozen wasteland."

Logan shrugged as a tiny sniggle of fear shot up his spine. Had he messed up in some way by telling the Professor about Europa? He shook off the strange feeling of uneasiness. How could telling the Professor about Europa be a bad thing? He was here, with Vagrants, not associating with the aliens or the Company. How could confiding this information to him be a bad thing? He couldn't see where the danger could come from, but that creepy feeling of uneasiness would not go away.

"I guess it's not." He answered the Professor with as little information as possible. Suddenly, he had no desire to share any of his thoughts, feelings or information with someone who had been his closest confident for years. If just felt weird. Anything that might even remotely put Shayna in danger, or put the resistance the Tong was mounting in trouble, he would avoid at all cost.

The Professor leaned forward. He had plopped his skinny butt on Kylie's cot after pushing the quilt aside. His glasses hung on the end of his brown nose, and his dark hair stood up in spikes. A fleck of spit dangled from the corner of his fleshy bottom lip. He looked and smelled as though he hadn't bathed in weeks. His white shirt was stained and one cuff badly torn. The frayed ends dangled loosely over his thin brown hand. He wore sandals that had been patched with duct tape and cut-off jean shorts. "What has the Tong built on Europa? Is it a real base? How many people are there? Do they have weapons or fighters? How many ships are there?"

The rapid-fire questions only made Logan's suspicions stronger. Was the Professor working for the Company? Such a thought was ridiculous. Professor Goswami had started the Vagrant resistance many years ago with Logan's father. He would never turn his back on them and work for aliens or the Company. Still, Logan didn't answer his questions. It felt wrong to do so. He made up his mind to talk to Corey immediately, smiled at the Professor and shook his head. "I don't know. Shayna hasn't said."

He rushed out of Kylie's tent and went looking for Raj and Corey. They'd found a comfortable tent made of hotel-room curtains hung on a framework of shower rods close to the cardboard shelter occupied by the Professor. The curtains were gold brocade and too long. There was a puddle of fabric at the bottom of each.

Raj was asleep inside the tent, but Corey was wide awake sitting on a folding chair reading the instruction manual for a portable generator sitting on the concrete floor next to him. He looked up and Logan was stunned at how young Corey appeared. His faded brown eyes were bright in his thin face under a mop of brown hair that kept falling over them. He brushed the hair out of his eyes and grinned. 'This will help out when the power goes off." He used a rag to wipe built up layers of grease off the faded green engine. "If I can get it to work."

"It's gas," Logan said. "The fumes will poison the air down here."

"They got a system rigged to draw the fumes off into the ducts. I understand small engines. Maybe I can make it run."

"Listen Corey," Logan squatted next to the boy and glanced into the tent to make sure Raj was sleeping. "I have a weird feeling about the Professor." Logan felt bad even putting his thoughts into words. It seemed almost treasonous and certainly disloyal. "Can you touch his mind lightly, you know so he can't tell you're there, and check to see if he's like normal."

Corey's face darkened. "I already tried to tell you there's something going on in his brain. I couldn't exactly figure out what, but there's an alien flavor running around the edges of his thoughts. Sometimes I see thoughts in colors or images. The Professor's brain is mostly blue, which is good, but there's a sickly yellow on one edge I don't like. When I see it, or feel it, I back away. It makes me nauseous to get too close."

Logan rocked back on his heels. "When he's talking to me, he stops and kind of disappears for a minute into his head. I've never seen him do that before. It's so weird I can't figure out whether he can be trusted or not, and I've known the Professor all my life."

"I just met him and in my opinion, well no, don't trust him."

"Trust who?" Raj asked as he climbed off the bedroll on the floor and scratched his wild hair. "My uncle? Are you being funny? My uncle is a most honorable man. He would never betray his friends or the Vagrants in any way. Surely, you know this, Logan. He's been like a father to you. You've known him all of your life."

Logan winced. He'd hoped to avoid confronting Raj and was certain the kid would tell his uncle. "We're just worried about the women here and all the Vagrants who work for the Company," Logan lied. "They seem pretty friendly with Company people and all."

Raj nodded and smiled. "I think they are trustworthy. They certainly took us in and provided us with every comfort. I slept deeply and feel most wondrously rested."

Knock appeared and grabbed Logan's arm. "Thanks, Corey," Logan said. He flicked his eyes at Raj and back to Corey in as plain a message as he could pass on without saying anything. Corey nodded as Logan stood up and turned to follow Knock.

"What's up?" He asked as the two of them wandered into the shadows. Huge concrete columns supported the floor above which was part of the parking garage. The ceiling was twelve feet above their heads. The corners were dark and dirty. Knock led him to a far corner and squatted next to the wall. Logan squatted beside him with his back against the rough concrete. "You see these chicks?" Knock finally said.

"You pulled me over here to talk about them?" Logan couldn't believe it.

"No, dude, I mean they're pretty sweet and Fang is green with jealousy, but I was just being, you know, opening a conversation like."

"And?" Logan said.

"And there's something wrong with the Professor. He's not right."

Logan shrugged. "He did almost die."

"Well Fang never knew him before and she says there's something wrong with him, and she's usually right on about everything. I, like listen to her, you know. And he did almost die. So, did you ask him how he got saved and who did the saving?"

"Good point," Logan said. "I haven't had the time. Let's go talk to him."

"Cool," Knock said. "I don't think we should blab anything important about us or what we're planning until we're sure he's okay. Just my opinion, dude, but Fang says he's wrong. I mean, where'd he come from? How'd he get here? I think we need to know the answers." Knock grinned. "Or at least Fang thinks so."

"So does Corey," Logan said as they walked back into the populated area. It was well-lit during operating hours by sodium vapor lights. They cast a yellow glow over everything from small lights set into the concrete ceiling. The two of them converged on the Professor together. The older man was leaning against one of the concrete columns next to Kylie's tent. He chewed on a stalk of wheat grass. The slender green piece of grass hung on his bottom lip and bounced as he chewed. The Vegas Vagrants grew the stuff under special lights for health and made juice out of it.

"Uh, dude," Knock began. "We got to talking and they're a few things we don't understand."

Logan nodded. "We trust you, of course, just want some details." Logan felt disloyal confronting his old mentor, but he had to know.

Knock rubbed the eyepatch over his missing eye, lifted it and scratched the open socket. "Yeah, we're just thinkin' and you know how that goes." He laughed.

The Professor smiled, his eyes crinkling at the corners. The expression reassured Logan. It was the same familiar smile he'd grown up knowing and loving. "Surely, ask me anything. I have no secrets."

"You know," Knock started. "We were wondering where you got cured? Logan saw you almost die so we know you were sick, but how did you get better and how did you get to Vegas? Did you like escape from the Company?"

The Professor's eyes turned inward. Logan could almost say it was as though the Professor was staring at his own brain. If that was possible which it wasn't. "Oh yes, I was in the cell with Logan when I had a heart attack. I believe it began when the evil mutant tortured me. The Company put me in one of those healing chambers in San Francisco."

Logan nodded. "Then what?"

The Professor's smile was no longer warm and fuzzy, it was creepy. Logan had never seen him smile quite that way. And his use of words was different. The Professor had always had a slight Indian inflection on his word choice and way of speaking.

"Then they took me to the base where the weapon is kept."

"Dude, why would they do that? Sounds stupid to me."

"Oh, they thought I could help them by pointing out Vagrant hideouts and targets for their weapon."

"I thought the weapon was like a planet-killing weapon," Knock said. "Not some lame weapon to use on Vagrant holdouts."

"It is, it is," the Professor said. "But it can be used on a smaller scale as well."

"So, did you?" Logan asked.

"Did I what?" The professor seemed confused.

"Tell them all you know about Vagrants and targets for their weapon."

"Oh, no, no, no," the Professor said with a small smile. "I would never."

"Professor, dude, none of this is making any sense." Knock stepped close to the Professor, stared into his murky brown eyes and poked him in the chest with a grubby finger. "Something ain't right with you and your story is total BS."

Logan pushed Knock back. "Give him a chance to tell the rest of the story." Logan stared at the Professor. "How did you get away and how did you avoid telling the Company and those aliens everything you know?"

The Professor patted Logan's arm and tilted his head. "Logan, my greatest friend, you should trust me. I escaped before they could use their nefarious methods of questioning on me. I had help. An old friend of your father was also imprisoned there. He and I escaped together. Sadly, he was killed while we were escaping, but he enabled me to get away. It was marvelous I made it here."

Logan shook his head. "I would call it miraculous. So, who was this friend of my father's?"

"General Mullins, Hector Mullins," the Professor said. He was in the Rangers with your father and had been promoted many times. The aliens held him prisoner. He was able to make an escape when the aliens were moving him to another cell. He was older but had many of his combat skills. The aliens were startled and he got away. I was luckily in a waiting room. The aliens planned to question me so they had me out of my cell. They believe me to be old and frail so I was not restrained. When General Mullins ducked inside of the room to escape the

Enforcers following him, he recognized me and took me with him. Yes, General Mullins had many skills. He got us out of the compound and into a truck. I'm afraid he killed several people while we were running."

Logan did not like any of this story, but asked a question anyway. "So, where's the General?"

"The Professor's mouth turned down in a sad frown. "As I said, he was killed. The truck he stole flipped many times and rolled into a ditch. He did not survive. I managed to crawl out of a window and hide. Then I made my way here."

Knock rolled his one eye. "Okay, so where's this terrible alien weapon?"

The Professor's smile was warm and genuine. "There is an old secret military base out in the desert. It's close to Nellis Air Force test range. Almost a hundred years ago, they tested nuclear weapons there. The base is directly north of here close to Crystal Springs, off of Highway 93. There's about, I mean there's a lot of buildings and hidden bunkers on this base. It's only about a hundred miles away. It took me four days to walk it. I would have died of heat and thirst out on the road if Kylie's people hadn't found me. They patrol up there."

Logan nodded. Even if the Professor was working for the aliens or the Company, the information he'd just passed on was critical. As long as it was accurate. "You're sure of this location?"

"The Professor smiled and nodded. "Of course. I was there."

Logan grabbed Knock's arm. "Come on, we gotta talk to Kylie."

As they walked away from the Professor, Knock shot Logan a questioning glance. "So?"

Logan shrugged. "I can't believe the Professor would ever betray us. I heard once that heart attacks, especially bad ones, change people. He's still the Professor and he was like a father to me when my dad was hauled off to work in the mines. I think we have to trust him. I'm going to send this information to Shayna so she can give the location of the weapon to the Tong."

"You sure of this?"

Logan stopped and stared into his best friend's one good eye. "We have to chance it. If the Tong can mount an attack on the weapon before it's fully operational, we can save our world."

"Knock rolled his eye. "Yeah sure, the Tong will attack. Right. Well, my money's on us, dude. I think we need to make a plan and head up to this secret base ourselves. We can't be waiting on the Tong. I mean, it's the Tong. You really trust them to save the day?'

Logan shrugged. "I can hope, can't I? But probably not."

"Then we make a plan of our own, get the Prof to guide us, and go get that weapon."

Logan nodded. "I'm down with that. Sitting around here is already getting pretty lame. I wanna go home. I need to see Shayna. She's gonna have my kid, dude. I should be there not hanging around Vegas waiting for something to happen."

Knock grinned. "You got that right. Get Corey, Raj, Bobby and some of the other guys if they wanna go. I'll grab Fang and go talk to Kylie. Maybe she can find us a couple of trucks and a van and some weapons."

"Explosives," Logan said. "We need some Nano-thermite, or some other super-high-tech explosives, and a couple of portable missile launchers. We need to seriously arm ourselves."

Knock rolled that one good eye again.

"Dude," Logan said. "If you keep rolling that one eye of yours, it might stop working."

"Can't help it. Where's this chicky group of Vagrants gonna get stuff like that? Did you look at them? Now if you want some glitter, a pair of six-inch high heels or maybe a G-string, I feel sure they can supply you, but weapons?"

Logan grinned. "Doesn't hurt to ask and that Kylie chick is a serious bad-ass."

Chapter Eighteen

The Tong base on Europa was crammed with people. Every Tong member within light years of Earth's system had showed up to fight the Company and alien control of humans. They were looking for a safe haven and Waterworld provided that.

The Tong traveled with their families on a variety of space craft, some of it old and some sparkling new with high-tech additions. They were a space-traveling society that had been the Company's choice for smuggling illegal items and drugs to Company colonies for decades. Their alliance with the Company had lasted until the Company recently joined forces with the Smugglers Guild and ruthlessly kicked them out.

The Tong was out of favor and being aggressively hunted across the known universe. This had driven them to ally themselves firmly on the side of the Vagrants. So far as Shayna knew, the Company had no idea the Tong had sided with Vagrants in an all-out war to eliminate alien and Company control of humanity, but she had no doubt they would know very soon. Time was running out.

Shayna's room in the women's quarters was full. There were over five hundred women and children staying on Waterworld. There were even more men, most warriors and pilots. Even the old men had positions in their war plans, and boys as young as ten trained with the adults. The landing field for ships had been expanded and held hundreds of fighters, star ships and freighters. The newest arrivals had to land outside the dome. Things were getting pretty crowded on Europa.

As she sat on her cramped bunk and worried about Logan and her future on this base if he never showed up, she rubbed her bulging belly. She hadn't heard from Logan in three days. If anything happened to him where would she go? What would she do? She was due to have her baby in four months. She had no marketable skills, nothing the Tong could use that would make her useful to them. Her only claim to fame was as Logan's wife. She was treated with respect because of that. If he died, who knew how long she could bank on that respect. If it hadn't been for Ju and Mark, the poor overweight kid they'd dragged with them off Gliese, she'd be alone.

The Vagrant colonists from Gliese all seemed remarkably able to care for themselves and hoped to go home to Gliese when the war was over. She felt apart from them and isolated. Logan had to live. Her life, or life as she knew it, depended on it. She didn't feel able to go on without him. He was the center of her life, the father of her child, and he held her heart forever.

Ju's bunk was above hers. There were three more above Ju's. The girl hung her head over the edge of the formed fiberglass bunks and grinned. Her one long braid hung almost to the top of Shayna's head. "This sucks," she said about the crowded dorm. "I wonder how long all these people will have to be here. Rations are getting thin even though they all brought food synthesizers and rice with them. Poor Mark has lost even more weight. He's glad, but he complains all the time about being hungry."

As if on cue, Mark stuck his head into the room. He had to thread his way between cots and pallets to reach Shayna. "Uh," he started speaking to Shayna even though his eyes were on Ju's face. Shayna could see the kid was in love. "Uh, Bat sent me to get you. There's a message in your box from Logan."

Shayna leapt to her feet. "Finally. I was starting to imagine all kinds of terrible things." She smiled up at Ju. "I was getting a little freaked out." She put her hand on Mark's thick forearm. The kid worked out twice a day and had developed some serious muscles. His old pants hung on his body cinched tightly at the waist with a piece of cord. He'd been given one of the black tops with no insignia. He still had a big belly, and since he was so tall, he seemed huge. Orientals were for the most part a small race. Waterworld was designed for smaller people. It made things harder for Mark. Ceilings were low, doorways small and low, and the Tong tended to cram facilities and furniture into tiny spaces making navigating inside of the buildings more difficult for a big person. "That's wonderful. Let's go to the Command Center so you can read it," Ju said."

They left the women's quarters clothed in cold weather gear. Mark had found pants that fit but so far, no jacket big enough to cover his broad shoulders and thick arms. He draped one around his upper body, but it didn't cover all of him, and he got really cold on the long walk between the women's quarters and the Command Center.

When they reached the third building, the common area for much of the base, they climbed the ramp and entered through the airlock to give Mark some time to thaw out. A crowd of people waited in a long line for rations. There was little talk just a mumble here and there and an undercurrent of expectation. Everyone on this base knew war was coming, though none knew how that would happen. They just waited.

Shayna followed Mark and Ju. Mark's bulk plowed a path between the milling crowd of mostly men. He stuck out and was easy to find, his head a full foot above most of the Tong. There were some women warriors. Everyone looked to be oriental and all wore the black uniform of a Tong warrior with the gold insignia of their individual Tongs on their left breast, over their heart.

No one noticed Shayna and her small group as they eased their way through the lines waiting for food and into the actual dining area. Hundreds sat at cafeteria-like tables eating their meal in haste. Amid the aura of excitement and anticipation, the warriors spoke in hushed voices and each face seemed to be filled with tightly repressed excitement. Shayna realized they wanted to fight, wanted revenge on the Company for killing their brethren and taking away the only means they had to make a living.

They left the common area and stopped at the airlock. Mark held out his arm. "Hang on a minute and let me check this storage locker. It's the only one I haven't been in. Maybe there's a bigger jacker there. I gotta find one that fits. It's amazing, but all these Tong guys are really small."

Ju laughed. "Not the issue, Mark. You're really tall and really, well, just large."

Mark was almost six feet five inches. Working out had made his bulk more muscular, but he was still carrying a belly."

He blushed and stammered. "I'm trying to reduce. I work out like twice a day now."

Ju patted his arm. "I know. I'll go with you."

He opened the storage locker and filed through the cold-weather suits, all were hung on hangers, and all were black, searching for a bigger one. "I saw some really fat Tong guys in the commons. Maybe I'll get lucky."

He yanked one out and crowed. "Look at this one. It's huge." He tried it on and it almost closed over his belly. It was a little short, not quite reaching the top of his pants, but it was better than what he had on.

Ju found another one in the locker and pulled this out. "I have an idea," she said. "Take that one off and put it on backwards."

Mark shrugged out of the high-tech, super cold weather jacket and put it on backwards. "Now," Ju said. "Put this one on like normal. "When Mark did that he was fully covered. The new layer wouldn't zip or snap over his belly but it covered the gap in back and gave him a complete suit.

"This will work," Shayna said. "Now you won't freeze to death if we have to go outside."

Mark grinned. "I was freezing. This planet is colder than the freezer in my house."

They pulled their masks on and went out through the air lock. This was the lock that exited on actual land. Land on Europa was rare, mostly small islands where rocks had thrust up and through the ice. The air was brutally cold eating into their skin. Overhead, a dome filled with warmed air covered the space craft parked closely together on the landing field. Even under the dome with the injected warm air, the temperature remained dangerously cold. A thermometer on the side of the building read minus thirty-four Celsius.

Shivering, Shayna walked up the ramp and into the Command Center airlock, waited while the doors shut behind them and the door into the building opened. The thick metal door closed behind her with a soft exhalation of air and Shayna stepped into the long hallway leading to the heart of the base. Doors on the side of the hallway led to offices and rooms filled with massive amounts of equipment needed to run the base. The building had an odd smell comprised of processed air, electronics, and too many human bodies.

Those in charge gathered in the Command Center itself, a large open space at the center of the building filled with computer stations, each manned by a Tong member. Both men and women sat hunched over a holographic keyboard as they stared at the screen in front of them. The walls were covered with high-resolution star maps, a map of Europa, a map of the solar system, and several maps of Earth with blinking lights to indicate bases and enclaves of Vagrants and aliens.

A group sat around a meeting table against a far wall. These were the leaders of the Tong plotting their next moves and the best way to capture the alien weapon and take back their planet. They came in all sizes and ages. Some were young men dressed like warriors in black. There were a few older men in spacer wear, tight pants tucked into boots with magnetic soles, tight tunics of every color with short collars and leather jackets. The collars had rank insignia on the corners. Many wore beards and stringy mustaches, their black or silver hair long and caught at the neck in ornamental clasps. Earrings were common. They looked like the ancient Chinese pirates they'd descended from.

Mark led the way, their footsteps quiet on the thick mat between their feet and the floor of the building. Shayna went right to the small cubicle housing the computer she used to access her mailbox. She quickly slid into the small rolling chair and awakened the machine. The keyboard appeared and she typed in her access code. It took only another minute to pull up her mailbox. There was the letter. She held her breath as she opened it. Every time she got a letter her heart raced with anticipation and dread. What if Knock or Fenfang were writing to tell her Logan was gone, dead or missing?

She took a deep breath and opened the letter. It was just a short note and it was from Logan. "Dearest Shayna, tell the guy in charge of the Tong there's an alien mother ship hiding behind the moon. From what I understand, it's heavily shielded and they have some way of cloaking the ship so it's hard to see. Also, tell him to be alert. I told the Professor about Europa. I hope trusting him wasn't a huge mistake, but it's the Professor. I've always trusted him and he's never failed me. He seems different and I'm not sure of anything anymore except I love you. Professor told me the alien weapon is at an old military base close to the Nellis bombing range in Nevada. Maybe the Tong has equipment they can use to pinpoint its location. He said it was directly north of Vegas close to Crystal Springs, off of Highway 93. Not much to go on I know, but it's a start. Be careful and take care of yourself and our baby."

Shayna pushed the print button and across the room Logan's letter shot out of a laser printer. Mark hustled over, retrieved it and gave it to Bat who stood reading it with one eyebrow raised. When he was done, he patted Mark's shoulder and took Logan's note to the table with the leaders. Shayna sighed. Logan had provided them with a lot of valuable intelligence. She hoped the Tong would make use of it.

Info passed on, she flipped the keyboard off with a wave of her hand and the screen slid into the console. "I hope this helps," she said to Ju.

Ju placed a small hand on her shoulder. "I know you're glad he's safe."

"He didn't say anything about being safe," Shayna almost sobbed. "He didn't say where he was or if Knock and Fang are okay. I want this whole thing over."

Bat's head appeared above the bowed heads of the Tong operatives concentrating on their screens. "That was some letter," Bat said as he stepped close to Shayna and Ju.

"Logan says the aliens have a mother ship hidden behind the moon, and he told me to tell you guys to stay alert."

"I didn't have time to read it all. I knew my uncle would wanna look at it ASAP. I read the part about where their weapon is hidden. We've been working on that for days. It really helps. You say they got a ship hidden behind the moon?" Bat lifted one eyebrow.

"He says they're cloaked. New technology I guess."

"I'll...." Bat started to say something but never finished his sentence. Alarms sounded all through the base. Loud claxons blared from every corner as the base suddenly shook and shuddered. "We're under attack!" Bat screamed. He grabbed Shayna, pulled her out of her chair, and pushed her toward the exit. "Find your group and stay away from the airlocks."

Shayna lurched to her feet. The floor suddenly rose and then dropped. "The ice is cracking," Bat yelled as he ran toward the table where the Tong leaders had jumped up and were pushing toward the exits. Another explosion hit the base. The leaders clutched the edge of the table as a surge in the ice under their feet shot part of the thick mat and the metal floor bulging upward. The floor of the building buckled, and jagged metal could be seen around a large crack. Shayna was knocked to her knees along with Mark and Ju. Bat was nowhere to be seen. A hole opened in front of her and Shayna stared into the deep blue icy water of Europa.

Mark grabbed her arm. "We gotta get on real land."

Ju stumbled to her feet and nodded. "How?"

"Jump," Mark said.

He took a short run up the bulging edge of the ripped metal and leaped over the yawning crevasse in the ice. He held out his hand. "Help her Ju. Hurry."

Ju dragged Shayna to the top of the rubber mat covering the metal floor and they looked down. "I can't," Shayna gasped. "It's too far."

A group of computer people and the Tong leaders surged behind them. One of the Tong, a muscular man with tattoos across his bald head and covering his bulging biceps, an earring shining from one ear, picked Shayna up and threw her across the opening. She landed with a grunt and started sliding toward the slit in the ice. Mark snagged the loose sleeve of her cold-weather jacket and dragged her up the bulging metal floor. "I got you. Come on Ju," he yelled.

Ju lightly and gracefully leaped the chasm as the remaining Tong streamed over the opening in the ice. The crevasse grew wider and one of the Tong women fell through into the water screaming all the way down. The line of Tong jumping the rift stopped as they struggled to lift her out. One man hung down over the edge with another holding his feet. He reached the girl whose struggles had died. She was freezing to death. "

Mark edged closer to the fissure. "Survive," he called. "Don't go to sleep."

The men holding the guy dangling through the hole dropped him far enough to grab her arm. They pulled her out of the water. Her soaked clothes were already freezing on her. "I have this," the big man said. He ran with her to the airlock where a knot was forming as everyone tried to get out of the Command Center. The big man and a woman shoved the girl, who was unconscious, into a cold-weather suit and zipped her in. They left the building with her.

Mark held Ju's hand and wrapped an arm protectively around Shayna as another explosion rocked the base. Behind them the opening in the ice widened and parts of the base began falling into the crystal-clear blue water. The ice actually groaned as it splintered under the base. Mark pushed Shayna into the airlock. "We need to get onto dry land now."

Ju was next out of the airlock. Most of the Tong had disappeared through the lock to their battle stations. Shayna was too frightened to look behind her. She was afraid she'd see men and women falling through the network of cracks rapidly expanding through the Command Center. Ju dragged her into the airlock and Mark shoved in behind her. They waited for the door to close. Mark slapped the red plate that opened the outside door of the lock and they rushed out.

The frigid air hit Shayna in the face like a brick. She stopped. "We can't survive out here," she wailed. "We have to get inside."

People erupted from the airlock in the common area on the other side of the rocky island and surged toward a storage room on the side of the Command Center. The doors were already open. The storage compartment contained hundreds of cold-weather suits and cold-weather gear. Everyone who didn't have a suit desperately grabbed for one. It was mass chaos.

Mark joined the people grabbing suits, searching for the biggest one.

"They're all too small," he said in a calm voice. The suits were rapidly disappearing as Tong members grabbed them and pulled them on.

"I know the ones you're wearing don't fit right," Ju said. "I think I can make them at least work better." She reached into her suit and pulled out a small flip knife. "Take your jackets off." Ju grabbed one of Mark's jackets and slit the sleeves and the back.

She smiled at him. His lips were turning blue with cold and he shook. “Here, put it back on.”

As Mark pulled the sliced-up jacket on, Ju fought her way into the storage room and emerged holding a suit made of a huge coat and pants joined together like coveralls and another large jacket. “Look, the jacket on this onesie suit is really big.”

Shayna almost laughed. It was more a bubble of hysteria, but little Ju was apparently no one to mess with. She’d pushed men aside to get that suit. She made more cuts in the new jacket and more modifications, and then handed it, now minus the pants part, to Mark. “Put it on backwards. I’ll zip it.”

Shayna helped her tug the suit over Mark’s bulk. Between the two suits, he was mostly covered. The pants he’d been wearing were tight, but fit, and the two jackets now covered him. They’d made it so the second jacket was the one zipping in the front so he could get in and out of it easier.

Ju held the other jacket she’d brought out of the melee at the storage locker to Shayna. “You put this one over your jacket,” she told her. “Two of your buttons aren’t buttoned because of your belly and the zip isn’t up at all.

Shayna grinned. “My gut is too big.” She pulled the bigger jacket over the one she had on, zipped it and snapped the final closures. She was finally completely covered. “This is great,” she told Ju. “I’m warm. Well, sorta warm. I don’t think there’s clothing manufactured anywhere that could keep you warm out here.”

“If you had the thermal underwear the Tong guys are wearing, it would help,” Mark said. “I saw sets of them in the men’s quarters. None big enough for me, but those guys are at least a little warmer than we are.”

These cold-weather suits were different from the warrior’s cold-weather suits. The warriors wore all black. These suits were light blue mottled with patches of white and faded into the background of Europa. Attached masks connected to a small pack that manufactured oxygen and fed it into the masks through a plastic tube. Europa's atmosphere contained oxygen just not enough to sustain humans for long periods of time. Shayna pulled the tight-fitting cap over her hair and the attached goggles over her eyes Suited up and reasonably warm, she stared at the devastation around her.

Beneath their feet was a thick layer of ice-covered solid rock. The dome above them was cracked, and more spaceships than Shayna had ever seen in her life crowded into the space under it. All of them seemed to start their engines at once and above them the cracked dome began rolling back. As it started moving, sections damaged by the attack, shattered and fell onto the ships and broke apart.

Europa didn't rotate, so the same side always faced the sun. The Tong had built their base on the sun side of the small moon which made it bright outside. Jupiter might be a long way from the sun, but there was still enough light and heat from it to make this side of the planet lit and a little warmer.

"Where do we go?" Shayna's voice quivered with fear and cold. With the dome rolled back, the air temperature was falling fast. The suits kept them from freezing to death but the actual temperature of Europa without the protective dome was minus one-hundred fifty degrees Celsius. They wouldn't be able to survive out here for very long.

A sonic boom sounded over their heads. Shayna looked up but saw nothing over the slowly opening dome. A ship or ships she couldn't see shot greenish-blue fire into the parked ships. "We're under attack," Mark said calmly. "We need to get to the women's quarters. It's the farthest from the space port."

Shayna could barely function or think, but one thought made it through the fog. She'd told Logan about Europa and now Waterworld was being attacked by alien fighters. It was her and Logan's fault. Logan had been right. Something was wrong with Professor Goswami. Either that or one of those hot chicks he was so interested in was a spy.

Something flying overhead fired into the parked Tong fighters. Shayna still couldn't see the enemy. Who was shooting at them? A small Tong ship exploded, and two Tong fighters took off. Bat suddenly appeared at Shayna's shoulder. He was dressed in a black flight suit with the faceplate of his helmet up. Under the black helmet, he wore a tight fighting hood covering his entire head. He put one gloved hand on Shayna's arm and stared into her eyes with a grim expression. "I guess your husband's friend, the Professor, isn't so much a friend. Looks like he's killed us all."

Shayna's voice was clogged with emotion. "I guess so." Her heart ached for Logan. He'd given them away by trusting Professor Goswami. "Maybe it was one of the Vegas people."

"It could be," Bat said as he grabbed Mark's arm. "Take care of Ju," he growled.

"Where are you going?" Ju asked, her eyes wide with terror.

"I fly one of the small fighters. I'm out of here."

"I can't see who's firing on us," Shayna said. "Are they invisible?"

"Cloaked with some new device. Our detection equipment picks them up, but they're almost invisible to the naked eye." Bat hugged Ju quickly and ran off leaving them shivering as the dome opened all the way and the bigger Tong ships started shooting into the sky. Shayna looked around and saw the Tong Command Center, smoking in places and sinking into the sea in others. Tong warriors, none of the women or children from the women's quarters that Shayna could see, struggled out of the commons and onto the only dry land available. She could barely see the men's and women's quarters through the smoke and water vapor and a kind of snow falling all around them. She held out her gloved-hand and caught some of the snow. "Look," she said. "It's not snow. It's tiny ice crystals."

"Where are all the women and children?" Ju cried. "We need to find them."

Mark held her arm as she tried to run toward the far buildings. "Wait until everything going down goes and everything that's gonna float is steady. The ice will refreeze rapidly and some of the buildings may be inaccessible."

"This is horrible," Shayna sobbed. "The aliens are monsters."

More sonic booms shook the base as the cloaked fighters flew over the dome and fired into the base before the Tong fighters could attack. The common area with the dining hall and kitchens exploded. A huge plume of blue water suddenly shot out of the ice in between the women's and men's quarters. The rock under Shayna's feet trembled. Ju, Mark and Shayna were knocked to their knees. The remaining ships on the rocky ground of the spaceport shivered and shook. Four more shot into the sky. Shayna looked up in time to see two ships overhead explode. Fireworks erupted all around as pieces of the two ships fell to the planet. One huge piece hit over open ice sending another plume of blue water high into the sky.

The ice of Europa surged into enormous hills, new crevasses formed amid creaking and groaning and thunderous cracking sounds. As soon as water was exposed, the frigid temperatures caused new ice to form. Shayna stayed on her knees as the remaining ships took off in blasts of flames and black exhaust. The rock under them suddenly cracked. A fissure formed between them and the building housing the sinking common area. Far on the other side of the dry land, the men's quarters slowly turned onto its side and was frozen like that, on its side. The women's quarters were the farthest away. Shayna shielded her eyes from the fumes of spaceship exhaust and tiny flying ice chips as she tried to see what was happening to the women's quarters. "Can you see the women's quarters?" She asked Mark.

He lifted his head, shielded his eyes and quickly dropped it. "No, can't see anything but a cloud of exhaust fumes and snow."

"I see it." Ju was on her feet. "It looks like it's floating away."

"We need to catch it," Shayna screamed over the sound of the last ship, a huge and ancient freighter taking off. "The children are in there."

Mark scrambled to his feet and stared off in the direction of the men's section. It was frozen solidly on its side blocking their view of the women's building "We'll never make it. The ice is cracking." To add emphasis to his statement, a jagged shard of ice shot straight up out of the water thirty feet between the men's section and the common area which was completely gone except for the antennas and a huge satellite dish array. It had sunk fifteen feet and then frozen in place. The ramp and airlock going into it were under the new surface of the ice.

"Look," Ju shouted. "There's someone on top of the building."

Several more people emerged onto the top of the tilted men's section. They scrambled out of a window onto its edge and clung to the tilted top of the building. "We have to help them," Shayna said.

"How?" Mark asked. "How can we get over the commons?"

Shayna grabbed Mark by the shoulders. He was shaking with cold and fear. "Think," she said. "You're strong and you're smart. Think."

"Look," Ju said. "Ice is freezing the buildings in. It won't take long for them to be solid. We can climb over the commons and the men's building and get to the women and children."

Ju was right. It was so cold, ice immediately formed around the buildings that were canted at odd angles making them solid again. "The women's building has stopped floating away. It's frozen into place" Ju said. "She looked up. "It's not snowing anymore."

Chapter Nineteen

Logan drove the ancient Land Rover across stark desert landscape. It bounced once, hit a huge bump, and began the climb up a small range of eroded mountains overlooking dry Groom Lake. At the top, Logan stopped. Professor Goswami sat next to him. In the back, Fang, Knock, Raj and Corey were squashed together as they held on for dear life. This mission was the most important mission of his life. They were here to destroy the alien's powerful weapon before it could be moved to the moon and used against humans.

A rusty-red Ford Ranger driven by Kylie pulled up beside the Land Rover and stopped. Below the mountains, in a small valley on the edge of a huge dry lakebed, lay the secret base known as Area 51. All the buildings were laid out in rows and covered with years of dust. Several long runways bordered the cluster of buildings. Three big star cruisers sat on the runways alongside seventeen smaller fighters. Four large hanger-type buildings were at one end of the group, and at the other end a bunch of what looked like containers but which the Professor said were barracks and mostly empty. Dozens of old American aircraft sat parked and falling to ruin on what Goswami said was the southern taxi-way. A runway ran beside a large building Goswami said was one of the newest hangers.

The Professor pointed. "Most of the base is underground. You can access it through that building on the edge of the runway. The one with the tower."

Logan grabbed the field glasses from Knock. "You don't need these," he said. "I don't even see how you can use them."

Knock rolled his one eye. "Hey, I still have one eye."

Logan ignored him and focused the glasses on the building the Professor indicated. He could see a guard walking the perimeter, some parked trucks, and human activity around the biggest of the hangers. "Not many people running around," he said to the Professor.

"They're all underground," Goswami said. "There are plenty of people down there. Believe me."

"Oh, I do," Logan said. He tossed the glasses back to Knock and opened the door of the Rover. It creaked and dropped open with a clunk. Logan stepped out and stretched. It was late afternoon and well over a hundred degrees. The sun was setting behind the mountains to the west. When the sun was gone, it would cool off. Neither of their two vehicles had air conditioning. Logan was hot, sweaty and tired. He was covered with dust. When he took a drink from his canteen, he had to rinse a layer of grit out of his mouth.

Kylie climbed out of the Ranger and walked over to talk to him. Bobby, Jordie and the Bakersfield Vagrants, Jesse, Fred and Midori, sat in the back of the truck with a strange assortment of weapons. Two of the Sweet triplets sat in the front with Kylie. The Sweet triplets were three of the most beautiful, blond, tall, hotter-than-a-forest-fire, women Logan had ever seen. They were identical and identically gorgeous with identically huge and bouncy sets of breasts. They wore as little as possible so ignoring these attributes was not something any man could be expected to do. They were Kylie's best spies and worked the Strip for information and for money, credit discs and anything else they could get their hands on. Ginger and Sugar had come on the trip. Candy had stayed behind to monitor the com.

The storage in the back of the Rover contained two rocket launchers and seven rockets capable of punching big holes in the buildings but not much else. Knock had been correct in assuming the Vegas girls could provide glitter and G-strings, but not much in the way of weaponry. They were all armed with a neurolizer and a personal hand weapon. A few of those were blasters, most old-fashioned handguns using bullets which were in limited supply.

"What do you think?" Kylie asked. A limp, sweaty ponytail hung to her shoulders. Her fair skin was mottled and red. She shoved sunglasses onto her head and wiped sweat off her face with a corner of her shirt. It left a streak of dirt.

"Not much," Logan said. "I guess we wait until dark and hike down there. I know we shouldn't drive. See those enormous dishes out next to the lakebed? I bet there's significant radar and detection for anything moving in that valley."

"Then they'll know we're coming even if it's dark," Kylie said.

"Professor," Logan stuck his head inside the Rover. "How good is their detection system?"

"Oh my," Goswami said. "I fear they would know if a rat crossed the runways or got near their space craft. Maybe there is not so much pointed toward the back side of the base. No one ever approaches from here. All visitors and supplies come in from Crystal Springs on the main road."

Logan drew Kylie away from Goswami and the Rover. They walked behind the Ranger and off to the side away from everyone's ears. "Let's hope Sugar knows what she's talking about," Logan said.

"The Sweet triplets are my best girls," Kylie said. "They hear more and find more stuff for us than any other members of my group. They've been through hell. They used to travel all over the world tag-team wrestling, but they got kidnapped by slave traders. They were just kids then, like eighteen. They never gave up and managed to get away. Nobody messes with the Sweets."

"We're putting a lot of trust into this device they stole."

"If Sugar says it's a cloaking device, I believe her," Kylie said. "She got it from one of the highest-ranking officers working out here. He had it stashed in the closet in his room. He told her all about it. Bragged about having it. He said his bosses had trusted him to take it to California. He was enjoying one night off before heading out there on the Loop."

Sugar Sweet and her identical sisters were six-foot tall Nordic blonds any man would give up his hope of redemption to have as a girlfriend. Sugar, along with the other sisters, Candy and Ginger, did most of Kylie's espionage work voluntarily. They knew what they did was dangerous and could involve distasteful situations and did it anyway. The Resistance was that important to them. Sugar and Ginger sat fanning themselves in the Ranger's front seat.

"I just don't want anyone knowing about it except Knock and Fang. At this point trust is a rare commodity."

Kylie nodded. "I think you're right to be careful. We'll use the device, but go in like the Professor said from the back side."

"After dark," Logan added. "Tell everyone to find a spot in the shade and rest if they can."

Kylie nodded and walked back to the Ranger. "We're going in after dark," she said to the five in the back of the truck. Kylie opened the Ranger's door and told the Sweet girls to find a shady spot and rest. Logan couldn't help himself. He stared as the tall women climbed out of the truck. They wore short shorts, combat boots, and tank tops covered by a white blouse knotted at their waist. Their legs were longer than most men were tall. He felt Knock move out of the Rover and stand at his elbow. "There's drool dripping out of your open mouth," Knock whispered.

"Sorry," Logan said with a grin. "I mean they're like Helga only real."

"I didn't think real women could actually look like that," Knock said in a voice filled with awe.

Fenfang grabbed Knock's shoulder. "I heard that."

Knock turned and hugged Fang. Logan heard him assure her. "Fang, you're the only woman in my life, but a man can't help but look. I mean seriously."

She smacked him in the back of the head. "If I didn't love you . . . ."

They all found a spot in the shade and waited for dark. If the radar and detection equipment in Area 51 were as good as Goswami said, and Logan believed the Professor about this, then it barely mattered whether they went at night or in the full light of day. Darkness would help their moral, Logan thought. If they were cloaked in darkness as well as the funny device, they would feel safer and maybe just feeling safer would help them get into the facility and destroy the weapon.

Logan couldn't rest. His nerves were dancing with crazy energy. He felt like he was jumping out of his skin. He got up and walked to a cliff overlooking Area 51. Night had fallen and lights winked on and off below in the facility. Most of it was dark, but there were lights on the spaceships, lights on one of the runways and blinking lights on six of the giant satellites. One yellow sodium vapor light shone from the building Goswami had said housed the egress to the underground part of Area 51. It illuminated the seventeen small fighters parked on the runway in front of the building. Logan wished he could take one of those fighters and fly to Europa to see his wife. It wouldn't take two hours and he would be there with her. He sighed. There was so much work to do here.

As he stared into the valley, he thought about Shayna and their unborn child. He was glad they were safe on Europa. If he died in the attempt to destroy this weapon, it wouldn't matter so much if Shayna and the baby were safe. He vowed to destroy the weapon, even if he had to sacrifice himself. His child would grow up in a safer world. Shayna had told him the Tong was siding with the Vagrants because of an action by the Company. Her message hadn't explained why the Tong had suddenly decided to work with them. Logan smiled. It didn't matter. He knew from experience the Tong was a strong force. Having them on their side could give them an edge they needed and ensure their eventual victory.

He found Knock leaning against a rock dozing with Fang next to him. He sat down and closed his eyes. It seemed he'd only been asleep for a minute when Kylie shook him. "Wake up, Logan. It's time."

Chapter Twenty

Logan rubbed the sleep out of his eyes and stood up. Knock held the cloaking device. It looked like a black plastic game controller. It had a toggle on the top and several buttons. Kylie and her group had played with it. She said it worked and there were several modes they could use.

"Will it cover all of us?" Logan asked.

"It should," Kylie said. "I've never tried to cloak this many people, but I know how to set it to cover the widest area. The amount of cloaking we get might not be as strong, but it will still be very hard to see us and radar won't be able to pick us up at all."

"You sure they don't know we have this thing?" Knock was skeptical.

Sugar Sweet stepped next to Knock and stood really close. Logan had to look away. Sweat beaded on Knock's forehead and Fang was bristling with resentment. Sugar spoke in a soft, thick Southern drawl. "I am the one who took the device. Ginger called me after her guest fell asleep. I brought an old gaming handset with me and we replaced the cloaking device with that. They wouldn't notice the switch unless they tried to use it because I doubt if the people in New LA have ever seen one. So far, we haven't heard anything on our networks about them discovering the theft. So, we should be clear to use it."

Logan gathered them all around. He knelt in the center of his troops and outlined the plan he'd come up with while resting. He pointed at the group of Bakersfield Vagrants. "You guys take the truck. Use the cloaking device and head to the dry lakebed. Use the rockets to destroy every satellite in the lakebed. Fire off two rockets. Get a couple of satellites and wait. That's our cue to run for the hangers. When we see the satellites go, we'll drive the

Rover down to the base and enter through the tower. Destroying just two might be a useless attempt to blind them, but it will provide a diversion for us. Wait for two hours. If you don't hear from us by then, blow the rest of the satellite array and finish your mission. You can bug out in the truck or wait for me to contact you on the two-way. Your choice. The explosions will draw attention, but you should be safe since you're cloaked. Got it?"

Midori, Jesse and Fred, the Bakersfield Vagrants nodded. "We can do this," Midori said. She glanced at her two companions. "If things look good, we wanna fight, so we'll join you." Fred glanced at Jesse. Jesse was an American Indian, a Sioux. He had long black braids, was tall with tattoos on his face imitating war paint. His eyes were outlined in black and there were permanent red and green stripes on his cheeks. "We got nothing left but fighting. All our people are dead. This is it for us. Fight or die."

Logan nodded. "That's great. You guys take the cloaking device. When we see the satellites explode, we go in in the Rover." He pointed at Bobby. "You drive us down there, dump us out and come back up here." He handed Bobby a walkie talkie out of his backpack then turned to Jordie. "You stay here with Bobby. You're a huge asset, a pilot, and a techie. We can't afford to risk you. When we're clear, we'll call for you." He held up another handset. "If you don't get a pickup message, wait until dawn and then bug out. Go back to Vegas."

Bobby took the hand set for the walkie talkie and pressed the button. Logan's hand set beeped. "Works," he said.

Logan grinned. "I know." He pointed at the Sweet sisters. "You can come with us or stay with Bobby. It's your choice. You two already did your part. This could very well be a suicide mission. We're going to destroy that weapon or die trying."

Sugar patted Logan's shoulder. He forced himself not to look at her chest. It wasn't easy. Her chest was impressive. "Before we were exotic dancers, we were tag-team wrestlers. Fighting is in our blood." She grinned and showed him her bicep muscle by flexing it. Logan glanced at it and looked away rapidly.

Knock burst out laughing and Fang punched him. "That's quite a set of muscles you got there," Knock said. Logan had to laugh at that. His laugh was more of a nervous titter. They were all on edge. This was the beginning of something great or a massive disaster that ended in all of them dying and the death of the world as they knew it.

"Corey, Raj, you guys can choose. Stay here with Bobby and Jordie or come with us. You're kids, so you shouldn't have to fight."

"You need me with you," Corey said. "I might be able to get readings from the bad guys and give you warnings."

"I'm coming with my uncle and you," Raj said. "I am not afraid."

Logan patted Raj on the back. "You've been in this from the beginning, little dude. You have the right to decide for yourself."

Raj hugged him. "Thanks, Logan."

Logan nodded and picked up his pack. A thermobaric bomb filled most of it. This was more of the Sweet sisters' work. They'd discovered a stash of the bombs using information secured by their devious methods. A thermobaric bomb used in an enclosed area would cause more destruction than any other type of bomb except a nuclear one. It would suck up all the oxygen in the area and the explosion would be sustained until all the oxygen was depleted. It was perfect for bunkers, foxholes, and caves. Using it would guarantee the destruction of the underground complex and the alien weapon. It would probably kill all of them as well if they couldn't get out fast enough, but that was the risk they had to take.

Under the bomb in his pack was something Logan had had for several years and used only when necessary. It was a jacket made from the skin of an alien amphibian. His father had given it to him. The skin was tough, almost bullet proof, and it had the qualities of a chameleon. It could change to blend into the background of anything. The jacket had saved Logan's life more than once. He touched the jacket and turned to find the Professor staring at him with an odd look on his face. Could Goswami read his mind? Logan shook this disturbing image off and stood up. "Time to get this show rolling."

The Bakersfield Vagrants gave him a fist bump and then a hug on their way to the Ranger. Sugar Sweet went with them and showed them how to activate the cloaking device. When she walked away, she turned to look back and all she or Logan saw was a cloud of dust as the Ranger headed for the dry lakebed with the rocket launcher and all of the rockets in the bed of the truck.

"Our turn next," Logan said. "Everyone load into the Rover. Crowd in any way you can. Bobby remember the walkie talkie." Bobby held it up. Logan hugged him and pointed. "You're driving."

They sat inside the truck waiting. The Ford Ranger with the Bakersfield people in it was impossible to see. The activated cloaking device was working. Ten minutes after it left, the first satellite dish exploded in a ball of fire, followed by the biggest dish. "Go!" Logan shouted to Bobby.

Bobby floored the accelerator on the Rover and they bounced and careened down the hill and into the valley heading straight for the tower on the edge of the runways. They passed a huge pit filled with melted slag. Professor Goswami pointed. "They used to burn toxic waste there many years ago."

Bobby drove the Rover by two buildings. Goswami pointed. "Security used to be in that one and that one is still some kind of lab. Bobby pulled the Rover up to the tower. "This is called the Janet Terminal. I have no idea why."

They piled out of the Rover. "Go!" Logan shouted to Bobby. Bobby turned the Rover in a tight circle, and he and Jordie took off back into the hills.

Sirens sounded all around them. Logan plastered himself against the side of the terminal and waited. A herd of Enforcers, guards, security people and soldiers raced out of the terminal and headed for the exploding satellite array. When the last one had gone, loading into Jeeps and fire equipment parked in one of the nearby hangers, Logan reached into his pack and removed the jacket. He shrugged into it and pulled the hood over his head. Goswami patted him on the back. "The chameleon jacket. You still have it."

"My father gave it to me. I would never part with it," Logan said.

Knock pushed close. "Time to party," he hissed. "It's like now or never, dude."

Logan nodded. "Let's go."

The door into the terminal was hanging open. The guards and Enforcers had left it that way in their haste to respond to the exploding satellite dishes. Inside the building, Goswami took over the lead. "This way," he said.

Logan ran after him, closely followed by Knock and Fang. Fenfang had a neurolizer in her hands and her swords on her back. Corey and Raj were next, each carrying a neurolizer. The big weapons looked funny in their hands. The Sweet sisters and Kylie covered their rear.

The Professor led them to a metal door. He glanced back and opened it. On the other side was an elevator with a black door. "It requires a level-five key," Goswami said.

Logan fished in his pack and pulled out his level-five key. It had gotten them into so many places. Logan hoped it would get them everywhere they needed to go inside this complex. He inserted the key into the circular slot and the elevator door opened. They squeezed inside. "Which floor?" Logan asked the Professor.

There were buttons for six floors. Each one was lettered not numbered.

"This elevator only goes down," Goswami said as he chose the button next to the letter X. "Bottom floor," he said.

The elevator dropped fast. It was a high-speed elevator dropping deep into the depths under the base. Logan thought about Shayna. She hated elevators. The elevator hit bottom and the door opened with no noise onto a short hallway. At the end was another heavy metal door requiring the key. Logan used it and glanced behind at his people. “Ready?”

They murmured agreement, all nervous, all slightly freaked out. Logan was ready to open the door when Corey spoke up. “Don’t. They’re waiting on the other side,” he whispered and closed his eyes. “I sense at least six Enforcers and one really weird mind. Must be an alien.” He froze, opened his eyes and slowly rotated to point at Professor Goswami. “He’s got two minds inside him. Crap, there’s an alien in his head. It warned them.” Corey’s voice was filled with horror. “It’s in his head, inside of him.”

Logan grabbed the Professor by the throat. “You’re a spy.”

Professor Goswami shook his head violently trying to loosen Logan’s grip. A high-pitched screech issued from Goswami’s opened mouth and his eyes rolled back in his head. He suddenly began shaking and then stiffened and bucked in Logan’s hands.

“He’s having some kind of seizure!” Raj shouted. “My uncle, let him go right this minute.”

Horrified, Logan dropped Goswami who fell to the ground in front of the elevator door in the grip of a strong seizure. Goswami kicked and tossed and the hideous high-pitched wail continued. Foam poured out of his open mouth. Everyone backed away. Knock pointed his neurolizer at Goswami. “Want me to end it?”

Logan held out his hand. “Don’t kill him yet.”

“There are aliens and soldiers on the other side of the door,” Corey said. “They expect him,” he pointed at Goswami, “to deliver us to them.”

Logan could feel the pressure of leadership tearing him apart along with crushing doubt and confusion. “What do we do?” he asked.

The Sweet sisters pushed forward. "We got this."

Kylie grinned. "Let them do their stuff. They're amazing."

Logan stuttered. "What are you two planning?"

The Sweet sisters smiled. "We'll provide a little distraction."

On the floor, the thumping and wailing from Goswami stopped, leaving a creepy silence hanging inside the small compartment. "Look," Raj whispered.

A hideous creature crawled slowly out of Goswami's mouth. It was red with yellow spots, looked like a slug but had a stinger. Fang took one look at the thing, stabbed it with the tip of her knife, and flicked it against the wall. Kylie immediately squashed it under the sole of her combat boot.

Sugar Sweet covered her nose. "What is that smell?"

"Gross," Knock said.

"Worst smell ever," Fang said as she pulled her T-shirt up to cover her nose.

"It was a terrible smell and it quickly filled the small room. "It's like rotting cabbage and sewer gas," Logan said. "I can't believe that thing was inside the Professor. What is it?"

Corey covered his nose, bent and stared at the splat on the linoleum floor. "It had intelligence." Corey looked up at Logan. "This thing was communicating with the aliens. Telling them everything we were doing and planning. They might even know about your wife and the Tong."

Logan ground his teeth. "I knew something was wrong with him. Knock, what do we do now? We're trapped in here. What do we do with him?" Logan pointed at Goswami.

Fang knelt and touched Goswami's chest. "I think he's dead."

Logan bent over and touched Professor Goswami's face. The man had been like a father to him. It felt weird and bad to leave him here, but that's what they had to do. "We can't carry him."

Raj began crying. "Uncle Depak."

Knock put his arm around Raj. "Sorry, little dude. You've had a rough time."

Raj straightened his back. "I must be strong. He'd wish me to carry on."

Logan nodded. "Now what?"

"We told you, we have a plan," the Sweet sisters said in unison.

"We have to complete the mission," Knock said. "If we don't everyone we know and love will die. Europa will go down. The Tong will be destroyed before they can help us. We gotta do something. We can't quit."

Kylie nodded. "It's do or die, people."

"You're right," Logan said. "This is our only chance to destroy the weapon. No matter what's waiting for us on the other side of that door, we have to face it. There's no going back."

Professor Goswami suddenly groaned and sat up. "What happened to me?"

Raj knelt beside his uncle. "Uncle Depak, we thought you were dead." He grabbed Goswami's neck and hugged him.

"Where are we?" Goswami asked. His face was filled with confusion. He looked a hundred years old.

Raj helped his uncle stand up. "You had a creature inside of your head that was controlling you. Do you remember?"

The old man grabbed the sides of his head. His thin hair was sticking straight out and his brown skin was a sickly gray-green. "I do remember. I was strapped onto a table and they put a most hideous slug-like creature onto my chest. It was red with yellow spots and wherever it touched, my skin burned."

Logan pointed to the remains of the squashed bug. "And there it is."

Goswami peered at it. His glasses had fallen askew and were cracked. "Is that what is creating the terrible odor?"

Knock grabbed Goswami under the arm. "Yeah, dude, that's stinkin' up everything. Come on. You ready? Because we're all about to commit suicide thanks to you."

Goswami shook off Knock's hand and straightened his back. "I will not allow you to die because of my treachery. Even though I was unaware of the thing inside of my head, I should never have allowed them to take me alive. I should have known they would try to use me to get to Logan." He pushed past the Sweet sisters, turned and stared into Logan's face. "I will lead."

"Give the Professor a weapon," Logan said.

Fenfang pulled her handgun and gave it to Goswami. "Here. Use this."

Goswami took the hand gun and stared for a second at the weapons in the girls' hands. "You must change the setting on your neurolizers," he finally said.

"What?" Sugar looked confused.

Goswami took the weapon from her and flipped it over. On the bottom was a small dial. He clicked it to the fourth position, the one indicated by a red arrow. "Neurolizers don't affect aliens unless they're set on the red arrow. You'd just tickle them."

"Well I'll be . . ." Sugar said. "Uh, what does it do to humans when it's set this high?"

"I do not know. I've never seen it used."

"I guess we're gonna find out," Sugar said.

"Thanks, Prof," Ginger said as she flipped her weapon over and reset it." You saved us."

"It was nothing," he mumbled. "They have a different kind of nervous system. The weapon is designed mostly to use on us. The red setting is dangerous to them and they know it. It is only used for emergencies or criminals of their own race."

The Sweet sisters gently pushed Goswami away from the door. "We got this." Sugar smiled and began unbuttoning her white shirt. Ginger did the same. The tank tops came off and Sugar's smile got bigger.

"Turn your heads, boys," Ginger said to Raj and Corey. "We wouldn't want you to grow up too fast."

Logan couldn't see exactly what they were doing, but he did see Sugar reach behind her back and pop the clasp on her bra. Sugar looked at her sister. "Think Candy will miss us?"

"We're not gonna die," Ginger said. "No man would shoot two women with a set of knockers like we got."

They high-fived each other and kicked the door open.

Chapter Twenty-One

Shayna, Mark and Ju clambered across the commons. Three Tong warriors ran pass them on their way to the airfield. The door to the men's section was now on the side of the building. All of the buildings had been frozen into new positions in the ice. The explosions and fire had melted the top layer of ice on Europa's frozen ocean long enough for the buildings to shift during the moments they floated. The common building with the dining hall had sunk three feet. There was no getting out of it for anyone trapped inside.

As they crawled across the building, Shayna prayed the same thing hadn't happened to the women's section. Cressy and Mai Li were there along with the other women Vagrants, Granny Hawkins from Gliese and any of the Tong women too old or too young to be fighters.

When they got across the common building, they had to climb. The men's quarters had rolled onto its side and was now higher than the commons which had sunk. Because of the height of the tipped over men's quarters, until they got on top of it, they couldn't see what had happened to the women's building. The designs of the building were super high-tech with stabilizing wings in a star shape. The buildings looked like giant flying saucers, their shape sloped to combat high winds, snow and shifting ice. They were covered in strange stippled metal to hold in heat and very slippery. Because it was on its side, one of the wings stuck up thirty feet into the air. Shayna realized they would have to go around it.

Mark, wearing his mix-matched cold weather suit shivered uncontrollably. If he wasn't so tall, his jackets would have covered him adequately, but there was a gap where the jackets ended and his pants began. Any uncovered flesh froze in these temperatures. Shayna was very cold, but her extra jacket was helping. Her face was covered by the mask and she breathed the additional oxygen from the pack on her back, and she knew she wouldn't die from the cold. Mark was another matter. "I don't think Mark can be out here much longer," Shayna told Ju. "I think he should go into the men's quarters and get warm."

"Not gonna do it," Mark said in a shaking voice. "Gotta help you guys save the women." He tugged his jackets down as far as they would go. "It's just this darn big belly of mine. Ugh."

Ju grabbed Mark's shaking arm. "You'll freeze if you're out here much longer. You'll die."

He shook his head. "Not die, just cold. Let's go." He pushed by them and jumped off the building onto the rough ice. They walked slowly around the jutting wing and then used ridges in the metal to pull themselves back up to the top. Shayna noticed they weren't so much ridges but diamond-shaped patterns cut into the metal. Mark helped Shayna get back onto the top and Ju followed. When they reached the top, which was really the side of the building, she stood up. The side of the building was flat and angled down to another of the wings. The windows were set into the aluminum in one long strip along the entire side. They were easier to hang onto than the aluminum so they walked carefully down the panels.

Mark refused to give up the lead. When they passed the open airlock door, Shayna felt warm air rising out of it. For a minute, they all basked in the warmth. Mark stopped shivering, gathered himself. "Let's go," he said. "We don't have time to sit here."

Shayna finally saw the women's building. It had sunk into the ice just like the commons. The airlocks were frozen under the ice. No one could get in or out. The top of the building was a windowed dome with reflective material painted across the reinforced glass to use the weak sunlight, from the sun that never set, to illuminate the exterior of the building and some of the surrounding ice. Lights from inside the dome lit up a narrow strip at the top directly under the heavy aluminum roof. Shayna stopped and looked at Mark. "What do we do now?"

"You go on ahead. I'll go back and get some tools. I understand tools. I worked with my father. His hobby was building furniture. There was a section in that closet space where we got these suits that held tools. I'll find something we can use to cut through the ice and access the door."

"Maybe we can get in through the dome or one of the windows," Ju said.

"I don't think anything will break this glass," Mark said tapping the material of the windows under his feet with one gloved finger. "We'll have to break through the ice. If I can hack far enough into the ice, the air lock is set into the walls. I should be able to work my way into the space and open the doors."

"If you can't, I can," Ju said. "I'm little. I can squeeze through."

Shayna smiled. "That sounds like a good idea. I'll try to start. The ice is fresh. It can't be that hard yet."

Mark shrugged. "Don't count on it. I'm just hoping we can chip it away with a crowbar or a shovel."

Shayna stood back and let him go. She grabbed Ju's hand when the girl moved to stop Mark. "Let him go," she said. "Maybe he knows what he's talking about."

Logan had a pretty good idea what the Sweet sisters were doing and so did Knock. Knock gave him a sly look and Fang growled. They moved to the very rear of the small room, knelt down low, and huddled in a corner as Sugar Sweet blew the door open with one solid kick of her booted foot.

When the door slammed open, the sisters were faced with four heavily armed Enforcers, a strange looking creature Logan realized was one of the aliens, and his two personal guards. None of them saw Logan, Kylie, Raj, Corey, Knock, Fang or Goswami crouching against the far wall. All they saw was two glorious

Scandinavian blonds with no shirts and a double set of amazing hood ornaments.

The men froze, mouths dropped open, and they stared as the Sweet sisters hosed them with the neurolizers. Blue electricity covered the entire group. They dropped as one, twitching and spasming in the throes of the neurological weapon's brain scrambling, shocking, electrical charge. Even the alien dropped to the floor. He seemed completely paralyzed except for the high-pitched screech coming from his small open mouth.

"Let's go!" Sugar yelled.

Logan and his group leaped up as one and poured into the hallway. Logan vaulted one shaking, shuddering Enforcer, stepped on the stomach of the second one and waved his group forward. They eased by Logan and followed the Sweet girls who had pulled their shirts on and were buttoning them on the fly. Logan stared down at the alien as they passed. The puffy, pale being had a round head, rubbery little lips bordered by stringy black hair you might call a Fu Man Chu, slanted black eyes that bulged as he lay frozen and unmoving except for the hideous wailing, and a corpulent body with four arms. Two of his hands opened and closed spasmodically, and Logan noticed he had two thumbs and long fingers on those hands. The other two hands were huge and had claws. Those hands were tightly clenched.

"Here," Corey said. He handed Logan the remains of the bug that had come out of Professor Goswami. The kid had used a rag to pick it up. The hideous red and yellow creature had magically reanimated, filled out, and was squirming in Corey's grip. "See if it will crawl up pig-face's nose."

Goswami hovered next to Logan's elbow. "Put it on his chest. That's where they put it on me."

"Happy to," Logan said. He dropped the bug on the alien's upper chest. Blue arcing electrical charges still shivered across the alien's stiff body. When the arcing electricity stopped pulsing across the alien's body, the worm crawled to a spot below the alien's throat, lifted its stinger and stabbed the alien. A drop of poison spread making a hole in the alien's pink skin. When the hole was a centimeter wide, the bug crawled into it and it closed behind him. The alien's hideous wail was abruptly shut off.

"Well," Logan said. "Maybe that will slow him down."

The Sweet sisters stooped and began picking through the guards' weapons. The two burley humans guarding the alien were armed to the teeth. Sugar picked up a sawed-off shotgun kind of weapon that Logan thought looked like a riot gun. "Now this is what I'm talkin' about," Sugar said. "I love me a real gun. One that will open up a huge hole in the enemy. I mean the neurolizer is okay, but this thing is awesome. When I kill someone, I wanna see blood and gore and know they're dead."

Ginger turned around and began a thorough search of the Enforcers. She found another riot gun on a tall, heavy, female Enforcer, and stripped off her ammo bandoliers. She handed one to Sugar and strapped the other leather ammo belt across her full chest. "Get his," she said to Sugar and pointed to the other guard.

Sugar flipped the beefy, muscled-up guard with the toe of her boot. He still shook and shuddered as blue electricity pulsed across his body. Sugar pulled two full bandoliers off that guard and handed one to Ginger. "Think we got enough ammo?"

"It's impossible to have too much ammo," Ginger said as she grabbed one more full belt and strapped it on. The shotgun shells were red and every belt was full. Each Sweet sister now carried the sawed-off, a neurolizer hanging on their Sam Brown belts, and three bandoliers of shotgun ammo.

"You got that right," Sugar said. "I feel good about this," she said as she cracked the shotgun and crammed it full of shells. "Idiots didn't even fire one shot at us."

Ginger laughed. "Men, they're all the same." She toed the alien. "Even the aliens have a weird obsession with knockers."

Logan rolled his eyes. "You girls done?"

Sugar tilted her head, batted ridiculously long fake lashes thickly coated with black mascara, and smiled. "I think so."

Ginger held out her hand. "Not so fast." She rolled one of the Enforcers. "They won't be needing this anymore." She unfastened his armored vest and pulled it off. The guard flipped over as she yanked his body armor completely off and held it up. "This we can use."

"Good idea, Sis," Sugar said. In seconds, both sisters were wearing their newly acquired ammo belts over body armor. "Anybody else want armor?"

"I got my jacket," Logan said. "It's bullet proof."

"I'll take a set." Knock rolled one of the alien's guards and took his armor. When everyone but Fang was protected, she didn't want to wear the bulky vests saying it would hamper her sword action too much, they got ready to leave.

"Which way to the weapon, Professor?" Logan asked.

Professor Goswami, now blissfully relieved of his venomous burden, led them deep into the underground bunker. When Goswami suddenly stopped, Logan ran into him knocking his glasses askew. "Sorry, Professor. What's wrong?"

Goswami straightened his glasses on his nose. "I just remembered. The door into the weapons bunker is protected with a retinal scan. Only the alien's eye can open the door."

"Can we blow it open?" Logan couldn't believe they had gotten this far and now would be unable to get to the weapon.

"Oh, no," Professor Goswami said with a moan. "It is most carefully protected. The door is made of alien metal that is extremely thick and impervious to heat. I have seen the alien leader put his eye to the scanner many times to enter the section of the bunkers containing the terrible weapon. It is the only way to unlock the door."

Knock stepped forward. "Uh, I got an idea." He lifted the patch over his missing eye. "Remember Humphrey Coleman's hand?"

Logan's mouth fell open. "Of course. Let's go. Professor wait here with the girls. Knock and I will be right back."

"What are you planning?" Goswami said. "I fear it is a horrendous idea."

"Let them go," Fenfang said as she laid one hand on Professor Goswami's arm. "They know what they're doing."

Logan and Knock ran back to the corridor where they'd left the neurolized Enforcers who were just beginning to move around and sit up. None of them looked in any condition to provide opposition to Logan or Knock. Logan eyed them, touched one and watched the man fall onto his back. His eyes rolled into his head and he had a seizure. "These neurolizers mess you up," he said to Knock.

Knock nodded. "Yeah, wouldn't like it much myself." He grabbed the alien's arm. The strange-looking humanoid still lay on his back with both eyes open. "You wanna do this or me?" Knock asked Logan.

Logan shuddered. "It's your eye, dude."

Knock dragged the alien into a sitting position and propped him against the wall. He pulled his K-Bar, Marine Corps special knife, out of the sheath on his belt, fit the tip of the blade into the side of the alien's eye socket and popped the eyeball out. A weird wail emerged from the alien's lips and then it fell over and started slapping at the floor with all four arms. Knock backed up rapidly. "Whoa, dude.' He held up the alien's eyeball. It wasn't as round as most human eyeballs. It was more oval-shaped. "Think it'll fit?"

Logan grinned. "Good enough for government work."

They ran back through the halls, found Goswami and held up the eye. Goswami shook his head. "Oh my. I thought you would just bring the alien back here. You've removed his eye. Oh dear, oh dear."

Knock laughed. "Dude was fat, Professor. I wasn't dragging him back here. He had to weigh over a hundred-fifty kilos. Besides, he's got that worm thing inside him." Knock shuddered.

"And, he was still out of it from the neurolizer. He'd be like dead weight."

The group reassembled with the Sweet sisters and Kylie leading, followed by Corey, Raj, Logan and Fang. Professor Goswami brought up the rear. "There's Enforcers ahead," Corey suddenly said. "And another alien."

"Vaerfeky," Goswami moaned. "It must be Vaerfeky."

Logan tapped Sugar on the shoulder. "Wait a sec." He turned to Professor Goswami. "Who or what is a Vaerfeky?"

"Alien base commander," Goswami said. "He's the one who put the bug in me and brought me here. He's in charge of the weapon and all of Area 51."

"Logan," Corey said. "Something else."

"What?"

"I can read the Enforcers better than the alien and they're thinkin' about a raid that is going on right now."

A bad feeling hit Logan in the chest. "Raid? Where?"

Sugar and Ginger crowded around Corey. The boy's freckles stood out on his white face as little orange dots. "Are they hitting Vegas?" Kylie demanded.

Corey shook his head. "No." He looked at Logan. "They just hit the Tong on Europa. They think they about wiped out the base."

"Shayna," Logan moaned. "Shayna's on Europa."

Chapter Twenty-Two

Mark returned to Shayna and Ju carrying a gigantic crowbar. Ju ran to him and hugged him. "You made it."

Mark's face turned red. "All the ships are taking off. Pretty soon we'll be on this planet by ourselves."

Shayna gasped. "All of them?"

Mark nodded. "It looked that way to me."

"What will we do?"

"Let's worry about that after we get out of the cold," Mark said as he began the arduous task of hacking his way through to the airlock. He dug the bar into the ice and pried out chunk after chunk. When he got to softer ice, he chipped it into flakes. In a few minutes, he had a hole big enough for Ju to slip into the declivity of the airlock. She hit the button to activate the door. It creaked, opened a hair and then slid open halfway.

Warm air rushed out as Mark kept hacking at the ice. The warm air melted some of the ice making his job easier. He had enough room for Shayna to fit through when multiple sonic booms resounded over the Tong base.

Shayna looked up. "Oh no, they're back."

She stuck her head out and looked at the sky. She knew fighters were up there, but saw nothing. When she squinted, she noticed shimmers in the hazy Europa atmosphere. The shimmers were moving. "I don't see them," she said. "But I know they're there."

"Cloaked, like Bat said," Mark grunted. "I heard the Company was working on a device that would hide their ships." He spoke as he furiously smashed the ice with the bar. He kept gouging off chunks and hacking flakes away until he had enough room to crawl into the airlock.

He squeezed through and landed with a huff on the floor of the airlock as multiple explosions announced the arrival of a squadron of Company fighters. Bombs hit the men's quarters and the commons. The commons exploded, the ice liquified and suddenly, they were floating.

"Get inside," Mark screamed.

Ju shoved into the space between airlocks followed by Mark and Shayna. They closed the door behind them and opened the connecting door. As soon as it slid open, they were met by Mai Li, Cressy, Granny Hawkins, the Vagrant women and many Tong women crowding towards the airlock. The group meeting them cried and moaned with terror as they pushed close and Mark waved his arms. "Go back. The base is under attack again. There's nothing out there but death."

The women backed away and screamed as the women's quarters lifted on a swell of melted ocean water. All of them dropped to the floor as the building rocked and started rolling. Shayna fell to her hands and knees as the floor tilted. "Hang on," Mark shouted. "I think we're going over."

He was right. The entire building slowly rolled to the left. The supports anchoring it to the ice must have broken loose. They were floating free on the rolling oceans of Europa. A huge explosion rocked the building. Shayna moaned. "I think that was the men's quarters."

"I hope it was empty," Ju said.

The women and children wailed with fear. Another explosion hit close and their building rolled again. Women and children tumbled across the tilting floor which was now one of the walls. The building rolled again and they fell onto what had been the ceiling. Shayna protected her belly with both hands as they landed on the ceiling in a wad of women and children. The building rolled slightly and then abruptly stopped. They all waited with their hands braced on the ceiling. No one moved, breathed or made a sound.

The building stayed in this position. An awful groan came from outside followed by a loud cracking sound. “That’s gotta be the ice freezing over again,” Mark said.

They waited for a few additional minutes. There were no more explosions and the building remained in the upside-down position. Mark slowly heaved himself upright. He was standing on the ceiling panels. Recessed light fixtures and air vents now dotted the floor. The lights were still on or they’d be in the dark.

Mai Li, still agile and with her wits intact, leapt to her feet. “Ju,” she said. “I’m so glad you’re alive.” She hugged her daughter close and cried on her shoulder.

Shayna struggled to get up. Her belly made doing anything awkward. Mark grabbed her hand. “Be careful. The ceiling ain’t a good floor.”

“Can we get out of here?” She asked him.

The women and kids huddled together. It was warmer in here than out there, but how long would it remain warm? “I think we should try to get to a ship and get off Europa,” Mark said. “The fighters could come back to finish us off. Anymore tumbling around and some of these kids are going to get crushed and die, or badly hurt.”

“Do you think there are any ships left?” Mai Li asked. “It would seem smart for them all to get off this cold rock of solid ice piece of….”

“Mom,” Ju said with a smile. “No cursing. There’s kids.”

“Well,” Mai Li said. “I can’t imagine any Tong warriors waiting to save the women. We’re not very important. And they’ll take every ship than can get into space.”

Granny Hawkins pulled herself slowly upright. “No, the men will worry about men things and fighting, not about us.”

Ju glanced at the huddled women. “Are any of you warriors?”

Three stood up. “We have trained,” one said. “My name is Rako. I can fight if needed.” She pointed to her friends. “Chani and Tsute can also fight.”

"The men will think we can take care of ourselves," Ju said. "And they are correct. We will." She turned to Mark. "We have Mark to help us. He is brave and strong and will do what is necessary. We're not stupid or cowards. We will protect ourselves, take care of our children, and we will escape."

Mark's ears turned red. "Uh, I'm no hero, but I'll do my best."

Ju grabbed his arm. "Of course you will."

"These pods are self-contained," an older Tong woman said. She was small with her dark hair in a knot on top of her head. She held herself with great dignity. "The power comes from a tidal generator and the pod is heated by the warmer water under the ice. The tidal action on this planet is great enough to create heat. It will keep us from freezing. I think we should stay here in the pod where we are at least warm and there is power."

Mark shook his head. "I think we need to get off Europa."

"I agree with Mark," Shayna said. "The men will not come back for us for a very long time. We'll run out of food."

A Vagrant woman stepped forward. She carried one infant and a toddler clung to her skirt. "I'm afraid to leave the pod. It's warm in here. Out there we'll freeze in no time. My children will die."

Shayna understood the woman's concerns. There were no cold-weather suits for the kids and few for the women. "Maybe a small party of us should try to get off the planet and bring help. If we split this large group into two, there will be more supplies for the ones remaining."

Mark nodded. "We should at least go out and see if there is a way to get more gear and supplies from the men's quarters and to check on the damage. We might not even have a ship here to escape in."

The women all began talking at once. Shayna, Mark and Ju pulled aside and watched as the women talked to each other. The older Tong women finally stepped out of the group. She held up a hand and the women became quiet. "I think this plan is good. You," she pointed at Ju, "go outside and see what's happening."

She pointed at Mark. “You go with her and see if there is a ship. We can’t really make a decision if we don’t know what our options are.”

Shayna nodded and shoved Mark gently towards the door. “Make it as quick as possible. Your cold weather suit won’t keep you warm long.”

She helped Ju and Mark get through the airlock, shut it behind them and turned to the remaining women and kids. “When they come back, we have to decide what to do. Until then, let’s gather all the supplies we can and see what we have.”

Chapter Twenty-Three

Logan grabbed his head in both hands. "Shayna is on Europa. I have to find out what's going on."

Knock and Fenfang huddled close to him. "First, we gotta destroy the weapon," Knock said. "That could take out our planet. If they get it to the moon or any other planet in the system, Earth will be destroyed. You know it's true, bro, we gotta take care of business."

"He's right," Kylie said. "You're here, in Nevada, there is nothing you can do for your wife right now. When we get back to Vegas safely, you can find out everything."

"First, we have to destroy the weapon," Fang said. "We've come so far. We can't turn back now."

Kylie nodded. "Too many people have sacrificed to make this happen. And failure is not to be considered. If we fail, our entire race could die."

Logan moaned. "I know. I'm just so worried, I think I'm gonna hurl." He bent over and grabbed his stomach. "Shayna," he moaned. "Why didn't you stay on Gliese?"

"Dude," Knock said. "You know she couldn't. The Company woulda destroyed her there, too. Come on, bro, pull yourself together and let's get this thing done."

Logan stood up and cracked his neck first one way and then the other. He squared his shoulders. "Dad would say soldier on. That's what he always did."

"You're right," Fang said. "Dek never gave up."

"You got your act together yet?" Sugar Sweet asked.

Logan nodded. "I'm good." He wasn't, but there was no time to worry or fall apart. He had to man up.

The Sweet sisters, holding their urban destroyers in front of them, led the way. When they came to a crossroad with four corridors, Professor Goswami stepped up. “Go that way,” he said pointing to the left.

They ran into the dark hall. The lights blinked on once and then went dark again. Without the recessed lighting, it was so dark you couldn’t see your hand in front of your face. Knock stepped forward and flicked on a powerful Maglite. He swept the beam back and forth across the hallway and suddenly shut it off.

“I saw a flicker of light ahead,” Knock whispered. “I think there’s guards or Enforcers waiting up there.”

“This is all my fault,” Goswami moaned. “I led you right here and now they’re going to kill you.”

“We got this,” Sugar Sweet said nodding to her sister.

“I can’t allow you to risk your lives. This is all my fault.” Professor Goswami took off running down the hall toward the flickering light. Logan could see it now. It looked like the narrow beam of a small flashlight. He tried to run after Goswami and was grabbed by Fang and Knock. “No way, dude,” Knock said. “No heroics. Come on, we just follow him.”

As a group, they trotted forward in Professor Goswami’s wake. The old man ran into the dark, tripped and fell over a rolling office chair that had been pushed into the hall along with a desk and two file cabinets to create a small barricade. It was impossible to see the stuff in the dark.

“Down,” Logan screamed as the beam of light focused on them and a shotgun blast hit the rolling chair sending pieces of it flying. The Sweets and Kylie dived to the floor followed by Knock, Fang and Logan. The Professor was already on his face. Logan reached behind and grabbed Corey. “Down,” he hissed.

“Where’s Raj?” Corey whispered. “You see him?”

“I thought he was with you. “Oh man, can’t you read him?”

Corey laid his hand on Logan’s arm. “No, it’s like he’s dead.”

Another blast hit the desk followed by a volley of AR-15 shots. The huge bullets tore into the furniture. Sugar Sweet, swearing a long string of curse words, leapt to her feet and began firing off shotgun blasts down the hall. They couldn't see a thing. Even the small flashlight beam was gone.

"I'm not sitting here waiting to get blasted to hell," Ginger said. "Sugar, let's rock."

"I'm coming with you," Kylie snarled.

The two sisters and Kylie leapt to their feet. Ginger fired the big shotgun, cocked the weapon and fired another volley of rounds. With each woman firing, there was a constant barrage and the sound in the underground hallway was overwhelming. Logan covered his ears and motioned for Corey to do the same

"Look behind them," Logan called. He pulled his neurolizer and held it ready, thumb on the trigger and grabbed Corey. "We'll have to wait to hunt for Raj. Keep trying to read him."

Down the hall someone screamed and the AR stopped firing. Sugar and Ginger kept the barrage going as they led the way down the hall. The only light was from the shotgun blasts. The smell of cordite, blood, human waste and burnt hair filled the hallway. The Enforcers had ceased firing anything. "Light," Logan whispered to Knock.

"You sure?" Knock whispered back.

"Yeah, we gotta see what's going on."

Knock switched the powerful light on. It illuminated a scene out of hell. The shotgun blasts had torn the walls up. Pieces of drywall covered the three dead Enforcers laying across each other, holes blown in them, limbs missing or askew, mouths open. It seemed like a gallon of blood covered the floor. Logan gasped. Sugar Sweet put her booted foot on one Enforcer and rolled him over. "Now this is what I call a weapon." She held up her riot gun.

Professor Goswami groaned. "This is so terrible. I have no love for these men, but the blood and the carnage, is it really necessary?"

"Would you rather it was you or one of us?" Kylie asked.

"No, of course not. It all seems very barbaric to me, but then I am an old man."

Ginger picked up the AR-15. "This thing fires 5.56 NATO rounds. They blow a bigger hole in you than the shotguns." She pulled the clip out and showed the Professor one of the bullets. It was almost three inches long. "Take your head right off."

"More men are coming," Corey said. "I can feel them."

"Lead on, Professor," Logan said. "Hustle."

Professor Goswami led them deeper into the tunnels. The lights came and went. When they were off, Knock led with the Maglite. "They're still behind us," Corey said. "They think we're going for the weapon. I believe Vaerfeky is with them, but I'm not sure."

Professor Goswami led them to a corridor that went down, deeper under the base. He finally stopped at a metal door. "This is the door I spoke of." Goswami pointed at a box beside the door. "The retinal scanner is inside of that."

Knock took the alien's eyeball out of his pocket. He'd wrapped it in a scrap of fabric torn from his Zombieland T-shirt. The one with the list of rules. "Hurry," Corey said. "They're almost here."

In the quiet, Logan thought he heard running footsteps. Knock lifted his patch and shoved the alien eyeball into his empty eye socket. He glanced once at Logan, stepped up to the scanner, flipped the lid covering it up, and placed his borrowed eye against it. A thin line of red light ran down the eye and back up. The scanner beeped and the door began to open. Knock backed away from the scanner and held his fist out to Logan. "Worked, dude," Knock said.

As they bumped fists, Corey hissed. "They're almost here."

"In!" Logan shouted as he smashed the retinal scanner. They rushed inside. Last one in was Knock. He slapped a red button closing the door as shots rang out. Professor Goswami screamed and fell to the ground as the door closed. Logan heard bullets hit the metal door as he dropped to take care of Goswami.

Professor Goswami had been hit in the chest. He opened his mouth to talk and blood bubbled out. "Quiet, Professor," Logan said. "Don't try to talk. He tore off his chameleon jacket and ripped off his shirt. The wound on Goswami's chest was huge. Even as he pressed the folded shirt into the wound, he knew with a feeling of intense despair that nothing could save Professor Goswami. Goswami lifted his hand and laid it on Logan's cheek. His soft brown eyes were filled with sadness and love. Tears ran down Logan's cheeks. "Find Raj," Goswami whispered.

"I will," Logan promised. More blood ran out of Goswami's mouth and bubbled from his nose. His eyes opened wide and then his head fell back on the concrete floor and his whole body shook. He was gone. Logan closed Professor Goswami's eyes, stood up and looked around. They were inside a huge hanger. The ceiling was high above their heads, probably at ground level or even higher. The weapon they'd been searching for sat in the middle of the hanger on a concrete floor surrounded by scaffolding and heavy equipment.

Knock punched Logan in the shoulder. "He was brave, dude."

Corey stripped off his poncho and laid it over Professor Goswami's face. "He's at peace," Corey said. "But we gotta find Raj."

"After we destroy this weapon," Logan said. "Professor Goswami lost his life to get us here. We can't let him down." A perimeter made of yellow caution tape had been set up around the weapon. Logan crossed the concrete floor to stand outside the caution tape and stared. The weapon was made of cold blue metal that glowed with inner light. Logan had never seen anything like it. The weapon was a gigantic ball easily thirty-feet high, set inside a metal dish. Hundreds of holes dotted the ball at regular intervals. The ball, as high as a three-story building, filled the hanger. When Logan stared closely, he noticed each hole was covered with a glass prism. "How does this thing work?" he wondered.

Corey edged next to him. I've been scanning minds. I touched the alien's. He knew I was there so I had to get out quickly, but I saw it, man. The ball spins. There's a hole in the top where it sucks energy from the nearest star and at its core is a tiny chunk of antimatter. The spinning is a little like a miniature cyclotron. You know a particle accelerator. When the spinning builds enough power from the antimatter, it shoots beams out of those little prisms and destroys anything it's aimed at. Even something as big as a planet."

"Wow," said Sugar Sweet.

"Dude," said Knock.

"We got this," said Fang as she pulled Logan's pack off his back.

Logan glanced at Professor Goswami's body. "Let's put the Professor next to the weapon. He'll be incinerated with it. He gave his life so we could destroy it."

"You sure it won't blow up and decimate the entire planet?" Ginger Sweet asked.

Logan shook his head. "Nope, not sure of anything."

"There is antimatter in there," Knock said.

"Gonna have to risk it," Logan said.

"I don't believe it will explode," Kylie said. "The core should be housed in a very stable and indestructible container like the nuclear heart of a power plant. But it is antimatter and in there to provide energy. I'm guessing when the weapon is gone, probably the only thing left will be whatever the antimatter is contained inside. I know you can blow up a nuclear weapon with an outside explosive, but the nuke won't detonate. You'd have to be really stupid to make a bomb using antimatter that might somehow cause the destruction of the universe because someone tries to blow it up."

"Should we come back and retrieve the core?" Logan asked.

"Your call," Fang said.

"Hmmm." Logan helped Knock set the thermobaric bomb beneath the weapon. They laid Professor Goswami's body under the edge of the dish-like structure and placed the super bomb on his chest. When they put Goswami's body there, Logan saw the dish holding the huge ball was on two rails. It was meant to be picked up by some kind of lift.

"They're coming!" Knock shouted.

Logan bent over the bomb and set the timer for ten minutes. He glanced at the door into the hanger and saw whatever metal the aliens had used to build the door was holding firm. It had a bulge in the middle but wasn't open. He looked at his friends. "So, I'm gonna hit the go button, then we got ten minutes to be far away. How we gonna do that?"

"I've been exploring," Corey said. "The ceiling rolls back. I think if we climb the weapon we can reach the roof. We just gotta roll back the ceiling far enough to climb through. Look, there's handholds on the side of the ball."

"Awesome," Knock said. "I always wanted to ride an alien weapon powered by a thermobaric bomb. Especially one with antimatter inside it."

"Roll it back," Logan said as he hit the button to start the bomb's countdown. "We got ten minutes. Let's do this."

Corey entered a small office in the corner and hit a big, red, flat button.

The roof shuddered and creaked as the whine of a motor filled the hanger. The ceiling rolled back revealing a small slice of the starry sky.

"We got company," Sugar shouted as she fired her riot gun.

The alien, who now carried the bug from Professor Goswami, entered the hanger through the big doors. He was closely followed by three beefy guards and held Raj in front of him like a protective shield.

"Damn!" One of the guards said. "It's the Sweet triplets."

"I am so sorry," Raj called. "Run away. Do not endanger yourselves or this planet on my account. Please do not worry about me."

The alien ignored the guard's comment about the Sweet girls and smacked Raj in the head. "Be quiet, insignificant child youngling."

When Logan saw the alien hit Raj, something inside him clicked. He hated bullies.

"The ceiling's open too far for us to climb up on it and get out that way," Kylie said. Logan followed her pointing finger and groaned. The ceiling was still rolling open. There was no way they could get out by climbing the ball. Exiting across the roof was now impossible and time was ticking away.

"We need a new plan," Kylie said to the Sweets. She and the Sweet sisters turned and ran to the outer hanger wall. It was made of corrugated steel. "Looks like we'll need an emergency exit," Sugar screamed as she opened up on the wall with the riot gun, jacking shell after shell into the weapon and firing until a ragged hole appeared in the metal. The sound of the roof rolling back and the riot gun's shells blasting the walls was deafening. Smoke rose from the guns filling the air with the stench of cordite.

"Stop or we'll kill him," shouted one of the Enforcers holding Raj. He held the boy up by his shirt. Raj's feet dangled in the air. The Enforcer holding Raj, shook him. The Sweets and Kylie stopped shooting. "What do we do, Logan?" Sugar shouted.

Logan had no idea what to do. Knock pushed past him, lifted his neurolizer and screamed. "I hate to do this." He hosed all of them, Enforcers, alien and poor Raj with his neurolizer. "But we're outta time," he finished.

Logan joined him, firing the nasty weapon. The alien, Raj and the guards were encompassed in waves of arcing blue and green electrical charges. The shimmering electricity raced across their bodies as they fell to the ground. Logan grabbed Raj and threw him over his shoulder. The kid weighed nothing, but was jerking and twitching so hard it was difficult to hang onto him. "Let's go," he shouted. "The bomb is ticking."

Knock backed away from the alien and the guards. He fired his neurolizer at them until it was empty, then threw the useless weapon away and ran after Logan. "Don't you think that was overkill?" Logan asked as they clambered through the hole Sugar and her sister had blown in the wall.

"Not in my book," Knock said. "No such thing. Where's Fang?"

Logan stopped to look behind. "I guess she agrees with you."

Fenfang had drawn her sword. With one swipe, she neatly decapitated the alien. When she caught up to them she was smiling. "I'd like to see him recover from that," she said.

Corey glanced over his shoulder. "That wasn't Vaerfeky."

"Who's Vaerfeky again?" Kylie asked.

"Alien leader," Corey said. "He was with them. Now he ain't."

"I'm sure he'll turn up," Logan said as he leaped through the hole and into the night.

Chapter Twenty-Four

When Ju and Mark came back from exploring what was left of the base on Europa, they carried boxes of emergency rations. Shayna met them at the airlock. "This is all we could get," Ju said. "The men's quarters are flooded and the commons sank."

"It sank?" Shayna couldn't believe it. "What about the Command Center?"

"A good portion is above the ice. I think we might be able to get into it," Mark said.

"Then I'm going," Shayna said. "I need to send Logan a message. If he knows about this attack, he'll freak out."

"Let's take the three girls who said they could fight, Rako, Chani and Tsute," Shayna said. "We need protection."

"Do we have any weapons?" Ju asked her mother.

The fighter girls stepped forward. "We each have a sword and a blaster," Rako said. "We know how to use them." She wore the blaster in a holster on a belt and the sword on her back in a scabbard.

"Got any extras?" Shayna asked.

The Vagrant woman with the baby and the small child pointed to a locker. "In there, but it's on the ceiling now. I don't know how you can get to it."

Mark piled loose furniture up and stood back to stare at his creation. "No way it's gonna hold me," he said.

Cressy stepped forward. "I'm little. I can climb that easily." Shayna boosted her to the top of the pile. She clung to an office chair wobbling on top of a desk, turned back and grinned at Shayna. "Easy."

She slowly climbed the mountain until she could reach the latch on the weapons locker. It was set into the outside wall. "It's got some kind of combination lock," she called down. "And the numbers are Chinese." Cressy looked thoughtful. "Or maybe they're letters. I wouldn't know and besides it's upside down."

"Allow me," Rako said. "I know the combination."

She scampered up the pile of furniture, helped Cressy climb back down, and opened the locker. Since it was upside down, the moment the door was opened, weapons, ammo, charges and body armor fell out. Shayna and Ju gathered the booty and sorted it into piles. She handed the three Oriental girls the extra blaster charges, took a neurolizer for herself and gave all of them body armor.

When they were suited up they looked like blimps. Body armor under cold weather suits equaled doughboy. Mark had no room for the armor under his two cold-weather jackets so he went without.

"We tried to get further into the men's quarters to look for survivors," Mark told Mai Li. "But water filled it and turned to ice. Anyone inside is dead and there's no way to get in it."

"Hopefully all escaped," she said.

When they were armed and as prepared as they could be, they gathered at the airlock. Mai Li kissed Ju goodbye. Behind her, Cressy and the Vagrant woman with the two babies stood in front of the remaining Tong women, Vagrants and kids. Shayna's eyes filled with tears. She had to save them. "We'll be back," she said to Mai Li. "With good news. You'll see."

"Just be careful," Mai Li said.

They climbed through the upside-down airlock and pulled themselves up onto the ice. The cold hit Shayna like a solid wall. She'd forgotten in the short time inside how intense the cold was. She put her mask on, her goggles over her eyes and tightened the hood covering her hair. Mark was the last one out of the airlock. He stood up and turned to hit the button shutting the lock.

A sonic boom roared across the ice shaking it. Shayna spotted a Tong fighter streaking toward them with smoke streaming out of its engines. Two more sonic booms followed and Shayna screamed. Two alien fighters were hot on the Tong fighter's tail. Shayna couldn't see them, they were cloaked, but she saw the bursts of blue-green fire coming out of their weapons. They fired shot after shot at the Tong fighter.

"Down!" Shayna screamed. One of the shots hit the men's quarters. It exploded and a tidal wave of melted water headed toward them. It rushed straight at the open airlock. The water hit her as she was dropping. She clung to a piece of the women's pod jutting up out of the ice. Mark ignored the water rushing around his legs to his knees and turned back to the airlock. The Tong fighter crashed into what was left of the dome wall and exploded sending a ball of fire across the airfield. The two shimmering spots marking the alien fighters turned, flew by and fired another shot into the crashed Tong fighter and the dome and then disappeared into space with another pair of loud booms.

Water melted by the explosion and fire in the men's quarters gushed into the open airlock of the women's quarters.

The Vagrant woman who had been standing behind Mai Li screamed. Cressy scrambled out of the airlock and turned around to help the woman and child behind her. Water had filled the airlock. Mai Li struggled to stay afloat and the small child was gone. The terrified woman holding the baby shoved the infant into Mai Li's hands. "Save my baby."

The melting ice suddenly set the women's quarters bobbing free on the liquified ocean. It rocked back and forth, tilted, and began sinking into the icy water. The water covered Mark's feet, rising to his knees.

Ju, Shayna and the three girls clung to chunks of ice as the water rushed around their feet, the ice groaning, creaking, melting and reforming in the intense cold. The salty water pulled at Shayna as she clung to a spike of ice that had formed next to her. A huge plume of water erupted from a hole in the ice ten feet away from her and shot a hundred feet into the air. "Save my mother," Ju screamed to Mark as she fell to her knees and clung to the reforming ice.

Mark was standing closest to the women's pod. He was like a statue among the heaving chunks of ice and water, a solid rock-like human. He leaned into the airlock as Cressy scrambled out, pulled the girl to her feet and shoved her toward Shayna as Mai Li tossed the infant to him. He caught the baby as the women's pod broke loose, tilted and rapidly sank.

Water filled the airlock until only Mai Li's head was above the rising level. She fought to keep her face clear and shouted to Mark. "Tell Ju I love her." Her last words were garbled as water covered her head. She stuck her face out of the water one last time, shrieked, and went under as icy water flooded the airlock and the entire women's section sank like a stone. In seconds it was gone, ice already freezing over the spot where only moments before the women's pod had been.

"Mom!" Ju screamed, tried to get up, fell, and crawled toward the sinking structure.

"No, Ju, don't," Shayna cried.

Ju rose to her knees beside Mark. "Mom," she wailed.

Shayna awkwardly pulled herself upright. She stood with her feet splayed in a wide stance as the ice beneath them rose and fell, cracked, groaned and split open. A huge fissure formed only feet away in the spot where the women's pod had been seconds before. Shayna wobbled to the edge of the fissure and stared into it hoping in vain to see the building rise again, but there was nothing, just more ice. The bottom of the fissure so deep it was black in its depths.

She pulled Ju to her feet. She, Cressy and the three girls gathered around Mark and Ju. The fabric of Shayna's cold weather suit dried rapidly and didn't freeze. Shayna knew it had been soaked by the meting water, but whatever it was made of repelled water and didn't freeze. If it had frozen, they would all be statues trapped inside layers of ice.

Chani grabbed the infant from Mark who stood staring at the spot where the women's pod had gone down. The baby was wrapped in a cold-weather blanket, but it would freeze soon if they didn't do something quickly. Ju looked at Shayna, pushed her goggles onto the top of her head and wiped her eyes. "What can we do with a baby? It's going to die in this cold before we can get somewhere warmer."

"I got this," Mark said. He opened his second jacket, took the baby from Chani in his big hands, and shoved the infant into the jacket close to his chest. The baby wore a knitted cap on its tiny head. Its thin wail was muffled against Mark's chest. Mark took off his mask and put it over the baby's face. "I'll get another one when we reach the command center." His voice was gruff with emotion as he awkwardly patted the infant's back and tried to zip up the jacket.

Chani helped him pull the jacket around the baby and then she yanked hard on the zipper, forcing Mark's extra-large outer jacket to cover the baby. When the zipper was all the way up to Mark's chin, she struggled to fasten the long row of snaps. Rako stepped forward to help her.

"Look," Shayna said and pointed. A single-wing flyer, with a man hanging in a harness under it, puttered out of the sky slowly making its way toward the smoking ruin of the Tong fighter craft. "The pilot must have lived."

Ju stood like a statue and stared at the spot where only moments before the women's quarters had stood. Her hands covered her eyes and she rocked back and forth. Her wails drifted into the icy atmosphere. Shayna gently took her arm and pulled. "We need to go, Ju. The baby can't be out here long, Cressy doesn't have a cold-weather suit, and Mark doesn't have an oxygen mask."

Ju's goggles were on top of her head. Her dark eyes gushed tears that quickly froze on her cheeks. The frozen tears sparkled in the weak sunlight of Europa. "My mother," Ju sobbed.

Shayna put her arm around Ju and laid her head against the girl's. "I lost my dad. I don't know where my mother is, whether she's alive or not, I'm pregnant, and my husband is far away. Come on Ju, Dek would tell you what I'm telling you, soldier on. You can grieve later. We can all grieve later. When this is over. Right now, we have to concentrate on saving ourselves and that baby. We're still alive. Don't let their deaths be without meaning."

Ju allowed Shayna to hug her. Shayna knew how the girl felt. So many had been lost and more would surely die, but they had to fight. Not fighting just wasn't an option. "Come on. Remember Zombieland's rule number twenty?"

A tiny smile flickered across Ju's full lips. "It's a marathon not a sprint."

"Unless it's a sprint, then sprint," Shayna finished. "So, let's go."

Shayna took off the second jacket she wore to cover her belly and handed it to Cressy. The girl could barely move and could not speak. She had ice crystals forming on her clothes. She had to force the little girl's arms into the large jacket. When it was zipped, it covered the girl to her knees and the sleeves hung six inches beyond her hands. At least they'd be warm. She still didn't have a mask.

They trekked around what was left of the men's quarters and over the rough, fresh ice covering the commons. The ruins of the destroyed dome lay all around. Its shattered pieces made traveling across the ice even more difficult. Because of so much fire, melt water, and destruction, the rocky ground the airfield and the Command Center stood on was covered with a fresh layer of ice. Some of it was slippery.

Half of the Command Center had been on ice and half on solid ground. The structure was canted at an odd angle with half of it sunk into the frozen ocean. The airlock was above their heads. The outside storage was above their heads as well. They were staring at it with stupid looks on their faces, partly from shock, and partly from having no idea how to get into the building or access the storage locker and get Mark and Cressy an oxygen mask, when Bat walked up.

Shayna couldn't believe it was him. "Bat," she cried and fell on his chest. Ju joined her hugging the fighter pilot. Bat gently set both of them aside. "I'm glad you guys escaped," he said. "Did anybody else?"

"We haven't been in the Command Center yet," Mark said. "But the other buildings are gone with no survivors."

Bat put his hands on his slim hips and stared at Mark. "Is it possible you got even fatter?"

Ju's eyes narrowed. "He's got a baby under this jacket. We need to get it out of the cold."

"A baby?" Bat pulled his mask away so he could talk.

"A baby," Ju's voice was colder than the air on Europa.

"A boy or girl?" Bat asked.

"We don't know," Shayna said. "Help us figure out how to get up there to the airlock."

Bat grinned and pulled his mask back over his face. His voice was muffled, but Shayna understood him. "There's a side door. It might not be ten feet in the air."

Mark was very quiet. Shayna was starting to worry about him. He looked a little blue. She tapped him on the shoulder. "Breathe some of the oxygen. You're going cyanotic."

Cressy was in the same condition. Ju took off her mask and put it over Cressy's face. The little girl wasn't talking. She'd gotten dangerously cold when she got wet escaping the sinking women's compound. Cressy had even stopped shivering. "I'm worried about Cressy," Ju wailed. "She isn't talking."

"Just keep feeding her oxygen," Shayna said. "Maybe that's part of her problem."

Mark took the mask off the baby, sucked down several deep breaths and put the mask back on the tiny face inside his coat as Bat led them along the outer wall of the Command Center. As they walked the ice groaned under their feet, shifted and the entire building sank lower into the ice. They reached an airlock on the side of the Command Center, which was the biggest of all the buildings on Europa. "This used to be the pilot's exit into the dome," Bat said.

A keypad inside a small box was set into the wall next to the airlock. Bat flipped up the lid and typed in eight digits.

The airlock began beeping. A red light over the top of it spun. "That's so pilots in ships taking off know the airlock is open," Bat said. He pushed Mark toward the open lock. "You first blubber-boy. You look like you could use some oxygen."

Ju poked him with her gloved finger. "Don't call him that. He saved our lives."

Mark moved into the airlock. Shayna turned to follow when a huge boom echoed overhead. Bat immediately spun and ran for the airfield. "It's a ship," he called.

Chapter Twenty-Five

Logan ran as fast as he could away from the hanger. It was set on the outside of a group of four hangers, all on a concrete pad with an access road leading to the runways. Logan examined his surroundings as he ran. They'd come a long way underground. The dry lake bed was ahead of them along with several small buildings and the huge satellite dishes.

"In here," Knock yelled. Knock was able to run faster than Logan who was burdened with Raj. He stood in the open doorway of a small building, low to the ground, with a flat roof. It looked like some kind of bunker to Logan.

They ran through the door which was made of solid core metal, down a steep flight of steps, and into what could only be described as a hideaway, a safe room, a bunker. Logan dropped Raj onto a bunk and fell onto it next to him. Above them, Knock slammed the door and leaped down the steps two at a time. As his foot hit the concrete floor of the safe room, the ground under them shook and shuddered. The door blew into the stairwell.

"Think we destroyed the weapon?" Logan asked.

"I have no idea about the weapon, but I'm betting the hanger is scrap," Sugar said.

Raj groaned and sat up. "Where the heck did you run off to?" Logan asked him. "We looked, but we didn't have time for a thorough search. We thought you were dead."

"Bathroom," Raj moaned. "My stomach was most distressed. You know I have a nervous stomach. I had to find a facility."

Logan slapped his forehead. "Dude, what's Zombieland rule number three?"

Raj dropped his chin on his chest. "Beware of bathrooms."

"You knew that and still went into one?"

"I had to go," Raj wailed.

Logan laughed. "I guess you'll remember next time."

"Better to crap in your pants, dude," Knock said. "You almost got all of us killed."

Raj nodded. "I don't think I could ever do such a thing. It would be most disgusting."

"Me either." Fang ruffled Raj's dark hair. "Stop worrying about it."

Knock opened a storage locker in the back of the room and began sorting through its contents. He suddenly chortled. "Look what I found."

Logan went to see and when he realized what Knock had found, he groaned. "No, man, you just got over that addiction"

"What's he got?" Fang demanded.

Logan took the small black box away from Knock and showed it to Fang. "Is that what I think it is?" She snarled.

"Could be," Logan said. He waved his hand over the sensor at the top and sure enough, a holo-maid appeared.

It wasn't Helga or Inga, it was an even newer model. She didn't wear a maid's outfit. She wasn't wearing anything at all.

"My name is Heidi. What is your pleasure, master?" The holographic woman said.

Knock's eyes were popping out of his head. "Dude," he whispered. "She's like naked."

"Shut it off right this minute," Fang said as she stepped between Heidi and Knock. "Stop looking at her." Fang snapped at Knock.

"I can't," he wailed.

"What model are you?" Logan asked Heidi.

"I am the very newest version of the Cherry Blossom series. I am a Cherry Blossom one thousand."

"Who owns you?"

"I have never been activated. You must be my owner."

Logan shook his head. “Uh, no, not me. I’m definitely not your owner. My wife would murder me in my sleep. You need to go back in your box. We’ll let you know when we find the right owner.” He waved his hand over the sensor and the beautiful, luscious, totally naked blond disappeared.

Sugar looked over his shoulder. “Well that was amazing. I’ve seen them before, but never a naked one. I wonder what she can do.”

Logan tossed Knock the box. “Stash this in your pack. You never know when we might need her. Been useful before, could be again.”

“He’s not carrying that thing in his pack,” Fang snapped.

“I’ll carry it,” Raj said with a cheerful smile. “I’ll put the tiny box into my fanny pack.”

Logan rolled his eyes. “Good plan. Here.” Raj took the box and stowed it away under Fang’s watchful eye. “Don’t even think about peeking,” she said to Knock. “Remember, I like sharp things”

Knock gulped and shook his head vigorously. “I’d never.”

Fang snorted.

The small bunker was crowded. Logan moved Raj slightly and sat at the end of the bunk. Everyone else either sat on the floor or crowded onto the other bunk. “I think we should stay here for a half hour or so,” Logan said. “Let things clear out up there.

They had just settled in to wait when another explosion roared above them. “Now what the hell was that?” Logan muttered.

“Sounded like it came from behind us,” Kylie said. “I’m going up to check.”

“Do you think that’s wise?” Logan asked her.

“Might be the satellite dishes, bro,” Knock said. “The Bakersfield people were gonna blow them. Remember?”

Logan brightened. “That would be awesome.”

“I think we need to check to see if the bomb destroyed the alien weapon,” Fang said. “I mean, what if it didn’t?”

Logan rolled his eyes. "That would suck. Let me talk to Jesse. He might be able to tell us what's going on." Logan pulled his two-way. "Ranger Two, you copy?"

"Static roared in the receiver and then a thread voice. "This is Ranger Two. Copy you, and the satellites are scrap."

Logan grinned. "Good news, Ranger Two. Can you see the hanger we blew? Is the weapon still there or did we get it?"

"Can't tell. Too much smoke."

"Is it clear? Can we come out?"

"Don't know where you are, bro. Can't help."

"Roger that," Logan said. "Sorry, I forgot. We found a bunker on the edge of the hangers. Over and out." He turned to Knock. "Let's go topside,"

Knock led the way up the stairs followed closely by Kylie, Ginger and Logan. Knock stuck his head out, looked both ways and ducked back in. "Hanger's gone." He stuck his head out again and craned his neck to see behind the building. "Satellites are gone."

Ginger pushed Knock aside. "What are the rest of you waiting for? An invitation?"

Knock shrugged. "Just being careful."

They slowly emerged from the bunker. The eastern sky was lit with orange and yellow. It was almost day. The weak light illuminated a scene of destruction. Hanger Four was a smoking ruin. Logan climbed out and looked behind the bunker toward the dry lake bed. All of the satellite dishes were down. The Vagrants from Bakersfield were parked on a hill overlooking the base in the old truck. Logan waved to them. "Think they see me?"

"Hell no," Knock said. "Too far away."

Logan keyed the two-way. "Hey, down here."

He got no answer. "Maybe the explosions are interfering with reception."

"I'll go get them," Kylie said, and then took off at a jog for the hill.

"I'm gonna walk over to the hanger and see if the weapon was actually destroyed," Logan said. "I can't tell from here."

There wasn't any cover between them and the burning hanger, but Logan was wearing his chameleon jacket. He blended into the background and was almost impossible to see. Nerves on edge, Logan looked over his shoulder and all around as he speed-walked toward the burning wreckage of Hanger Four. He didn't see a living soul and needed to know the weapon was gone. That was the mission. He wanted to make sure he'd completed it.

Fang and Knock followed along with Corey and Raj. Ginger squatted on her heels beside the bunker with Sugar and lit a cigarette. "I didn't know she smoked," Logan said to Knock.

"I don't think she does," he answered. "Hey, if I had a cigarette on me, this would be the moment to smoke it."

Parts of the hanger were spread over a wide area. Logan stepped around a smoking truss, a piece of twisted siding and more roofing. One of the buildings supports still stood. It was peppered with scraps of metal. Logan pointed. "Shrapnel."

The roof had collapsed onto the foundation. It was hard to tell whether the weapon was dead or not. Corey suddenly stopped. "Someone is alive in there."

Fang snorted. "Well it's not the alien."

"Nope," Knock said. "You made sure of that."

"Whoever it is, is barely alive," Corey said. "I'm getting pain and confusion."

Logan picked his way over the smoldering debris to the center of what used to be the building. The twisted metal and smoking supports suddenly moved. Logan stopped. "Something's going on," he whispered.

It was the biggest pile remaining in the building. The weapon had to be under it. Screeching and scraping erupted from the pile. Metal and burning lumber shifted and fell away. The metallic-blue ball of the weapon gleamed beneath more twisted roofing. The glass prisms sparkled. "Holy crap," Knock whispered

The ball rocked and spun on its base. The cup-like base tilted, the ball rolled out, and took off across the debris field, rolling faster and faster as it crushed everything under it.

They turned and watched it roll toward the dry lake bed. "Well that's a hell of a thing. What now?" Knock asked.

"It rolled over whoever was left alive," Corey informed them. "The spark I was reading just flickered out. It's gone."

"Where's it going?" Fang asked what they all were thinking.

"I don't know," Logan said. "But we gotta follow it."

The red truck roared up and Sugar leaped out. "Did you guys see that?"

Logan stuck his head in the cab. "Have you got any rockets left?"

Jesse nodded. "Two."

Sugar leaped into the bed, got the rocket launcher out and quickly loaded it. "This is a long shot," she said.

"It's not rolling that fast," Jesse said." "Wanna get closer?"

Bobby was driving. He braked the Rover inches from them. "We have to destroy it," he yelled. "Load up."

They scrambled into the vehicles. Sugar and Ginger were their best shooters, so they sat in the back of the truck with the rocket launcher and two of the Bakersfield Vagrants, Fred and Midori. Jesse, the American Indian, drove.

Bobby followed the red truck as it took off in a cloud of dust after the rolling weapon. "Think one of those rockets will destroy it?" Logan asked Bobby.

Bobby looked thoughtful for about a second, tilted his head and twisted his mouth into a rueful grin. "No."

Knock was squished in the cab along with Fenfang. "What about you?" Logan asked Knock. "Think we can blow it up?"

Fang leaned over Knock. She was halfway sitting on his lap. "Not a chance, but we need to try."

"What we need to do is follow it," Logan said. "Some force, no doubt it's alien, is pushing it or driving it with a clear destination.

Look." He pointed. "It's headed southeast toward Vegas. It's even skirting the mountains like it knows it can't roll over them."

"Indian Springs Air Force base is that way," Jesse said. "Maybe there's more aliens there."

Logan leaned back in the seat one shoulder behind Jesse's and one in front of Knock's. "Let's try to blow it up first. If we can't, then we follow it."

"Can you see what kind of ship it is?" Shayna asked.

Bat shaded his eyes against the eternal daylight on this side of Europa. It was brighter than you'd expect, because of reflected light off the ice. "I think it's one of ours," Bat said. "If it is, it's coming in hot and it's probably one meant to stay in orbit, because it's really big."

"The baby is crying," Mark said. "I need to get it somewhere warmer."

Shayna nodded. "Bat, you and Ju stay out here and see what happens with that ship."

"But Shayna," Tsute said. "If it crashes, it'll melt a lot of ice and then the Command Center could sink, or flip over. I don't mean to be negative but . . ." She pointed at the common building, or where the commons used to be, which was now a sizable mound of ragged ice.

Bat waved them on. "Look it's slowing like it might be gonna use its thrusters and make a decent landing."

Shayna snorted. "We aren't that lucky."

But Bat was correct. The big spaceship slowed, held its position above what used to be the packed spaceport and slowly started to descend. Smoke billowed from the rear of the ship and every few minutes a small burst of flames spurted from a port in the ship's aft sections. "I think it's damaged, but it looks like they can still maneuver it." Bat stared at the ship hard. "I think it's one of my cousins. Stephen Huang is Triad, but, I mean, we're still related so we talk. His Triad owns an interstellar trading ship just like that one."

Shayna patted Bat on the shoulder. "Awesome, you and Rako and Tsute go check it out. I need to send Logan a message and the rest of us need to get out of the cold for a few minutes."

"Why can't Ju come with me?" Bat smiled at the girl and held out his hand.

"Because I'm going with Mark to help take care of the baby," Ju answered in a cold, flat voice. "He needs my help. And Cressy is frozen. I'm worried about her."

"I need your help, too," Bat said as he shot her his most charming smile, even white teeth flashing from full lips, eyes snapping with that rakish sparkle. Even Shayna felt the pull of his charm. He was just a spectacularly good-looking guy.

Ju was having none of it. "You can take Chani if you need more help," she said.

Shayna was secretly proud of Ju. She'd seen a side of Bat she didn't like and was turning toward Mark, the sweeter and more considerate guy, even if not the hottest guy. She put her arm around Ju. "Let's get Mark, Cressy and that baby where it's warm."

The Command Center was tilted at a funny angle. The airlock they went through was about six inches above the level of the rocky, ice-covered ground. Once inside, the warmth encompassed them like a blanket. Immediately, the cold weather suits became a burden and too hot. Shayna peeled hers off and hung it on a rack beside the lock. Mark shrugged out of his outer jacket and handed Shayna the baby.

Shayna had never held an infant before. She took the baby from Mark and had no idea what to do with the tiny human. Instinct finally kicked in. She laid the baby against her chest and it snuggled its head against her. Feelings she'd never experienced flooded her. She knew intellectually she was pregnant. Suddenly, the reality hit her. In three short months, she would be taking care of an infant just like this one. Her and Logan's child. Tears gushed out of her eyes as her heart filled with all kinds of conflicting emotions; love, terror of the unknown, and an indescribable longing.

Ju saw her crying and put an arm around her. Ju seemed to understand exactly what she was feeling. Their eyes met and Ju hugged her hard. "You'll make a great mom," Ju said and burst into tears. "My mom is dead," she wailed.

Shayna did the only thing she could think of. She handed the baby to Ju. "Cressy isn't moving. We need to get her into the infirmary and into some hot water."

Cressy stood like a statue, not moving, not crying, not talking. "I'll help Mark get that other jacket off," Shayna said. "If you can take care of the baby. It's wet. Oh my god, where we gonna get diapers?"

Ju dried her tears on her sleeve. Her moment of painful loss passed as she took the baby in a practiced carry and said, "We'll find something." She began rocking the child who had woken up and was grumping.

"Do you think it's a boy or a girl?" Mark asked as Shayna helped him get out of the jacket he wore backwards.

Ju held the baby out in front of her. It squirmed and its blanket slipped. "It's a girl," Ju said smiling. "Look. Her onesie is pink."

"She has no mother or family. We'll have to name her," Shayna said. "Any ideas?"

Ju stared into the tiny infant's face. The baby had soft blond hair, blue eyes and apple cheeks. "Can we name her after my mom?"

Shayna closed her eyes. Would that be a good thing or a bad thing for Ju? She had no idea. "What do you think, Mark?"

Mark had shucked his cold-weather pants and was hanging them up. He turned his head and smiled kindly at Ju. "I think it's a fine idea. If Ju wants to name the baby after her mom, she should be able to."

"Mai Li," Ju said. "You are now little Mai." Tears ran down Ju's cheeks. "I think my mom would approve."

Shayna refused to be drawn into any more emotional scenes. She was pregnant and afraid one more tearful moment would send her over the edge into a full hysterical meltdown. "Let's find the infirmary and see if anyone is alive in here."

The hallways were lit with emergency lights and the building was still being warmed by the ocean currents. Energy for the base was provided by a plant using the tides. Europa was so close to Jupiter the tidal movement was huge. Strong enough to provide energy for warmth, it kept the seas from freezing solid, and energy for electricity. They never stopped and when Europa was closest to Jupiter, the tides became so powerful, geysers erupted in the ice and the giant fissures formed.

They made their way to the heart of the base, searching for the infirmary. "Look," Ju said. One of the closed doors was labeled infirmary. "Nice of them to label everything." Ju shoved the door with her hip. Lights automatically switched on. There was a medical chamber against one wall. It looked like a coffin. Tsute waved her hand over the control panel and a keyboard appeared. She hit a button on the keyboard and the lid of the coffin-like medical chamber opened.

"This is going to be close," Mark said. Cressy had collapsed. She lay on the floor, unmoving. Mark put his hand on her chest. "I'm not sure if she's breathing."

Shayna grabbed the girl and removed her jacket. "Help me get her into that thing."

"I got this," Mark said. He gently lifted Cressy and placed her in the chamber. Tsute typed something on a floating keyboard at the end of the chamber and the lid dropped. Fog filled the coffin-like container. "This thing is mostly used for hypothermia," Tsute said. "It's already set for it."

"Nothing else we can do for her at the moment," Shayna said. "I need to get a message to Logan. If he knows Europa has been attacked, he'll be freaking out."

As she ran down the long hall to the heart of the Command Center itself, all Shayna could think about was Logan. She hoped her small cubby was still operational so she could access her mailbox and send him a message.

All Ju was worried about was finding a diaper for the baby. “This kid stinks,” she said to Mark with a tiny smile on her tear-stained face.

Shayna hoped taking care of an infant would direct Ju’s mind away from sad thoughts about her mother. Both the tiny girl and Ju were essentially orphans. Hopefully, Ju would realize this and bond with the child. It would be the best thing for her.

When they walked by one of the break rooms, Ju ducked inside with Mark. “You go on ahead,” she said to Shayna. “There’s a paper towel dispenser in here. Diapers.” She said that with a lot of satisfaction in her voice. Mark followed her inside. “I’m gonna help Ju, if that’s okay with you, Shayna.”

Shayna already knew Mark was head-over-heels in love with Ju. She certainly wouldn’t stand in the way of that. She laughed. “After you two figure out a diapering system, come find me. I hope there are other people in here somewhere.”

“All of them weren’t pilots,” Mark said.

“Where’s Cain and Tom?” Ju asked. “Wouldn’t they have stayed behind?”

That’s when they heard the cries for help. “Help us,” issued from the depths of the Command Center. “Is anyone in here? Help!”

Chapter Twenty-Six

Sugar aimed the RPG, rocket propelled grenade launcher, by hoisting it onto her shoulder. It was a sophisticated weapon, tube-shaped, military green, with a pistol grip and a trigger just like a handgun. It launched a missile-like grenade that was designed to destroy tanks. Logan hoped it would destroy the alien weapon, but seriously doubted it. If the thermobaric bomb didn't blow it up, how could an RPG round do the job? But they had to try. Maybe they could at least stop it.

Jesse pulled the truck up close to the rolling sphere. The diamond-shaped crystals embedded in the alien weapon all glowed brightly with flickering blue lights. The entire globe-shaped weapon glowed with a bluish halo. Up close it was enormous, almost forty-feet in diameter.

"Here goes nothing," Sugar screamed.

"Aim for the port," Logan called to her. There was a square door in the side of the sphere that was visible every time the weapon rolled. It might be an access to the workings, or even a way to get inside the weapon. It was certainly large enough to hold the aliens or humans.

"Yeah, sure," Sugar called and fired the RPG. The missile flew straight at the weapon. They all held their collective breaths, hoping against all hope that it would blow up the sphere. The missile hit the door exactly where Logan wanted, and exploded. The sphere didn't blow up. The door didn't blow in. The explosion was absorbed in the eerie blue glow which burned brighter for several seconds, and then the weapon stopped rolling.

"What the heck?" Ginger Sweet screamed. "It stopped."

"Go for it," Bobby," Logan said and smacked Bobby on the shoulder. "Jordie, get ready. Maybe we can get that access panel open."

"You're nuts," Jordie said. "It could go off, fire at us, explode, or a zillion other crazy things. We should turn around and drive the other way at a high rate of speed."

"You're right," Logan said. "But we can't. We gotta try to stop it. If we die, then we die trying."

"Oh god," Jordie moaned. "This is insane. I don't wanna die. Why did you guys have to drag me off Gliese? I was happy there."

"We just plain love your company," Logan said. "You gotta admit we've had some amazing experiences."

"If you call almost dying every day for weeks, then yeah, pretty amazing."

"Hangin' with Logan is a blast, ain't it?" Knock chortled.

Logan laughed with him as they pulled close to the weapon and Bobby stopped the Land Rover in a cloud of dust. The red truck spun out as it circled the sphere, sending up more clouds of dust. Logan jumped out of the Rover, dragging poor Jordie with him. "You're all we got, man," he said. "You gotta figure out how to disarm, destroy or disable that thing."

Jordie hung back. "Seriously? I'm so scared I probably won't poop for a year." He thought for a minute. "Or maybe I'll poop right now."

Logan grabbed him under his left arm and Knock picked grabbed his right. "Balls to the walls," Knock said. "It's time to nut up or shut up."

"We're all gonna die," Jordie moaned.

The sphere still glowed with blue light but it was dimmer. The access panel Logan had spotted was close to the bottom. Next to it was a blue ocular reader. Logan smiled. "Knock, you still wearing the alien eyeball?"

"Haven't had time to take it out," he said and lifted his patch.

"Dude," Logan gasped.

"What?" Knock asked.

Fang stepped close to Knock and peered into his borrowed eye. "I think it's grown into your eye socket," she said. "Can you see out of it?"

Knock blinked a few times and tilted his head. "You know, I sorta can. The world's a little fuzzy." He held her face between his hands, looked into her eyes, and giggled. "Your skin is see-through. I can see some of your veins." He looked down and gasped. "Holy crap! I can see right through your clothes."

"How about me?" Logan demanded.

"Dude, I refuse to look at another man's junk." Knock slowly and deliberately turned his head to gaze at Sugar Sweet.

Fang spotted the move and yanked the eyepatch back over Knock's borrowed eye. "Don't even think about it."

Logan stifled a snort of laughter. It came out as a cough. "Come on. See if the eyeball will open the hatch."

Knock squatted to press his alien eyeball against the ocular reader. A red line of laser light scanned the eye. Everyone was hovering behind him. They all stopped breathing as they hoped and waited to see if the hatch would open.

The light coming out of the crystals flickered in a strange pattern and the hatch creaked. "It's opening," Logan whispered. "I heard it."

Sure enough, the hatch moved to the right, the metal screeching as it sent tan dust dribbling down the side of the sphere. "Dust can't be good for the insides of this thing," Jordie whispered.

Knock stepped away and dropped the eyepatch over the alien eyeball. He fingered his eye under the patch and squinted his good eye. "You know," he said to Logan. "I think this eye is starting to do the same thing."

"Do not tell Fang," Logan hissed. "Be very bad if you had to wear two patches." Logan put his hand on Jordie's shoulder and pushed the young man toward the open hatch. "Go on, I'm right behind you."

The door was big enough to squeeze through. Jordie kept glancing over his shoulder. His eyes were wide with fright. "You know we're gonna die."

"Yeah, we're all gonna die. You're gonna die, I'm gonna die, just praying it's not today."

Jordie crawled into the hatch and Logan followed. Inside the sphere strange panels blinked with red and green lights. Words in a language Logan had never read or heard of, and he'd seen and heard many under the city of New Washington, scrolled down twenty screens built into the walls, the ceiling everywhere but the tiny square of floor they stood on. A row of switches, each labeled in the weird writing sat under one huge screen. A controller like for computer games sat under another screen which showed the Orion Arm of the Milky Way galaxy. Their solar system and the sun were highlighted. Another panel showed a completely different galaxy. Logan didn't recognize it but Jordie did. "That's the Libra constellation. That's where Gliese is."

More screens showed more galaxies, some with highlighted systems. Logan rotated around the circular cabin which was barely big enough for the two of them. Jordie was frozen in front of one of the screens. "Logan, uh, that's Jupiter," he said in a shaking voice. "Aren't the Gliese people on Europa?"

Logan shoved close to Jordie and examined the screen he was pointing at. There was Jupiter shining big and bright with its brown and red striations and the big red storm that rotated right in the middle of the enormous planet. In front of Jupiter, Europa was a small white dot crisscrossed with red lines. "Oh no, they were gonna use this weapon to destroy Europa."

"You could be right," Jordie said. The space inside the sphere was as round as the orb, but beneath their feet there were no panels or screens. "Did the sphere rotate while we were in here?" Jordie asked. "Cause it looks like we're standing on a floor."

"I didn't feel it move," Logan said. He couldn't take his eyes off Europa. Shayna was there and they planned to blow his wife up with this weapon.

Jordie pressed a button and Logan freaked. "What are you doing?"

"You wanted me in here to figure out stuff. Well, I think this should bring up some blast chairs."

Sure enough, two chairs, shaped for the aliens who were kind of round, popped out of the flat floor under their feet. Logan was knocked into one and Jordie into another. As soon as they were seated, the hatch ground shut and the sphere started rolling. "Now look what you've done," Logan snarled. "We're moving."

Jordie was suddenly calm. "I think I understand this panel here," he pointed to one that had descended when the sphere started rolling and spread across Jordie's lap. "I think this controls a kind of flight mode. It's like nothing I've ever seen or even imagined, but you know, I think this thing flies."

Shayna heard the cries for help. Mark and Ju were busy with the baby. Cressy was in the medical bed. Chani had gone with Bat. She glanced at Rako and Tsute. They nodded. "We'll go with you," Rako said.

Tsute and Rako led as they jogged down the corridor to the center of the command center. The building was a four-point star just like all the buildings on Europa. The center was filled with computer stations, star maps and a big table. All loose furniture was piled against one bank of screens, all blank. The entire building was tilted at a twenty-degree angle, which is pretty steep for a floor.

"I'm going to send a message to Earth," she called after the girls. "Find where those voices are coming from."

The calls for help had grown weaker. Shayna wanted to help, but she needed to try to contact Logan. It was imperative he knew he had a spy, a mole, someone who had blabbed about their existence on Europa to the aliens and the Company, and if he'd heard about the attack on the Tong base, she needed to reassure him she was okay.

She found the little cubby holding the computer she'd used. The chair was gone, probably in the pile of furniture against the lowest wall. She had to squat to activate the screen. She waved her hand over a sensor and the keyboard appeared. The screen had just popped up before. She stared at the keyboard and saw an icon that looked like a screen. She tapped it and the keyboard disappeared. Crap! She waved her hand over the sensor again and this time the screen slipped out of its slot on the desk. Sighing with relief, she opened her mailbox. There was no new message. She typed a quick one to Logan telling him he had a spy and she was safe and if he had a way, could he send them help.

As she hit send, she had no way of knowing whether the message would go anywhere. Most of the satellite dishes had been on the roof of the Command Center and could be damaged. She'd heard they had an entire building back behind the Command Center dedicated to communications, but she'd never seen it, and it could be at the bottom of the European sea There might be no way to get messages off Europa. They might be totally alone.

She shut down the IT and followed Tsute and Rako. They'd disappeared down the corridor leading out of the central command room on the right. As she entered it, she heard muffled voices. She'd walked ten feet when the floor dropped. The end of this section of the building had broken off and shot down, probably into the icy ocean of Europa.

She had to be careful. There was a rail. She hung onto it as the slope of the floor increased. It was like sliding down a steep hill. The overhead lighting was gone, but further down the corridor, she spotted a beam of light. "Rako, you guys okay?"

"We're good," the girl shouted. "We found four guys."

"Shayna! Is that you?" It was Cain.

"Cain, you're alive."

"I guess you could say that." His voice was weak. Shayna inched forward heading for the beam of light. The end of this arm of the building was crushed. Rako and Tsute had high-powered flashlights. They were trying to disengage a man from the ruined metal of the building. It was freezing cold down here. Water had seeped in at the bottom of the building's arm where it was crushed and ripped open. Cain Hollyroad was trapped by a broken support.

Tom Curran and two other Tong leaders, Shayna thought one was Bat's uncle Sammy Lee, the other was the leader called Muuno-something, Manu for short. Lee and Tom were struggling to free Cain. The Manu leader guy was injured. He sat in a dry spot against the wall shivering. His leg looked broken to Shayna.

She crouched low. "Cain, how badly are you hurt?"

"I'm not," he snapped. "My damn foot is caught between two pieces of the support structure and it's under water. I've lost feeling in it and I'm cold."

Tsute shined her light into the dark around Cain's lower body. "I see the problem," she said.

"There's a tool locker in the second room up there," Manu said.

"I got this," Lee said. "I know the locker."

He ran back up the corridor, hit a switch to open the door, and nothing happened. "Power's out," Lee said.

"There's a manual override in the panel beside every door."

Lee found it, hit the button and the door clicked. Lee fit his fingers into the crack when it unlatched and pulled it open. He appeared seconds later with a crowbar which he held in front of himself like a trophy. "Low tech as you can get. Thank god we still have real tools."

Using the crowbar, they quickly freed Cain. His foot was undamaged, but probably had frostbite. "I can't feel it," Cain said. As he spoke the entire structure groaned and shuddered.

"We need to get out of here," Manu said from the floor. "It feels like the entire building is destabilizing."

"You got that right," Tom said. He put his arm around Cain's waist as Lee and Rako linked their hands together and lifted the leader, Manu, in a chair carry. "Let's go," Rako said. "I can't do this forever." She turned to Manu and grinned. "You need to lose some weight."

Manu's face was white with pain. "Yeah, I'll get right on that . . . next week."

The small group limped up the inclined arm of the building to the central part. "We have to go out the way we came in," Shayna said. "Through the pilot's exit."

Mark appeared in the corridor, saw Rako struggling to hold the large man, and ran to help. Ju appeared with the baby in her arms. "We can't stay in here," Shayna said. "The building isn't safe."

"What about Cressy?"

Shayna grabbed her head. "So many problems. It's making me crazy. If we leave the building, we'll freeze." She closed her eyes and took a deep breath.

"Let's hole up in the infirmary until we just have to leave," Mark said. "If we take these guys outside without suits on, they'll die anyway."

"Mark's right," Shayna said.

They piled into the infirmary. Ju had explored every corner of it. She pulled out some hot packs. Cain sat on a chair and Ju wrapped his frozen foot with the heated packs. Mark and Tom Curran put the leader, Manu, on a bed and gently lifted his broken leg. Ju examined it without actually touching it. "He needs to go into the medical chamber. This isn't something I know how to fix," Ju said.

Shayna nodded and popped the lid open. Cressy's light-brown eyes stared into hers. The girl smiled. "I think I'm fixed," she said brightly.

Shayna helped her out of the chamber. It took Mark, Cain and Rako to lift the heavy base commander into the chamber. He stopped them before they could close the lid. "If the building starts to go into the water or if we get another attack, run. Just leave me in here. These things are supposed to be bomb-proof. It should be," he mumbled. "I paid enough for it. They can find me later."

Shayna hit the button, the clear polymer lid closed, needles shot out of the walls of the chamber and injected Manu with painkillers. A mask fell over his face and fog floated out of jets in the walls of the coffin-like box. "That's all we can do for him," she said.

"We can't take the baby out into the cold," Ju said. "She'll die." Her face crumpled into tears. Mark immediately grabbed her in a bear hug and comforted her.

"I'll carry little Mai under my jacket," he said into her hair. "We'll get another mask. She'll be fine."

As he spoke, the building shifted again. This time, it rose a foot. "We can't stay in here," Cain said. "I can feel my foot. I can wiggle my toes. Let's roll."

Chapter Twenty-Seven

"Make it stop," Logan said. "Hurry."

Jordie played with one panel, touching it in the middle and dragging a weird icon to a spot in the corner. Then he fiddled with the joystick. "Got it," he said.

The sphere had stopped rolling. Logan felt it settle. "You know, we stayed stationary in these seats even when it was rolling."

"It's got stabilizers," Jordie said.

"Of course it does."

Jordie was fascinated by the device Logan could no longer call a weapon. It was much more. He was so wrapped up in checking out the maps, the controls and the various screens, he didn't hear the screams and yells from Knock. "Dude, someone's coming." Knock stuck his head in through the hatch and yelled. "Looks kinda like an army truck, a hummer."

Logan punched Jordie on the shoulder. "Someone's coming. We gotta do something."

Jordie shook his head. "No, man, I'm just starting to figure this thing out. Lock me in here."

Logan rolled his eyes. "I really think that's a bad idea."

Jordie pushed him. "Go see what's shaking. I'll be fine. I'm inside an impenetrable weapon for crying out loud."

"Well alrighty then," Logan said. "But don't say I didn't warn you."

Logan scrambled out of the sphere in time to see a desert-camo hummer crest a rise about half a mile away and head toward them. "Should I blow it up?" Sugar asked as she hefted the RPG and knelt to take aim from the back of the red truck.

Logan held his hand out flat to stop her. “Wait a second. There’s an alien driving it and he looks alone.”

The hummer pulled up and stopped. An obese alien clambered out and waddled toward them with all four arms in the air. “I Vaerfeky,” he called. “I was base commander.”

“Okay,” Logan said. “We get that. So, why are you here?”

The alien started sobbing. “I in very much bad trouble with my bosses. I so in bad situation. They want to kill me very much badly in terrible way. Probably put me in a pain amplifier first so I scream and die horrible death after longest amount of suffering ever recorded. I loses their most valuable weapon which we stole from Rigellians. Please . . .” He stopped in the middle of his statement to stare at Sugar who had stepped forward smiling.

“Well, well,” she said, her smile growing broader. “If it isn’t titty boy himself.” She turned and yelled for her sister. “Ginger, look who dropped by. It’s Fecky.”

Ginger strolled up in her signature strutting walk and stood beside Sugar. “Well, as I live and breathe. Fecky.”

The alien’s small mouth turned up in a huge grin that revealed pointed teeth, lots of them. “Yes, yes, it be me, Fecky. I remember yous.” He glanced around at all of them as though seeing them for the first time. “I thought there were three.”

“Candy stayed home,” Ginger said. “She had to work. What do you want, Fecky?”

The alien squared his round shoulders still grinning. “I wants to be a human like all of you. I could tell you lots of important stuffs.”

“Like what?” Logan demanded. He’d been watching the show and decided this alien liked women and had the same general obsession they all did for blonds with big hooters.

The alien’s eyes narrowed and he twitched his round head in the general direction of the sphere. “Like how to fly that thing. We steal design from Rigellians. They much older race. Know much stuffs we steal from caches all over the universe. Or we sometimes catch one and torture for information. They live very long lives. Not too many left." He smiled an evil leer. "We kill most, destroy their home world with their own technology." He then burst into a fit of giggles but never took his eyes off Sugar's chest.

"What would you want in return for helping us?" Knock asked. "Aside from a hot chick. We can see you like Earth girls."

Vaerfeky's eyes narrowed and a crafty expression, if you could call it that, he was an alien, crept across his round face. His drooping black mustache twitched. "Yes, I be wanting my own woman with nice, large breastsesses." He pantomimed a full chest with his two top hands. "And yellow hair, long leggies, round bottom, too. And I would like to be safe with big suite of rooms on top floor of the MGM Grand."

"Look," Logan began. "We can't just give you a woman."

Kylie stepped forward. "Women are not objects in our society. We're warriors." She growled the last line. Fang stepped up to stand beside her and growled with her.

"Wait, wait a minute," Knock said. He pulled Logan aside. "He's got a lot of info we need. If this thing can fly, like into space, we can get to Europa and see if Shayna is okay. Maybe help rescue her if she's needing it. And what if it can go interstellar? I mean this could be the discovery of the century. We gotta deal. Figure out something we can give him."

"I'll give him something all right," Logan said between gritted teeth. "I'll torture him until he tells us everything he knows."

"Yeah and a bunch of crap he just makes up. Torture never works. We gotta deal."

"Well, we can't give him a woman and that seems to be his chief desire. Look at him. He's drooling over the Sweet sisters and he's even peeking at Kylie, which is a very bad idea, and Fang, which is an even worse idea."

"I've never seen one of their women," Knock said. "They must be dog-butt ugly."

"Seriously, what do we give him?"

Raj tapped him on the back. "Logan, sir, I hate to interrupt, but I have a very wonderful and good idea."

'What?" Logan snapped.

Raj unzipped his fanny pack and pointed to the black disc inside. "You think he might be satisfied with Heidi?"

Cain called up to Shayna. She was hanging on the very edge of the main airlock into the command center. "Drop the suits," he yelled.

She carefully shoved the pile of cold-weather gear, masks, gloves and helmets over the lip of the floor. The stuff fell onto the ice where Ju, Tom Curran, Rako and Tsute gathered it up and started sorting it. The building had tilted to such a degree, the pilot's exit was no longer above the level of the ice. They'd had to climb a steep incline up the corridor to the regular exit which was now at least twelve feet above the ice.

"I'm gonna lower Cressy and then the baby," she yelled.

"I got her," Cain called back.

Cressy climbed over Mark, who was holding Shayna's feet, over Shayna and then Shayna grabbed the girl's hands and dropped her into Cain's waiting arms.

She rolled onto her back and Mark passed her little Mai Li. The baby was wrapped and then tied inside the sleeves of two cold-weather jackets. Shayna used the empty sleeve to dangle the infant. Cain grabbed the baby and passed her to Ju who pulled her close.

"Now you," Cain called.

Shayna looked back at Mark. "You going to be able to get down by yourself? Nobody can catch you, you know."

He nodded. "I'll fall onto the pile of cold suits," he said with a grin. "I can do it. No problem."

Shayna turned around and backed out the exit. She clung for a minute to both of Mark's hands. "Let go," she finally said. He dropped her hands and she fell six feet into Cain's waiting arms.

They piled the suits up and called to Mark. "You now."

He crawled to the edge and looked. Shayna could see he was terrified. "Jump," Cain yelled.

"I will," he snapped. "Just give me a minute."

The command center suddenly creaked and groaned. It shuddered and the ice beneath it rose three feet, then dropped suddenly. "Oh crap," they heard Mark scream. He was going to back out and drop slowly. Shayna had talked to him about how to get out safely. With the sudden movement of the command center indicating it was going down, maybe for the last time, he had to jump.

Cain and Tom tried to catch him. They were standing on the edge of the pile of suits when Mark hurtled out the open airlock door. They all tumbled together, Mark landing on the ice on his belly with a loud smack. Ju thrust the baby at Shayna and ran to Mark. He lay groaning on the ice. "Mark, Mark," she sobbed. "Don't die."

He rolled over groaning. "I won't, I think."

She grabbed his broad shoulders and hugged him. Rocking back and forth, clutching him close, she kissed the cap covering the top of his head over and over. He finally pushed her away. "Help me up." He reached his hand toward Cain.

"Sure you want to get up?" Cain asked.

"No, but we need to get to the ship where everyone will be warm and safe."

The spaceship they'd seen landing was now parked in the center of the old spaceport. Several smaller Tong fighters buzzed overhead and they all looked up at once. A dark-clad figure ran towards them out of the ship. "I think that's Bat," Shayna said.

Cain and Tom hoisted Mark to his feet and they started toward the ship. Bat met them halfway. Shayna's teeth were chattering when she asked. "Is it warm in there?"

"Half of it was burning, so yeah, it's warm."

"Will it fly?" Cain asked.

"Needs some work," Bat said with a grin. "Might be able to get it going. Gonna take a while."

"I don't care as long as it's warm," Ju said. "I have to get this baby somewhere safe."

"Safe for now," Bat said. "Won't be if the aliens come back." He stepped toward his uncle. "Uncle Sammy," he said and bowed.

His uncle grabbed him and hugged him. "Our entire family is getting slowly killed off. We gotta fight 'em, Bat. It's on us. Our poor leader, Muunokhoi. He's floating around somewhere in that." He indicated the destroyed Command Center.

"He dead?" Bat asked.

"Base commander is in the wreckage," Cain said. "We put him in that medical chamber thing. He said no matter what happens to the building, he'll survive."

"Manu's in that?" Bat stopped and pointed at the destroyed Command Center.

"He had a broken leg," Sammy Lee said. "He's too heavy for us to carry, especially with the bad leg, so we had to stow him in the medi-pod."

"I'll talk to Chen. He's in charge now. He can send a search party out to find him."

"Chen as in Chen Wang, leader of the Black Dragon Triad?" Bat was stunned. "They hate us."

"Not anymore. We're all in this together, and he's in charge now. He's the one who brought in the ship. His entire triad got involved in a pretty hot space battle with the new Guild. Took place at the edge of the system between Pluto and Hydra. Chen says there's parts of two Triad ships and one Guild ship on Kerberos and Charon, two of Pluto's moons. According to him it was a crap show. He'd never imagined being in a space fight and there they were being attacked in Earth's solar system. His own ship, Black Dragon II, was practically destroyed. They left it, all of them in space suits, and boarded the Guild ship through a hole they punched in it with their laser cannons before their own ship started cartwheeling toward Kerberos. He said, it was no contest after they boarded. I mean fat, lazy Guild dudes fighting us." He giggled. "No match for our trained warriors."

"I hate to interrupt this fascinating discussion," Shayna said. "But we're freezing to death and there's a child and a baby to consider."

"Let's head for the ship," Cain said. "Got to get these women and kids out of the cold. Will the ship fly again?"

"We're working on it. It's kind of in bad shape," Bat said. "But we'll be safe there for now."

"Yeah, for now, but we need to get somewhere safer like off this planet," Cain said.

"That's the plan," Bat said. "Get her on the dark side of Europa and hide. Fix it for interstellar travel and then haul ass."

"Who did it belong to?" Mark asked.

"Bubble boy, no one needs your input." Bat snapped.

Cain lifted his hand. "Enough of that. Who did it belong to?"

Bat grinned showing those white teeth. "Smugglers Guild. And now what's left of it is ours."

Chapter Twenty-Eight

"That's the best idea you've ever heard," Logan said to Raj. He took the black disc. "Let's introduce him to Heidi."

"Uh, Mr. Vaerfeky, sir," Logan began when they were back in the group surrounding the sphere. "We can't give you one of our women. You'd have to probably hook up with one like we humans do, convince them of your sincere admiration, and possibly get some in return. Or, I guess, in Vegas you might be able to purchase female companionship. We can put you in a nice suite and protect you. We don't run Vegas, we do have some sway there, but the Company still runs the place. So, MGM Grand might be beyond our ability, however, he grinned, we do have an alternative for you while you meet your own woman or find one to hire." He held out his hand, opened it, and revealed the disc.

"What is that?"

Logan took a deep breath. "Meet Heidi."

He paused before passing his hand over the sensor and turned to Knock. "Tell Raj and Corey to go stand behind the sphere and under no circumstances are they to peek."

Knock grinned and hustled the two very interested boys off. When they were gone, Logan passed his hand over the sensor and Heidi appeared in all of her naked glory. Vaerfeky gasped and reached for Heidi's chest. Logan took a step back. "No, no, not so fast."

Vaerfeky's eyes were alight with what Logan knew had to be lust. He shuddered and shook it off. "Heidi could you please dress yourself?"

"Yes, master," she said. "What would you like me to wear?"

"Mr. Vaerfeky, how would you like her to dress?"

"No clotheses needed. I like her fine way she is."

"We have children here. We need her dressed."

Vaerfeky's lust-filled grin disappeared and his face fell. His mustaches drooped to his chest. "Oh well, make her wear red dress with sparkles and high heels. Make dress show some of her bosoms and be tight. Yes, yes, very tight."

"Did you hear that, Heidi? Red dress."

Heidi was immediately clothed in a shiny red dress with sequins, very high heels, dress as tight as a second skin. Logan waved his hand in Heidi's direction. "Does she work for you?"

"What can she does?"

Logan had to force himself not to roll his eyes. "I truly don't know. She's uh, a newer model. The last holo-maid I knew of had been modified to touch, but I don't know if you'll be able to touch her, or if she has the same ability to touch you. You'll just have to find out. Is it a deal?"

Vaerfeky held out one of his top hands. "Yes, yes, gives her to me now."

Logan passed his hand over the sensor and dropped the disc into one of his cargo pockets. "Not until we know the full capabilities of this weapon and how to operate it. Then the Sweet sisters will take you to Vegas, find you a nice room, and give you Heidi."

Vaerfeky's lower lip thrust out in a parody of a human pout. His eyes narrowed and he sighed. Knock whispered into Logan's ear. Logan smiled and said to Vaerfeky. "She apparently speaks your language, too."

The alien's eyes lit. "She could then understand my instructions?"

"Yup, and you can password protect the box so no one else can open it. And as I understand it, from my previous experiences, you might be able to reprogram her to do more than her original instructions allow." The thought made Logan wince.

"Yes, yes, is deal."

"That's great," Logan said. "Show us how to work the sphere."

The inside of the starship smelled weird. Kind of like garlic, burning electrical equipment, scorched plastic and rubber, and human sweat blended into a musky funk. Shayna wrinkled her nose as Bat led them to a forward section. He opened a door and ushered the women into a large room filled with bunks, a desk with a built-in computer, table, four chairs and a servo unit against the wall. A large vid screen filled one wall. "Chicks can stay here. Dudes come with me."

Mark shook his head. "I stay with Ju. She needs my help with the baby."

Bat smirked. "What can you do for an infant?"

"I know a lot about babies. My parents had twins when I was twelve. Believe me, I saw a lot."

Bat snorted. "You just wanna stay here and move in on Ju. I ain't stupid."

Cain stepped between them. "Let Mark stay here and help out with the women. They could use a man's help and he is very good with the baby. I've seen it myself." He winked at Mark. "Us guys will go do guy stuff with you. No problem. Tom here is good with machinery. I feel sure he can help with repairs."

"I want to go with you," Shayna said. "I need to see if Logan got back to me. You know after that last message he might figure out a way to send us some help. And maybe we can get some news about the weapon."

Cain nodded. "Sure. The com center must be operational. That's a primary consideration for everyone."

Bat took Ju's hand in his, bent over it and kissed it. Shayna thought she heard Mark growl, but when she glanced at him he was bouncing the infant on his chest like an expert. Ju's cheeks reddened when Bat kissed her hand, but she didn't jerk it away. Shayna shot her a *look* as she followed Cain out of the room.

The ship was filthy. Shayna had never been on a spaceship that wasn't organized and neat with everything stowed in its proper place. This one was a rat's nest. Garbage littered the corridor. When she looked into rooms, the crews' personal spaces were disordered with clothes, belongings and food detritus everywhere. Whoever had inhabited the ship before the Triad took it over lived like pigs. She tapped Cain on the shoulder. "Are you seeing this?" She pointed into a particularly filthy room.

He grinned at her. "They're criminals. Not too organized and definitely none too clean."

"I still don't understand why the Company went with them and dumped the Tong."

Cain rubbed his thumb and forefinger together. "Money, it's all about profits and the Guild will haul anything. I mean anything no matter how dangerous or how disgusting. And they'll fly into any planet, even ones that rain fire and have storms the size of Earth every second of every day. They're crazy. The Tong have standards."

Shayna nodded. "Well it shows."

There were signs the Triad and the Tong people were organizing and cleaning. They saw piles of trash and smelled heavy-duty cleaning products as they grew closer to the center of the ship. "This is a star ship and not meant to land ever," Bat said. "Some of its operating elements had to be jettisoned so it could land. That's just a small part of our problems. Getting it back into space is going to be a lengthy process."

"But we could be attacked again," Shayna said. "We'll all die if they attack us even one more time."

"Not if we can help it," Bat said. "We're working on generating the ship's shields. This thing had some pretty high-tech protection. And," he paused and smiled. "The hold was full of fighters, all with these high-tech shields and the new cloaking equipment."

Shayna groaned. "But that means we're still stuck here."

Cain put a comforting arm around her shoulders. "We'll be warm and dry and you'll be able to have your baby in a safe place."

Shayna shook off his hand. "This ship is a disaster." She turned on Bat. "Does this piece of junk even have an infirmary?"

"We're working on it," he said. "Chen knows our needs and he's a good commander."

Sammy Lee snorted. "Since when is a Triad worth the sweat off a Tong's butt?"

"We need to work together, Uncle," Bat said. "The time for petty differences has to be over. It's us against the Company now, and the Smugglers Guild, and even aliens. We need to be as one unit, one entity. We'll join with Shayna's Vagrants on Earth, and we'll send these aliens and the Company straight to hell."

Shayna nodded. "We'll see. Now, can you find me a working com unit? Does this hunk of space garbage have one?"

"Be nice, Shayna," Cain said. "We're guests."

"Sorry I'm a little cranky," Shayna's apology issued from between tightly-clenched teeth. "I'm feeling like I'm a hundred months pregnant right now. My back hurts, my feet are swollen, I have a migraine, I almost froze to death, and now I just found out I'm indefinitely stuck on ice world where I will no doubt die in child birth."

Bat grinned at Cain. "I remember my mother when she was pregnant with my little brother, Arban. She was grumpy the entire time." He patted Shayna's shoulder softly. "Don't worry. We'll take care of you. There's a working com unit right here." He opened a door and ushered Shayna through. The room was clean and filled with six busy people. There were screens on the walls and banks of IT stations. Bat pulled out a seat. It was built into the station on a swivel that stowed into the bottom of the desk.

Shayna sighed with relief. At least she could send a message. She thanked Bat who took off with Cain and his uncle, then pulled up her message box and waited for it to load. There was no message from Logan. Tears filled her eyes. There was nothing she could do to change her situation or help him. It was so hard to be separated. So hard to wait.

She wrote him a long note telling him about the attack and the Triad fight with the Smugglers Guild and the filthy ship, trying to make a joke out of it even with tears running down her face. Maybe he would read this and respond. The best thing about being on this ship, aside from the fact it was warm, was she could communicate. Now if only Logan would answer.

Chapter Twenty-Nine

Getting Vaerfeky, Logan and Jordie into the sphere was tight. Jordie made the seats disappear and there was just enough room. "He's gonna show you how to operate this thing," Logan told Jordie. "Get everything out of him you can. I mean peel his brain. Suck him dry."

Jordie winced. "Wow, that was kind of a gross mental image."

Logan closed his eyes. "Sorry, I'm a little stressed out and falling down with fatigue. I haven't heard from Shayna in what feels like forever, and everybody wants a piece of me."

"I figured out the com on this bad boy," Jordie said. "When old Fecky here gets done showing me all the bells and whistles, I'll hook you up."

"That would totally rock," Logan said. "I know she's up there on this terrible planet, pregnant and alone. It's making me crazy."

Logan figured Vaerfeky really wanted Heidi, because he went over every detail of the sphere, explaining the controls for flying it, and for destroying the odd planet or super spaceship. He even showed them the terraforming functions. "Now, if yous use this to terraform a planet, it will be absorbed by the antimatter and become part of the new world," Vaerfeky said. "It will be gone. Poof, no more sphere. No more weapon."

Jordie took extensive notes by typing them into an IT console that came out of the control panel. "This thing has it all," he said to Logan. "The technology is light years ahead of anything I've ever seen."

"Rigellians' technology," Vaerfeky said. "We capture them and torture them to reveal to us new ways to kill." He giggled. "Rigellians peaceful race. Live hundreds of years. Been around for millions, but we working on wiping them out." He seemed very proud of this. "They no believe in war, no eat the meat, love only." He made a gagging sound deep in his throat as though just the thought of a race of peaceful creatures was revolting.

Vaerfeky worked his way around the sphere explaining everything in great detail. "I's the only one who knows all of this," he bragged. "I get all the bestest information. Did you know, we even got brand new star cruiser at base just a few miles from here? We planning on launching it in two days and sending it to Europa to wipe out nasty infestation of Tong."

When Logan heard this, he had to struggle to contain his fear. They couldn't allow that to happen. Shayna was there. It was unthinkable. He immediately tuned out the alien's running commentary on the sphere and started thinking about how to deal with this new threat.

Vaerfeky showed Jordie another panel and explained it contained life support controls for the sphere or pod, or whatever it was, when in space. There were even space suits. He seemed to be having a great time. He punched Jordie in the arm. "Space suits will adjust to your shapes which are so primitive with only two arms." He made another gagging noise. "But you know, we been coming to this planet for many of centuries and when we first came here, yous people were like monkeys living in caves." He giggled. "But you womens always have the big round breastesses, so we mated with them. Big joke on you. Ha ha," he laughed this time. "You descended from us."

Jordie's head snapped up and his eyes were huge. "What?"

"Oh yes," Vaerfeky said. "Just looks at the girl out there." He pointed out the sphere's door at Fenfang. "And all the Tong and oriental-type peoples on this planet. They all descendants of us. Hahahahaha," he burst into laughter. "For some reason, only born with two arms. Probably not capable of our extreme advancement. Four arms so much better to grasp yummy frontal ornaments." He seemed to think this comment was hilarious. He went off in gusts of loud braying laughter.

"No way that could be true," Logan said. "How could your race breed with ours? I mean is that even anatomically possible?"

Vaerfeky was wearing a skirt-like garment, kind of a kilt, over his skinny lower body. He grinned and flipped up the front. Logan gasped in horror. Vaerfeky's sexual equipment was right there in his face and very similar to their own. Logan put his hand over his eyes to block the vision. "Cover yourself. Please."

"I think I'm blinded for life," Jordie said as he rubbed a hand across his eyes. "Vaerfeky, dude, never do that again. Human males NEVER show each other their junk. Never." Jordie shuddered. "Now what the heck was I doing? My mind is blank."

Vaerfeky giggled and pointed to the wall of the sphere. "Suits are in there. I was telling you about them. Easy to uses, fit to your two-armed bodies, no problem. Designed by Rigellians. Two armses is all they have. Like you."

Right," Jordie said.

All Logan could think about after Vaerfeky's crazy revelation was Shayna. She had oriental blood. His own child was going to have Kruellian blood running through its veins. How could he tell her? How could he deal with it? He shuddered. Life just kept getting weirder and weirder.

Vaerfeky continued to talk about the Kruellians early space travel adventures. "Yes, very much happened in ancient times," Vaerfeky said. "We got us star travel from Rigellians and started roaming the universe."

"Why'd it take you so long to come here and try to take us over?"

Vaerfeky nodded and his mustache jumped up and down. "You got star travel, duh," Vaerfeky said. "If yous going to run all over universe and dig holes in planets, not yours by the way, we need to take over. Makes sense. No?"

"None of this is ever gonna make sense," Logan said. "I can't believe it. I'm going outside." Logan left the sphere and went hunting for Knock who was leaning against the Rover kissing

Fenfang on the neck. Logan narrowed his eyes and looked at her closely. When he thought about it, he saw the resemblance quite clearly. Why hadn't he seen it before? They were all blind. He shuddered and shook himself. *Get over it, Logan. It happened a long time ago. Orientals are not Kruellians.*

"What's happening in there, dude?" Knock asked. He leaned back and stared at Logan. "You okay, man? I mean, you look like you seen a ghost."

Logan closed his eyes and shook his head. "I'll tell you later. We got more problems to worry about. Vaerfeky said there's a star cruiser close by they're preparing to launch at Europa. Shayna's there, man. I gotta figure out a way to stop them."

"No kidding?" Knock said. "We'll have to think about that, but in the meantime, we need to move on here, get back to Vegas and all that. It's freaking hot and the Sweet sisters and Kylie wanna go."

"I think, from listening in to Fecky's little tutorial in there, that I'm gonna be able to fly this thing to Europa and get Shayna, or at least help her. Take Fecky back to Vegas, give him the holo-maid, and show him how to use the controller." He handed Knock the black disc. "He says the star cruiser is over at the Indian Springs Air Force Auxiliary Field. It's only about twenty miles that way and it's on the way to Vegas. Maybe you guys can make some kind of plan and capture it. Just saying it would be nice to have a star cruiser for our very own, and even nicer to know it wasn't heading toward Europa to destroy it."

"Dude," Knock said his eyes lighting. "I like it."

Fang nodded. "Me, too. We could use one of them for the Resistance. Give us some real fire power."

Vaerfeky had clambered out of the sphere. He leaned against it and wiped sweat off his round face. "Knock, is the alien eye still working?" Logan asked. "Can you still see out of it?"

Knock flipped the patch onto the top of his head. The eye was even more settled into Knock's empty socket. His face appeared to have reformed around it. The strangely shaped orb now looked like it was part of Knock's face, as though Knock had been born with it. Fang held Knock's head in her hands and stared at his alien eye. "Looks like it's permanent," she said.

Knock squinted. "I can see through it like it was my normal eye. Even got better vision than before." He blinked a couple of times and gasped. "Wow, I can control it. When I think hard enough, I can see through clothes and skin right into people's bodies."

Logan sighed. "What's the alien look like inside?"

Knock turned his head slightly and stared at Vaerfeky. Suddenly he closed his eyes. "Well, he's hung, that's for sure."

Logan shuddered. "I know. I've seen. I meant his organs. Are they like ours inside?"

Knock narrowed his eyes. Wrinkles of concentration appeared on his forehead. "You know, they kinda are. His heart is on the other side and as far as I can tell, he's got no liver." He glanced at Logan and then back at Vaerfeky. "What exactly are you sayin', dude?"

"He said oriental people and many others we think are completely human, descended from his race when they first came here centuries ago."

Knock's eyes flew open. "Say what?"

"I know. My thoughts exactly."

Knock looked at Fenfang and grinned. "No wonder Fang is so epic."

"Shayna and Ju and Mai, too," Logan said. "It's a tough nut to swallow."

Knock patted him on the back. "Don't worry too much, man. You'll have a freaking stroke. Take the sphere thingy and go rescue Shayna. You'll feel better."

Logan nodded. "Right."

"Vaerfeky, you sure that star cruiser is at Indian Springs?" Logan asked. "Is there some way you can check? I mean, what if they've already launched it? Things are moving pretty fast right now. We just stole the sphere and you're defecting. Is there anyone you can contact to make sure?"

Vaerfeky looked at the palm of his upper left hand. It lit up and he touched it in several places with one of his fingers. "I can contact my cousin, Udhi, he working on ship. He probably don't know I'm running off with blond womens from Vegas yet."

"Do it," Logan said.

Vaerfeky's palm turned red, then blue, then green and a voice issued from it. "Look," Knock said to Logan. "Dude has a phone built right into his hand."

Logan nodded. "I see that."

Vaerfeky's narrow, slanted eyes flew open to their maximum width followed by a string of words in his language. Logan thought it sounded like a long series of burps and grunts. The alien shook his head and muttered into his hand. The light in his palm went out and Vaerfeky looked up. "Sorry, ship just took off for Europa. They in big hurry for some reason. So sorry, boys, so sorry." He brightened. "Udhi, he did say they got another ship, this one not that big but still battleship, landing later today. That one to be taking CEO to mother ship for visiting with wives." He snickered. "He goes to see his wifes." Vaerfeky made a gagging noise and then pinched his nose with two fingers from a top hand. "Stinky, flat-chests, womens with no nice hair."

"Damn! Holy crap." Logan felt the fear for Shayna start in his stomach and burst in his head. "We gotta fly."

Knock pushed him toward the sphere. "Go, man, go do whatever you can."

Logan nodded. "Jeeze, this is terrible. Shayna."

"I know, dude," Knock gave him a quick embarrassed hug. "Don't die, okay?"

Logan was so freaked out he could barely think. "I gotta go."

Knock pushed him again. "Then go, dude. Me and the chicks are headin' back to Vegas. We'll make a plan, or Kylie there will, she's the one with the smarts in this group, and we'll go get that battleship. Count on it. We'll either capture it or destroy it. And when we get it, we'll head to Europa."

Fang hugged Logan. "Don't worry so much. You'll get gray hair or have an aneurism. We'll get that battleship and then we'll go kick some ass."

Logan nodded. He was so tired. He needed to get his head back in the game. "You're right," he said. "Gotta go. Gotta save Shayna."

Logan put his head inside the sphere. Jordie had the seats out again and was touching the screens with a finger, swiping across them to change to another screen. "You figure this out yet?" Logan asked him.

"Ready for lift off any time you are."

Logan glanced once at Knock and his group. They'd loaded the alien into the Rover between the Sweet girls. Logan sighed. Vaerfeky must think he'd died and gone to heaven. Logan climbed in beside Jordie and the seat formed automatically to his body. Straps shot out of the seat and tied him tightly to it. "You sure you know what you're doing?"

"Did I not fly a strange ship here? Newest, most high-tech ship ever? I did, didn't I? I can fly anything," Jordie said proudly. "And besides, this thing is like got a super autopilot. All I had to figure out was how to input the desired destination."

"And you did, right?"

"Yup, next stop Europa. I set it to orbit, and we should be there in six hours."

"Well punch it," Logan said. "That Kruellian starship left a couple of hours ago and it's on its way to destroy Europa."

"I doubt if it can travel at the speed this sphere can achieve," Jordie said. "From what I've been able to figure, this thing is super-fast. I mean faster-than-light-speed fast." A low hum built around them. Jordie touched a spot on the screen in front of him and the door slid shut. The hum grew louder and Jordie's grin filled his entire face. "Who would have thought I'd pilot something like this. Man, this adventure just keeps getting better and better. Never thought I'd be glad you kidnapped me, but dude, this has been the trip of a lifetime."

Logan closed his eyes and nodded. "That's not what you said when we were chasing this thing."

Jordie grinned. I know. I get pretty cranky when I'm doing my best not to go number two in my pants." He shrugged sheepishly as he touched a sequence of spots on the lighted screen and the sphere took off. While they were streaking out of the atmosphere, Jordie dropped a screen in front of Logan. "I know you want to contact Shayna. Just touch on that weird little icon shaped like an exploding star. It'll open up a screen and you can connect to the net with it."

Logan managed to get into his mailbox. There were two messages from Shayna. As he read them, anxiety raced up and down his spine sending his brain reeling. "The Tong base on Europa is destroyed," he told Jordie. "The Tong and the Triad are now working together, and the Triad stole a ship from the Smugglers Guild. She says they're all hiding in it, trying to get it back into orbit. It's pretty damaged and she says the Smugglers lived like pigs. The ship stinks and it's filthy."

"Are your people okay? The people from Gliese?"

Logan shook his head. "Most of them are dead including Fang's mother, Mai Li. Shayna says Cain and Tom are good, most of the men who could fight died in battle, and Fang's sister Ju is safe, but all the rest of the women and the kids are dead. She saved one little girl and a baby."

Logan felt tears running down his face. The sadness threatened to overwhelm him.

"Logan," Jordie shoved his shoulder. They were sitting very close together. "Snap out of it. This is war, man. People were gonna die whether on Gliese or in space or on Europa. Concentrate on getting some rest. You and I got six hours to sleep before we get to Europa." He smiled. "Just think, in six ours, you'll see your wife. Hold onto that thought, man. Hold on to that."

Logan nodded and closed his eyes. "You're right. I'm exhausted." He tried to smile through his tears. "I'll see Shayna soon."

'That's the ticket," Jordie said softly. "You'll be together soon."

Chapter Thirty

Shayna heard the baby crying and sat up. It was hard to sleep, hard to get comfortable around her belly. Ju was standing beside Mark watching as he changed the baby. Cressy saw she was up and sat on her bunk. "You feeling better?" Cressy asked.

Shayna tried to smile. "I feel like a cow," she muttered. "I can barely see my feet."

"You look beautiful," Cressy said and laid her head on Shayna's shoulder. "Let me braid your hair."

Shayna pulled her loose hair forward over her shoulder and grimaced. "I need to wash it. I hope they get us a hygiene chamber working soon. We all need to bathe."

Mark left Ju playing with the baby's feet and walked the three steps to Shayna's bunk. He looked macho and strong which was a far cry from the way he'd been when they first found him, clothes all torn, crying and bleeding, fat and terrified of everything. "I think they're more worried about getting the ship back into orbit," he said. "And getting some kind of shield working. I heard Bat tell Cain this ship has the cloaking technology, it's just broken. I could help if they'd let me. They treat me like I'm one of the women. I know a lot about the IT systems on these ships. But Bat thinks he knows everything and won't listen to me."

"I'll talk to him," Shayna said.

"Take Ju," Mark said. "He listens to her." He turned to stare at Ju whose face was lit with joy as she played with the baby. "Just look at her. Any man would listen to her. Any man would love her," he mumbled.

Ju crossed the room bouncing baby Mai on her shoulder. "Go with Shayna," Mark said. "Talk to Bat and tell him I'm not an idiot and I can help with the technology on this ship. I might not be able to weld or fix the outside of the ship, but I know computers. He seems to think I'm stupid."

Mark had lost even more weight. His face had been round and he'd had a couple of double chins when they first met him. His chin was now clearly defined, square, with a dimple. His eyes glowed and were a startling blue-green. He had freckles on his nose, which was sharp, and he had chiseled cheek bones. Ugly duckling Mark had blossomed into a swan with thick sandy blond hair. He'd always been tall, now he had a waist, broad shoulders and slim hips. He still had a barrel chest, but his belly was slowly going away.

Ju hugged him and handed him the baby. "I'll go with her if it's what you want me to do." The look she gave Mark was one of complete understanding. Mark and Ju had formed a special bond over the baby. A bond that could blossom into love, Shayna thought, though clearly it had already for poor Mark.

They left their quarters and walked toward the center of the ship where the bridge for this massive interstellar spaceship was located. The center of the ship was surrounded by circular modules containing living quarters and life support systems. The propulsion systems were located below the bridge. Some of the outer modules had been destroyed. The Tong workers were attempting to cut away the damaged sections and make the ship functional.

Mark led them as they cut from their module into a connecting corridor that ran straight through two more modules to the bridge. Everything still smelled like burnt hair and wiring, but less like garbage and unwashed humans. The command center was a hive of activity. Men and women were under the consoles and working inside the walls and ceiling of the ship. Every few minutes a sparking noise flared as someone used a soldering iron to fuse wires together. The odor of burning wires was strong in here. Shayna spotted Bat standing on a ladder working on something inside one of the ceiling panels. The panel leaned against a bank of computer screens that had strange writing running in a constant stream up the black background in blue and red.

Bat spotted Ju and jumped off the ladder. "Ju, how's little Mai Li?"

Shayna tried not to frown. Bat was using a fake interest in the welfare of the baby to get to Ju and Ju was too innocent to see it.

"She's so adorable," Ju gushed. "She smiled at me today and yesterday she rolled over."

Bat's eyes glazed over for a second and Shayna had to look away. The kid was no more interested in what the baby did than he was in growing flowers in the greenhouse section of the ship, or learning how to bake a cake. The Tong men were warriors, or they were mechanics and electricians when needed. "We do need a bathroom of some kind, Bat. When do you think we'll have sanitation?"

"Not soon," he said. "Gotta get this tank into orbit and worry about stuff like that later."

"You don't have to deal with dirty diapers," Ju snapped. "Water, toilets, showers, we need them now."

Bat shrugged and fought to control his eyes. He had a hard time not rolling them. Shayna could read his every emotion. "I'll talk to my uncle."

"Did you recover Muunokhoi? I haven't heard anything." Shayna was worried about the base commander. He was in that medical chamber floating around under the ice or trapped in the crushed command center.

"We got a team that thinks they've located the medi pod," Bat said. "We won't leave Europa without him one way or another."

Shayna nodded and was about to say something when an explosion rocked the ship. She fell to the floor and tried to balance on hands and knees with the floor bucking wildly under them.

"What was that?" Ju screamed. She'd been flung into a bank of computer terminals against one of the walls. The panels under the terminals were off exposing a mass of wiring.

Bat lay under the collapsed ladder. He tossed it aside and leaped to his feet. "Go back to your quarters," he yelled.

Ju jumped gracefully to her feet and grabbed Shayna's arm. She helped Shayna up and together, they ran out of the command center toward their section of the ship. People were running everywhere at top speed. They had to hug the walls to avoid getting trampled. The crew members seemed to know exactly where to go, they ran with a purpose. Shayna saw Sammy Lee and grabbed his arm before he could race by. "What's going on?"

"We're under attack again. Big star cruiser is in orbit around Europa. It's sending a squadron of fighters against us. We gotta get ours launched before we get destroyed on the ground."

Shayna immediately visualized the last attack, cloaked fighters shooting into the base. This ship was their only hope of getting off Europa alive. They'd die if it was destroyed. They had no other shelter.

Another explosion rocked the modules farthest from the central command center. "Mai!" Ju screamed.

Shayna pushed Ju ahead of her. "Run, I'm right behind you."

Ju took off like a gazelle, racing for the module housing the crew and where Mark waited with the baby and Cressy. Shayna followed at a slower pace. Another explosion hit the ship. The floor under Shayna's feet tilted sharply and she fell, rolling down one of the connecting corridors toward the module they lived in. A loud creaking was followed by another shift. The outer module, the one the Tong had been trying to save, the one Mark was in with Cressy, suddenly broke away from the ship and fell. Shayna tumbled down the connecting tube landing against the module's outer wall. When she looked up, she saw the hazy sky of Europa. The module was no longer part of the ship. Frigid air rushed into the new openings. Shayna picked herself up and ran for their quarters.

A terrible urgency filled her. They had to find their cold weather suits and oxygen immediately. She rushed into their quarters to find Mark calmly helping Cressy into a suit that almost fit her and Ju gathering more cold-weather gear for all of them.

"What's happening?" Ju gasped.

"I don't know exactly," Shayna said. "Bat's Uncle Sammy says we're under attack. That's all I know. This module's come loose. We need to move closer to the ship's bridge or we're gonna freeze."

Mark tucked the baby inside Ju's roomy cold-weather suit and zipped it over the baby. He tenderly snapped the outer closures and fit a small mask over the baby's head. "You two head to another module. One closer to the bridge. I'm going out. I want to see what's happening out there."

Ju grabbed his arm. "No, Mark, don't leave us. What'll we do if anything happens to you?"

For a moment, a look of wonder filled Mark's eyes. It must be the first time he'd ever been told he was needed. "Don't worry," he said gently. "I just wanna see what we have out there. Who's attacking us this time. I'll take a quick peek and come find you guys."

He dressed in a suit he'd found that fit him perfectly, pulled the mask over his head, and ran out of the room. Ju watched him go with an expression of horror on her face. Shayna grabbed Ju's arms and stared into the girl's frightened eyes. "He'll be fine. Come on." She turned to Cressy. "You warm enough?"

The little girl nodded. Her answer was muffled by the layers and her mask. "I'm good. Let's get the poor baby someplace warmer."

When Shayna was dressed, they left the sinking module and clambered along the corridor which was now tilted down at a forty-five-degree angle. Shayna hung onto the rail along the inside wall as they passed one of the connecting tubes heading toward the center. It was the one Shayna had literally fallen out of. When she looked up the tube, she saw it had come completely away from the main body of the ship.

The kept going. The module tilted down again and Shayna felt like they must be at ground level. A huge crack in the wall showed blue ice with black rock under it. Shayna pointed. “That’s bad.”

The crack was open so Shayna stuck her head out. Black fighters were shooting out of the belly of the ship as they headed for battle. Shayna shaded her eyes against the glare off the ice and the shiny metal ship as she struggled to see who or what was attacking them. She saw the blurry images of cloaked fighters and knew it was the Company. She was following one cloaked fighter as it headed toward them when suddenly a blue sphere with bright, glittering lights all over it, boomed into Europa’s atmosphere and headed for them. Green light shot out of the sphere and one of the cloaked fighters exploded into dust.

Shayna jerked her head back inside the module. “There’s something weird out there. It blew up a Company fighter.”

“Explain weird,” Mark said.

“It’s a sphere, like a big ball, and it’s shooting the bad guys.”

Chapter Thirty-One

"We made it," Jordie crowed.

Logan was concentrating on the weapons' console and controllers wearing a headset with a microphone. He grunted. "Got another one."

Jordie moved his hands across the shiny plate placed flat on the console. The sphere rotated and headed deeper into Europa's atmosphere. "There's too many of them," he said about the Company fighters. "I see a crashed ship below us, but the base is gone."

Logan fired the sphere's crazy weapon and one of the Company's cloaked fighters exploded. "I can't understand why the Tong fighters are doing so poorly."

"Company fighters are cloaked," Jordie said. "Our screens show them clearly, but you see their outline is a little blurry? That blurry stuff completely obscures them from Tong fighters."

The sphere shot low over the crashed spaceship. "If Shayna is still alive, she's gotta be inside that ship," Jordie said. "There's no other place people could survive on this iceberg."

A Company fighter fired into the helpless starship sitting useless on the planet's surface, hitting the body of the ship at its center. A hole appeared in the starship's skin. "We have to stop them," Logan screamed. "Shayna must be in there."

Jordie took the sphere back out of Europa's thin atmosphere chasing the Company fighter. Logan fingered the controller and green fire consumed the small aircraft. "Got him," Logan muttered "Find me another one."

Jordie turned the sphere and they chased two more Company fighters toward Jupiter. The planet loomed enormous and glowing in their viewing screens. Jordie guided the sphere deeper into space where they spotted the Company's gigantic star cruiser hovering behind Jupiter. Cloaked fighters still issued from its belly. There were hundreds of them. "The Tong fighters are screwed," Logan said. "There's no way they can handle that."

Jordie nodded. "So, what do you want me to do?"

Logan closed his eyes. He'd feared the Company would get their new ship here fast and they had. "We can't save anyone with this thing," Logan moaned. "It's too small. Keep chasing Company fighters. At least we can destroy them."

"Won't last long out here," Jordie said. "Our shield's hot and getting hotter. Every time we get hit, it absorbs more energy. Eventually, it's going to shut down and we'll be sitting ducks."

Logan stared at the view screen. "Where's Knock? I was hoping he'd show up with Kylie and Fang in that battle cruiser."

Jordie shook his head. "Even if they did manage to capture the battleship, it had to be slower than the star cruiser. That big sucker is the aliens' newest ship. Old Vaerfeky seemed to think it was something special. It should take Knock at least two Earth days, and maybe more to get here."

Logan groaned. "I don't know, Jordie. Got any ideas? Should we attack the star cruiser? We supposedly are riding around in the biggest, baddest weapon ever created. What if we use it?"

Jordie swiped his finger across the screen in front of him. It brought up a vertical row of icons Logan had never seen before. "In theory we could use it, but the star cruiser is parked so close to Jupiter, the result, and I'm not going to say explosion here because I don't think exploding is what this weapon does, the result might affect Jupiter which would be very bad."

Logan rolled his eyes. "Like how bad?"

"Like we create a black hole that sucks this entire system into it. Earth included and possibly even the sun."

"How can you know this?"

"Well, that's the thing. All I have is what Vaerfeky told me about the weapon and all of that was pretty horrible. If it can be used to destroy an entire planet, which is, apparently, exactly what the Kruellians used it for, then it's going to create either a black hole, which would suck us all into it and spit us who knows where if we survived, or it will instantly obliterate everything in our solar system. Like cosmic dust or maybe we'll get spit out in some galaxy on the outer reaches of nowhereville and be lost for life. We're too close, dude and Europa will get sucked into anything the weapon does because it's so close. And Jupiter is like this giant mass that will affect everything. Sure, the star cruiser will be gone, but in all likelihood, so will all of us, and maybe even Earth if it starts a chain reaction. Which it could, from what Vaerfeky said. That's why it was designed to terraform. That's its major use according to what these screens say. Most of the controls and screens I been looking at deal with terraforming. You know, what kind of air to generate, oxygen carbon ratios, how much water like oceans, how much land, stuff like that."

Logan felt like screaming. More Company fighters were bunching up in a weird formation on the other side of Jupiter. "Looks like they're getting ready for another attack on Europa. Can we land and build some kind of shield around that wrecked spaceship? Then we could at least save the people down there including Shayna and whoever else survived."

"We can try," Jordie said. He waved his hands across the screens, the strange one disappeared, another appeared, Jordie touched two icons and the sphere dived for Europa. They sped away from the gathering fighters. Six black Tong fighters hovered above Europa. They didn't even see the sphere. The alien technology made them almost invisible. Company fighters could penetrate their cloak to a certain degree, but they were invisible to the Tong.

"Look," Logan pointed at the Tong fighters. "That's all they got left."

"I see that," Jordie said. "They're history, man. The Company outnumbers them ten to one."

Jordie passed his hand over another screen to his right "Woah, dude, we got a major disturbance over here. I think another ship is arriving."

"Let it be Knock," Logan breathed.

Jordie did something and the sphere slowed. Suddenly what Jordie had noticed disturbing space, arrived. It boomed out of hyper drive so close to the tiny Jupiter moon, Lo, the moon shot out of orbit and headed straight for the Company's monstrously huge star cruiser. Logan and Jordie watched it with their mouths hanging open. "Did they do that on purpose?" Logan asked.

"Don't know," Jodie breathed. "Looks like it's going right through the Company's fighters. The moon crashed into several fighters sending them spiraling into the enormous gravitational pull of Jupiter. When it hit the fighters, the group split in an effort to escape. The moon itself continued on in a straight line for the star cruiser.

"This looks good," Jordie said.

He spoke too soon. The star cruiser fired a huge green blast of plasma energy at the moon. It didn't explode, but its course changed and it headed away from Jupiter and the star cruiser, straight out into space toward Neptune or beyond. Jordie shook his head. "Spoke too soon. Think Knock's driving the battleship?"

"Hope so."

It did look as though Knock, Kylie and friendly forces were in control of the battle cruiser. It began firing on the starship immediately. It didn't have the plasma gun the starship had. Its laser cannons splattered harmlessly on the shields of the Company's starship. "I got chatter," Jordie said.

He touched a small screen, it enlarged, and he touched an icon with his pointer finger while swiping another across the bottom of the screen. Logan was continually amazed at how fast Jordie had picked up the alien technology. Suddenly voices erupted inside the sphere. "Can anyone hear us? Logan, you out there? Jordie, Cain, anybody?"

"That's Fang," Logan said. "How do I answer her?"

"Logan? I hear you. We can see you, man. We're late to the party, but we're gonna make a difference."

"I think Shayna is trapped on Europa," Logan said. "We can land, but we have no room to save anyone. Can you guys get something down there to haul off survivors?"

"Kind of got our hands full," Knock's voice issued over the speaker system. "We can try."

"They got some kind of awful plasma weapon," Logan said. "We just saw it deflect a moon."

"Yeah, we saw that, too, but according to the vast amount of info given us by our good buddy Vaerfeky, we know it's gotta recharge. We got about an hour and we're gonna do our best."

"Their shields are strong," Logan said.

"Can't you guys shoot it down with the planet-killing weapon? You're the one packing all the fire power."

Jordie says it will create a black hole that will suck us all in because we're so close to Jupiter. The gravitational issue and all these moons. Looks like the sky around here is full of them."

Knock laughed. "I see that. We're gonna go hide behind Ganymede and try to launch a shuttle to Europa. Can you guys cover us with some kind of fire power? And where the hell are you? We can't even see you on our radar."

"Sure thing," Jordie said. "We're cloaked."

"We can see cloaked ships."

"Not ours," Jordie said. "It's different, I guess."

The battle cruiser began a sharp banking turn toward the outer orbits of Jupiter's many moons. Ganymede's orbit was second to the farthest with Callisto being the one orbiting on the edge. The turn made it vulnerable to the huge star cruiser's weapons, but as yet, they didn't have the plasma gun back on line so they opened up with laser cannons. Six shots were fired at the battleship. The shields absorbed all but two which hit the ship in the tail section. Small explosions blossomed on the skin of Knock's battleship, but did no real damage as Logan and Jordie began firing their crazy energy cannon. They weren't close enough to hurt the big starship, but the last shot hit the core of the ship's central mass. It loosened one of the connecting tubes from the central core to the outer rings. It broke away tearing a hole in the ship's skin and leaving the ring, which was probably living quarters and life-support systems, partially disconnected from the main core of the huge ship. Loose chairs, equipment and three people exploded out of the opening in the ship's side. A Tong fighter screamed past and shot the three floating humans which was probably a blessing because they were all dying horribly.

"That should keep them busy," Jordie said. "Let's land this thing and hunt for Shayna."

"Give them one more shot while they're wounded," Logan said.

"I think Knock's got that covered," Jordie pointed to the view screen.

Sure enough, the battleship hiding behind Ganymede accelerated toward the gigantic star cruiser. It came out from behind the moon with cannons blazing. The shield on the Company's starship must be damaged because Knock's cannons were connecting. A big hole was blown in one of the rings and more junk flew out of the hole. "They got this," Jordie crowed.

Logan shook his head. "Oh no."

A glob of green fire erupted from a tube on the top of the control section. It seemed to have a gelatinous mobility. The green glob formed and reformed, poison-green and glowing, as it headed for Knock and Fang in the battleship. It hit the ship's nose. The battleship was shaped more like a huge land-based jet than one of the starships. The lime-green goop slid across the nose leaving a glowing sheen of luminescent slime behind. When the ship was completely covered with slime, it swelled.

"This is bad," Jordie said. "Very bad." He spun the sphere and headed for Europa, away from the battleship as fast as it would go.

"Can't we help them?" Logan cried. The battleship was behind them, but they could still see it on one of their screens. It kept swelling.

"How?" Jordie asked through clenched teeth. "I don't even know what that crap is or what it's gonna do."

A pod shot out of the swelling battleship. It looked like a lifeboat or possibly a shuttle. Lime-green slime coated it, but the pod seemed to be losing some of the slime as it shot toward Europa. The battleship suddenly stopped swelling, turned yellow, then gold, and then it just disappeared.

"Where did it go?" Jordie screamed.

Logan just shook his head. The small pod shot toward Europa leaving a green trail. "I hope Knock got away," Logan said.

"They look out of control to me," Jordie said as he homed the sphere in on the wrecked Tong base on Europa. Company fighters swarmed them but couldn't seem to pick them up on any shooting radar or shooting systems. They could see the sphere, that was obvious because they were shooting at them, but their shots went wide every time. Tong fighters dived into the swarm of Company aircraft, shot up a couple and jetted off before the Company fighters could destroy them. One of the Tong fighters took a hit, but kept going.

Suddenly, the Company fighters spotted the escape shuttle streaking toward Europa. It really did look out of control. The fighters began shooting at it. Every hit caused a burst of green slime. The Company fighters seemed to have a healthy respect for the plasma or whatever it was because when the poofs of slime shot off the shuttle, they dived for cover.

Jordie aimed the sphere for the wrecked Tong base and they burst into Europa's thin atmosphere in the wake of the escape shuttle from the battleship. "I'm praying Knock and Fang got out of that ship," Logan said.

"I'm praying the Sweet sisters are in there," Jordie said.

Logan almost smiled as Jordie set the sphere down in a crater in the ice-covered rock next to the crashed spaceship. "You would."

"What man wouldn't?" Jordie grinned briefly, then sobered. "You do know we'll freeze to death if we get out. It's minus one twenty out there."

"Space suits," Logan said. "Remember? Vaerfeky told us there were suits stashed in here and they would form to our bodies even though we only have two arms. He said something about the Rigellians only having two arms."

Jordie began scanning his screens. "You're right. All I have to do is figure out how to make them appear. They're stored somewhere in this thing."

He swiped two icons and the smell of cooking food filled the sphere. A tray erupted from under the console. It contained two amorphous globs of brown stuff and tan biscuit-like things. Logan picked one of the biscuits up and munched. "Not bad, but not a space suit."

"Wrong icon," Jordie mumbled. "It looked like a space suit. Musta been a human or a sentient being, though why it meant food I'll never know." He pulled up another screen and smiled. "There it is. Plain as the nose on your face." He swiped an icon into a container on the side of the screen and a door opened up behind them. Inside were two head-sized silver globs in a wrap of some kind. Jordie reached back and grabbed one. It opened when he took it out of the cupboard and swelled into what looked like a helmet. Jordie put it on and a protective shield formed around him. It looked insubstantial, but when Logan tried to touch Jordie, his finger hit something hard.

"That is very cool," Logan said. He grabbed one of the helmet-like things and put it over his head. He was immediately surrounded by a protective layer complete with breathable air. "Can you hear me?" He asked Jordie.

"Perfectly. Let's get out of this thing."

Chapter Thirty-Two

"We can't stay here much longer," Shayna said to Ju as they huddled in the damaged section of the wrecked space ship. "It's getting colder and colder. Pretty soon we'll be frozen."

A huge explosion rocked the wrecked ship. The module they huddled inside creaked and broke away from the tubes connecting it to the ship and started sliding. "Hold on," Shayna said to Ju and Cressy. "We're moving."

The section of the module slid over the ice toward what used to be the men's quarters of the Tong base. When it stopped, Shayna screamed. "Out. Get out now."

Ju was carrying the baby, so Shayna herded Cressy out of the ship. The little girl was shaking with cold. Shayna couldn't pick her up. She was just too pregnant, so she wrapped a protective arm around her and helped her out of the destroyed module. Once outside, the frigid air hit them like a granite wall.

They ran for ten steps and stopped. Shayna looked back at the wrecked Triad ship. It was in pieces, most of it burning. "Well we can't go back there," she said.

As she spoke a Tong fighter streaked by. Behind it a blurry Company ship shot blue fire at it. "That looks like Bat's fighter," Ju said. "See it has a falcon on the front under the cockpit."

"If it's Bat, he's in trouble," Shayna said. "Come on. We have to find shelter or we're in just as much trouble."

Six hours ago, the men's quarters had been under a layer of ice. The attack by the Company, the explosions and all the bombing had caused the water under the structure to gush upwards and it had pushed the men's quarters out of the ice. A large section was visible, the metal siding shining in the weak European sunlight. "Let's see if we can get inside." Shayna pointed at the building. "Maybe one of the airlocks is accessible. I swear if we can't we're gonna freeze to death in the next twenty minutes."

They humped across jagged rocks, chunks of ice, and a debris field littered with parts of destroyed fighters. The building that used to house the men was canted at an odd angle. Supports jutted out to the left and the row of windows was at ground level, or the level the ice was at now. Shayna led them around the building to the windows. "If one is broken, we can get inside," she said to Ju.

They found three broken windows in a row. The windows ran in a strip completely around the top of the structure. Each window panel was six-feet wide and two-feet high. Shayna laid down and slithered into the building through the broken window. She helped Cressy inside and Ju followed, sliding in on her back to carefully keep the baby inside her jacket safe. When the three of them were inside, Shayna looked around. The destruction was awful. There were dead men everywhere, frozen into stiff corpses.

Cressy burst into tears. "We can't stay here. There's dead people."

"We'll wait here until this battle stops," Shayna said. "It's at least fifty degrees warmer than out there. Sometimes you gotta do what you gotta do. Just don't look at them."

They found chairs and mattresses from the bunks and set them on the floor. Shayna and Ju pushed and carried the bodies off to the side and tossed blankets over them so Cressy couldn't see them, then they sat on mattresses wrapped in more thermal blankets under another layer of thin Mylar blankets they found in an emergency bin. The combination of blankets and Mylar had them warmer than they'd been in a while. Cressy peeped out from under hers and smiled. She wasn't shivering. The angle of the building had them sitting on the outside wall. The bunks were sideways. They'd piled the mattresses high enough to see out of the windows. "Look," Ju said. "Here comes Mark."

The relief in her voice was easy to hear. Shayna saw Mark coming and gasped. “He better run. There’s a small spaceship shooting straight at him and it’s green and glowing.”

Ju thrust the baby at Shayna. “Keep her warm. I’m going out to get him.”

“Don’t,” Shayna tried to stop her. “There’s no time.”

Mark was running toward the men’s quarters as fast as he could. The small ship looked like some kind of shuttle. It was covered in green stuff that it rapidly shed as it shot through the atmosphere toward them. As more of the weird goopy-looking green stuff came off, the spacecraft left a strange luminescent trail and Shayna realized it was a Company shuttle. “It looks out of control,” she screamed to Ju who had already scrambled out of the building and was running toward Mark. She met him and grabbed his hand, towing him toward their refuge. The Company shuttle hit the ice, bounced and began sliding and skidding straight toward Mark and Ju.

“Hurry,” Shayna screamed. Mark pushed Ju through the broken windows and clambered in after her as the shuttle skied by inches from their refuge, bumping over rocks, chunks of ice and through the debris field of destroyed starfighters. It barely missed the men’s quarters, finally crashing to a shuddering halt against the remnants of the dome.

Mark panted like a dog in hundred-degree weather. “I found this place,” he said between breaths. “It used to be the men’s quarters.” Pant, gasp. “And I was coming to get you guys,” wheeze, pant. “And then I saw this weird round, ball, sphere thing heading out of space. It landed over by the Smugglers Guild’s ruined ship. I don’t know what or who’s inside of it.”

Ju cuddled Mark’s head on her lap as they both lay on one of the mattresses. She stroked his face. “I was so scared for you.”

He reached up and touched her cheek. “I was afraid you guys had frozen. When I saw the module break off, I thought you guys were dead. I was going to try to rescue you when I saw the shuttle coming at me."

They all stared out the window at the crashed shuttle. "It's still green in spots and the luminescent-shiny-lime-color looks like it's spreading. What do you think the creepy-green stuff is?" Shayna asked him.

"Company's been working on a plasma weapon," Mark said. "My dad knew all about it. He was working for a research organization that was developing some of the plans for deploying the weapon. Maybe the shuttle is escaping from the Company. Maybe there's good guys inside." He paused for a second. "Or it could be full of Company soldiers and they're here to kill us."

"Don't think they're Company," Shayna said. "Look." The door on the shuttle had opened and people were hesitantly emerging. They didn't have cold weather suits. Shayna immediately recognized Fang. She grabbed Ju. "That's your sister."

Across the ice-covered landscape two more figures stumbled toward them from the direction of the wrecked Guild ship. They wore crazy space suits made from a glowing red material, complete with helmets. "Who are they?" Shayna asked.

"I don't know and I don't care," Ju said. "Hold little Mia." She thrust the baby at Shayna and climbed out of the windows onto the ice.

The people who had come out of the shuttle were going back inside it. The cold was impossible to handle without the proper gear. Ju ran toward them waving. "Fang! Fang!" She screamed as she ran and Fenfang stopped heading back into the shuttle and turned. She seemed hesitant, then she ran for her sister streaming puffs of breath behind. They met fifty feet from the shuttle and hugged. Shayna's heart swelled with happiness for them even as she prayed Logan would be in the shuttle, too.

When the two figures hiking toward them in space suits suddenly started running and waving their arms, Shayna turned her attention to the shuttle. It was slowly turning from a sickly lime-green color to a golden hue. Ju and Fang weren't paying attention and the rest of the shuttle passengers had retreated into the craft to escape the cold. "Hold the baby," Shayna snapped at Cressy. She handed Mai to the girl, clambered awkwardly out of the broken window, and started running toward the shuttle with Mark right behind her. "This is bad, isn't it?" He said.

"I think it's really bad," she yelled over her shoulder.

The spacecraft had begun to swell. A terrible sense of foreboding filled Shayna. Swelling, turning colors, none of that could be a good thing, not to mention the two suited guys running and pointing at the shuttle.

"Ju!" she screamed.

The girl turned and stared at Shayna. Mark ran past Shayna shouting. "Run!" He ran past Ju toward the shuttle. The two space-suited guys met him at the shuttle door. One of them pushed back his helmet and stuck his head inside. "Out, out, it's gonna blow."

Shayna had reached the shuttle. Ju and Fang crowded behind her. "Get everyone out," she screamed and backed away from the door. The craft was still swelling and Shayna heard an ominous pulsing rumble coming from it, like whoomph, whoomph, whoomph. Suddenly she was grabbed from behind. She turned and found herself locked in Logan's embrace.

Chapter Thirty-Three

"Logan," Shayna breathed as she grabbed him and hung on.

He hugged her quickly and took her hand. "Everybody out of the shuttle," he yelled. "Hurry. Chop chop. Fast as you can. Run."

Knock leaped out and grabbed him. "Is it really you?"

"Yeah, and me and Jordie saw the battleship you guys came in covered in this same green crap. After you abandoned ship, it turned yellow and swelled like this, and then it just disappeared. Like it was vaporized or zapped into another dimension like maybe dragged through a worm hole."

"We knew it was bad when it hit us," Knock said. "Bobby told us to get out so we evacuated. We didn't see what happened to it."

Logan pounded on the side of the shuttle. "Out. Now." The entire Vegas group erupted through the doors. "Run," Logan yelled. He stared into Shayna's eyes. She wore a mask and breathing gear along with a cold weather suit that made her look like the Goodyear tire guy. "No time to talk now," he whispered as he squeezed her hand. "Let's go."

She hung onto his hand as they raced toward a cock-eyed building with a strip of broken windows. The building's legs stuck out to the far side. On the side closest to them, a dome glittered gold in the glow from the shuttle. "Faster," he yelled.

The Sweet triplets ran past him dragging Raj and Corey. Fenfang, Kylie, and Knock ran beside him shivering uncontrollably. "We're gonna freeze to death in like two more minutes," Knock said.

"Company fighters!" Shayna screamed.

Two Tong starfighters sped toward them chased by a host of Company ships firing steadily. The Tong fighters split and doubled back. Blue fire exploded all around them, many blasts landing on the rocks surrounding Logan and his group. The ground shuddered. Ice groaned and creaked and the building they'd been aiming for rose.

"Cressy!" Ju screamed. Ju and a big guy in a huge, black, cold-weather suit took off for the building which was slowly rising out of the solid ice. Blue water exploded from a hole right in front of them and shot fifty feet into the air. Logan leaped away from it. Shayna pulled him along as she kept running. "We see this kind of thing all the time," she said over her shoulder. "We have to get Cressy. She's in that building."

Ju and the big guy reached it first. "That's Mark," Shayna said as they slid toward the men's quarters on brand-new, slick-as-snot ice. "We found him on Gliese."

Mark scrambled into the building through one of the broken windows, which was now at least six feet off the ground and still rising. His feet dangled for a second, and then he dropped out of the window holding Cressy and a wrapped bundle. Ju snatched the bundle from Cressy, unsnapped and unzipped her jacket, stuffed the bundle inside, and then refastened the layers.

The rest of the group had caught up. The fighters had made one pass and were regrouping to make another. "If those two Tong fighters can't stop them, we're dead," Shayna said. "Unless you have any ideas."

"Look," Sugar Sweet said. "Do you believe that?"

The shuttle had swollen to twice its size and was golden. "It's gonna go," Logan said. The shuttle suddenly disappeared. A sucking sound swirled around them and anything loose hurtled toward the empty place where the shuttle had been. Cressy screamed as she was swept off her feet and carried along with all the loose debris toward the spot where the shuttle had been only moments before. The big guy with Ju took two giant steps and tackled her. His weight kept her from being sucked away with all the debris from the destroyed base and crashed fighters.

"We're screwed," Knock said. "No place to get out of the cold." He was shaking so hard his words were difficult to understand.

Ju looked back at the building they'd just pulled Cressy out of. It still rose, climbing high on a wave of water and ice. A sudden enormous surge in the ice sounded like the roar of a tornado. It creaked, cracked and groaned, the building rose onto its legs, hung like that for one minute and then sank. The ice under it collapsed. The two supports that had been on the solid rock tilted and the entire building dropped into the sea. A wave shot into the air and then the building was gone.

"Can't go back there," Shayna said. "What do we do?"

All the people from Vegas, Shayna and her group, Logan and Jordie all huddled in the middle of the Tong's wrecked spaceport. The starship on the edge of the field was burning. "Might be warmer over there," Logan said.

"We'll never make it," Knock could barely talk. His arms were wrapped around Fang, the Sweet triplets huddled with the rest of the people from Vegas. The kids were inside their huddle. "We're gonna freeze and there's not enough oxygen."

Shayna shot Logan a pleading look filled with desperation and fear. "What did you come in?"

"Two-man alien craft." Logan pointed. "Small, it's tiny inside."

"Maybe we can put the kids in there," she said.

"Come on," he said. "I'll carry Cressy." He poked Knock. "Dude, get up. Try. Don't quit on me, man."

Fang slowly pulled herself upright. She grabbed Knock's hand. "Gotta move," she said. "Can't quit. Moving is our only chance to stay alive."

Another string of explosions rocked the Guild's wrecked ship. "Three figures stumbled out of it toward them. "Cain!" Logan shouted. "Tom!"

The man in the lead started running. Double sonic booms rocked the ice. Two Company fighters, cloaked, but still distinctive because of the distortion caused by the cloaking device, shot toward them. A third boom quickly followed, and a Tong fighter screamed into the space above them firing on the two Company ships.

Another man caught up to Cain. He carried an armful of breathing equipment and a few cold-weather suits. He looked up when they heard the booms and grinned behind his mask. "That's my nephew, Bat."

"He's in trouble," Shayna screamed. The Company fighters had looped around and were now firing on Bat's un-cloaked fighter. Explosions rocked the ice-covered rocks next to them.

"Take cover," Logan yelled as he grabbed Shayna's hand and ran toward the burning Guild ship.

"Not there," Cain yelled over the sounds from the battle raging overhead. "Ship's ready to explode. The fire has reached the energy core."

Logan stopped and looked around. There was nowhere to run to, nowhere to hide, no cover, no safety. It was hundreds of degrees below zero, lack of oxygen would kill those with no breathing equipment if the cold didn't. They huddled next to the burned-out wreck of a Company fighter while Cain and the two new guys handed out the breathers and suits. They put Raj and Corey into one by splitting it in half. The two boys had to share a breather. The Sweet triplets stood up and declined any suits or breathing gear because there wasn't enough for everyone. "Help them," they said pointing at the women from Vegas, Kylie, a mother with a half-grown son about Raj's age, and an old woman.

Logan huddled next to Shayna. "This is so hopeless," she cried into his shoulder as the Company fighters made a pass over them. Blue fire rained down exploding holes in the ice sending a wave of water toward them.

"Run," Sugar Sweet yelled as she grabbed the hands of her sisters and Kylie and dragged them toward the burning Guild ship. The water washed over the older woman struggling to put on a cold weather suit, knocked her down, and covered her. In seconds, she was frozen solid.

Overhead, Bat fired on the Company fighter. The Company ship blew up in a bright ball of flames as it streaked toward the burning Triad ship. When it hit the ship, it exploded. Cain waved his hands. "Stop."

The Sweet sisters turned to look at him. He was gesturing wildly. "Drop," Cain shouted. "Down." He fell to the ground on top of Raj and Corey. Logan had known Cain long enough to listen. "Down," he echoed as he pulled Shayna to the ice and shoved Knock and Fang over. They all fell to the rocky, ice-covered ground and covered their heads as the huge Guild starship exploded. It was horrible. The Company fighter and Bat were both caught in the explosion and incinerated. A wall of fire blasted over the huddled survivors. The noise was deafening. The rock under them began to splinter and shatter. Logan hung onto Shayna, but in his heart, he knew they were all going to die. They had nowhere to go, and it felt like the small island of rock beneath them was disintegrating.

Chapter Thirty-Four

The splintering rock suddenly stabilized. The roar of the blazing Guild ship disappeared. A deathly silence descended over the huddled group. Logan lifted his head. "What in the heck?"

The entire rocky, ice-covered island glowed with an unearthly green.

Shayna lifted her head. "What is it, Logan?"

Ginger Sweet looked up and pointed. "This could be either very bad or maybe good," she whispered. "What do you think?" Her question was just tossed into the air and not aimed at anyone in particular.

Knock and Fang rose to their knees and stared at the sky. "It's not cold anymore," Cressy said.

Ju put her arm around Cressy. "What is it?"

"I have no idea," Logan said.

Hovering above them was the strangest spaceship Logan had ever seen or even imagined. It looked more like a butterfly than a spaceship. The wings didn't flutter, but they were covered with blue-green spots. The center of the ship had windows that glowed with emerald light. That green glow spread to cover the entire landing field including the burning Triad ship. Everywhere the glow touched, it was warm. Steam rose from icy rocks that had never felt anything but sub-zero temperatures. Ice started melting and the water was warm.

When the ship hovered only ten feet above them, it stopped, and a beam of white light emerged from the center section. A creature rode the beam down. It was humanoid with two arms and two legs. It was pale, and dressed in a tight-fitting, blue-gray spacesuit with no helmet. The being touched down on the ice and walked toward them. Logan stood up to greet it.

"Who are you?" Logan asked.

The humanoid held up a hand to quiet Logan's questions. The hand was covered with a glove and had long fingers with four joints. "I am a Rigellian," it said. "My name is Harkony. My race has been at war with the Kruellians for many and many more of your years. They steal our technology and destroy using it. We know this and have developed ways of following them and foiling their plans. Rigellians do not kill. We do not eat the flesh of any creature. We seek only peace. To this end, we have come to save you. The killer ship orbiting this small moon is manned by people of your species and one Kruellian. Though the Kruellians intend to conquer the universe, in actuality, they are spread thinly across the galaxies. They use the species they plan to subjugate to implement their nefarious crusade of domination. Unfortunately, greed and hatred are universal emotions in most species and the Kruellians have learned to capitalize on them."

He gestured to them. "Come with me. You will be cared for and transported wherever you would like to go."

Logan moved between the alien and his people. "We could be jumping out of the frying pan into the fire," he said to Knock. "What do you think?"

Knock removed the patch over his alien eye and stared at Harkony. "Under the suit, he's like naked," Knock said. "But he's got no, uh, no sex things, organs, you know. He's like an it."

"I can hear you," Harkony said. "Our species have been unisexual for many arrans of time. We live longer than any other species and rarely reproduce. For all of our time we've been historians, saving and documenting the history of not just our species, but all species we've come in contact with. Even yours."

"That's terrific and all," Logan said. "But what do we do now?"

"You brought the sphere with you," Harkony said. "With it, we can terraform a planet to fit all your needs, a planet outside of the known Kruellian domain, and then we can place you there."

"What about our race, our world, all the people down there on Earth?"

"We will help all we can, but you must understand, the Kruellians have declared war on our species, and it is against our code to kill, even Kruellians."

"Well that sucks," Knock said. "For you guys and for us."

"For the moment, we will go aboard my ship and warp out of this system to a safe one."

Logan gathered his people around him. "Then get us out of here," Logan said as the ground under their feet heaved, cracked and rumbled. "This is about the worst place I've been in my entire life."

"You got that right," Knock said.

Chapter Thirty-Five

"Think it will be a boy or a girl?" Ju asked Logan. Logan, Ju, Mark, Knock and Fang sat in what the Rigellians called an infirmary. Everything on the Rigellian ship was so strange and so off-the-wall as to be downright weird. The infirmary was no different. Shayna lay on a bed that floated, covered by a blue-green fog. They couldn't see her or hear her. A Rigellian dressed in a filmy white garment stood over her. Shayna was delivering their child. Logan was so nervous, he felt ready to barf at any moment.

"I don't know or care," Logan said. "I just want Shayna to be okay."

"Well I hope it's a boy," Ju said.

"Me, too," Fang echoed.

Baby Mai Li sat on Ju's lap playing with a shiny toy provided by the Rigellians. The toy spoke to her in a baby language the infant seemed to understand even as she stuffed one edge of it into her mouth. "If it's a boy, could you name it Deklan?" Ju asked.

Logan was gnawing on a fingernail. He looked up. "Sure, that's a great idea. I mean it's great as long as Shayna says it's great."

Tears suddenly ran down Fang's face. The tough-as-nails warrior woman was crying. "I can't believe both of our parents are dead. I never got to say goodbye to Mom."

"Her last act on earth was to hand me this child," Ju said. "She was a wonderful, brave and loving person."

"Well Dad was brave," Logan said. "Loving, not so much."

"He did love us," Fang said. "He showed it by teaching us to survive. We learned that from him, and we're stronger, better people because of him."

"True that," Knock said. "He was like epic."

Sammy Lee stuck his head into the room. "How's the delivery going?"

Logan glanced up. "Good. I mean I think it's going good." He grabbed his hair. "But I really don't know."

Lee smiled. "You'll be fine. The Tong has decided to go wherever the Rigellians take us and reform there. We will continue to fight the Company and the Kruellians for as long as it takes to defeat them, and with our last breath."

Ju put a hand on Lee's arm. "Bat was so brave. You should be very proud."

Lee's smile vanished. "I am proud. He probably saved our lives by keeping those fighters from destroying the Smugglers' ship before we got out."

"Look," Logan said. "Something's happening with Shayna."

They all moved to the edge of their seats, and Logan held his breath as the Rigellian hovering over Shayna reached into the cloud of blue-green and pulled out a baby. It cried once and the Rigellian passed a calming hand over its tiny body, wrapped it in a silvery cloth, and headed for Logan. Logan stood up, shaking with emotions he could barely put a name to. "Your son," the Rigellian said and handed Logan the baby.

Logan turned to Ju and Fang who crowded close. "It's a boy." Unashamed, tears flowed down Logan's cheeks. He stared into the infant's face for one long moment. The baby's eyes were blue and his hair black just like Logan's father, Deklan. He kissed the baby's forehead and handed him to Fang. "I need to see Shayna."

The Rigellian led Logan to the bed, the mist disappeared, and there was Shayna lying in a soft cocoon of fluffy white stuff with her head propped on a pillow. When she saw Logan, she reached out with both arms and he pulled her into his embrace. They hugged silently for a few moments, then Logan leaned back and smiled at her. "You look beautiful."

She laughed and touched his cheek. "So do you."

"How you feeling?"

"The Rigellians are amazing. No pain, nothing but a wonderful sensation like I was floating in heaven, and then the baby was just there. Not inside of me anymore."

"We have a son," Logan said.

"I know. We should name him after your father."

Logan nodded. "Fang and Ju want that, too."

"Are the Rigellians gonna get my mom?"

"They're gonna try. She's with that weirdo group under the Denver airport. I know they'll take care of her, but I'd like all of our people to be together."

"Where will we go?"

"The Rigellians picked up the sphere me and Jordie rode to Europa, and they said they know of a perfect planet to terraform for us. I don't think Gliese is an option. The Company and its new stooges, the Smugglers Guild, they have too much control. Bat's uncle, Sammy Lee, says the Tong will come with us."

"I don't care where we go as long as we're together," Shayna said.

"The rest of our guys are happy with that," Logan told her. "All except the Sweet sisters. The Rigellians seem to be fascinated by them. Something about them being identical triplets. Or at least that's what the Sweet girls say. They want to stay here and hang with the Rigellians. You know, travel the space lanes, and go back to Earth to get more of our people."

Shayna started laughing. "Oh, don't make me laugh. It hurts. There isn't a male in the universe that wouldn't find the Sweet triplets fascinating."

Logan tilted his head. "But the Rigellians said as a race, they're asexual."

Shayna burst into more laughter and grabbed a handful of his shirt. "Stop, you're killing me."

Meanwhile, in a luxurious three-room suit atop Caesars Palace in Las Vegas, Vaerfeky lounged in a comfortable La-Ze-Boy recliner drinking a tall, icy glass of Hawaiian Punch. Alcoholic beverages were very bad for Kruellians. The alcohol turned Kruellian urine into highly flammable liquid. When they'd first landed and had tried drinking alcohol, one Kruellian, sadly now deceased, had discovered the flammable nature of alcohol when he'd gone to the men's room and voided his bladder onto the urinal cake. The resulting explosion was still talked about in hushed tones and alcohol strictly avoided.

Vaerfeky took a sip and sighed. The red dye in Hawaiian Punch had much the same effect on Kruellians as alcohol did on humans. "Heidi," Vaerfeky said. "Tickle me beneath my left leg one more time."

The tall, blond holographic maid smiled. "Yes master."

About the Authors

Gabe Thompson

Gabe lives in Florida with his wife and son, where he teaches school, but he's traveled the world. He draws upon his experiences in life as fodder and inspiration for writing.

He retired from the military because of medical reasons, but regularly flies around the world on military Space A, AMC and MAC flights. He states that the military has bases in some of the best places and plans on venturing to most of them before he dies

Janet Post

Janet writes books with her son, Gabe, who has a degree in journalism because they have many of the same interests.

She's a self-described military brat from Hawaii.

She worked as a reporter for years before retiring to write